Notebook Mysteries

Notebook Mysteries

~∞ Emma ∞~

KIMBERLY MULLINS

NOTEBOOK MYSTERIES -EMMA

Book 1 of the Notebook Mysteries Series

Copyright © JKJ books, LLC 2020

First edition: March 2021

Mailing address for JKJ books, LLC: 17350 State Highway 249, STE 220 #3515 Houston, Texas 77064

Library of Congress Control Number: 2020920824

ISBN 978-1-7360104-0-2 (hardcover)

ISBN 978-1-7360104-1-9 (paperback)

ISBN 978-1-7360104-2-6 (ebook)

This is a work of fiction. It is based on historical events within Chicago during the time period 1871-1881.

Edited by Kaitlyn Johnson; Cover Art by Miblart

To Claudia, the person who believed in me and my books.

To Joshua and Jonathan, thank you for being in my life and giving me the support I need at all times.

PROLOGUE

here to start, the Narrator thought as she sat drumming her right fingers against her lips. *Where to start*, she thought again, glancing around the brightly lit room, looking for inspiration. The room she chose to start her writing project was in the attic space of the old Victorian she and her family called home. The house faced east, the room's dormers caught the bright morning light, and it washed across the writing desk where she sat. She chose the early morning hours to work on her book because she liked the feel of the sun on her face and the peace it gave her.

The room was large and furnished with an old dark brown leather chair stationed next to a lighter brown antique desk on the east wall. Located across the room from the desk was a tall white dresser with brass handles, two white iron twin beds covered with patchwork quilts, and aged lace throws. The floor was whitewashed and a large colorful area rug lay under the beds.

It was a place where she could be away from the noise within the house. Her family was usually in high spirits about something or another and could be quite loud. *Family*, she thought with an exasperated shake of her head. *I'll have to get to them soon enough.*

She moved her hand from her lips to where the pencil laid on the desk, absently rolling it back and forth, while she continued to concentrate on her book plans.

A shuffling of shoes on the steps caught her attention, and her mouth quirked up in a quick smile. She looked toward the door and saw her dear-one walking into the room.

Dear-one was a tall, slim man—so tall that he had to duck under the doorway to enter the attic. He wore his usual brown suit with a pressed shirt and vest. His face rested in an absent-minded expression as he carried a battered brown box under his left arm and (of course) an open book in his right hand.

He dropped the box onto her desk, startling her, and then settled himself into the leather chair nearest her. He relaxed back, put his feet up on the edge of the desk, and continued to read. He hadn't glanced at her the entire time, but that wasn't unusual.

He didn't look up until she tapped his battered brown leather shoe.

"Where should I start?" she inquired, tilting her head toward her writing paper and typewriter.

The reader of this might wonder why the Narrator chose not to inquire about the box. Well, Dear-one was always moving things about and working on projects; it got tiresome asking what was in one box or another, so she just nudged it out of the way.

He acknowledged the question by lowering his book, brushing a thick brown curl back off his forehead, and then, finally meeting her eyes with his, stated rather brusquely, "Well, at the beginning, of course. Where it all started."

She glanced down at her desk, again nudging the brown box so she could glance at her notes. *The beginning*, she thought. She reflected on how life as an investigator had begun. The long and varied career with many highs and lows, that affected everyone who came into contact with it. She did not know it would eventually lead to this point and writing a book, but she wouldn't have changed it for the world. "But the details of it. How to remember everything?" she fretted aloud.

Dear-one didn't look up from his reading this time when he said, "Look in the box. Something in there might help." She didn't notice a sparkle in his eyes, as he kept them averted toward his book.

She glanced at him suspiciously, stood up, and folded back the lid. She realized what was in it almost immediately and knocked the heavy desk chair back as she moved closer. She sighed into a long smile. Looking at him, she said, "The notebooks, where did you find them?"

He glanced up and, with a smile, said, "I had them put away. I thought you might want to keep them to look at one day."

Her eyes filled with tears as memories began flooding her senses. She pushed back the tears and, with a deep breath, started pulling items from the box. As she kept removing notebooks, she was taken aback by the sheer number of them. They were small black scribble books that fit easily into a pocket, full of years' worth of data, detailing the life of an adventurer. "So many," she murmured, "so many adventures."

Dear-one agreed quietly. "A lifetime's worth, to be sure."

He had suggested the beginning. *I might as well start there*, she thought. She dug until she found the oldest notebook and the earliest case. The black leather crumbled a bit as she handled it, but the papers inside were not damaged.

She took one in her hand. "I'll call it Case 1, The Office."

He interrupted again to say, "Love, there is another case to discuss, a very important one," he reminded her. "It should be the first one."

She knew the case of which he spoke, and finally agreed with a nod of her head. "Yes, you are quite right. I should start there."

She started organizing the notebooks into piles, stacked by date. Though, for this case, she could almost go from memory. She opened that first notebook and saw the title. She picked up her pencil to start the work.

CHICAGO, 1871 - LATE NIGHT

"Wake up, Dora, Sister," Papa said as he nudged their shoulders. He reached over to turn up the gas lamp above the sidetable.

The two girls had been asleep for hours and were groggy.

Dora yawned as she opened her eyes and saw Papa standing over them. Intuitively, she knew something wasn't right. "Papa? What's wrong?"

Sister woke, rubbing her sleep-filled eyes, then laid silent and watchful, waiting to hear how Papa would answer Dora's question.

"No questions now. You must get dressed," he said as he handed each of the girls their clothes and sat on the edge of the bed.

They quickly scooted to the side where Papa sat and started pulling their dresses over their nightshifts.

He knelt in front of them to help with their buttons.

They watched Papa silently and noticed his hands shaking. His hands never shook. Sister's hand reached out for Dora's; they held tight to each other, staying silent, ready for Papa's next direction. Dora and Sister were little girls of eight and six and would do anything their beloved papa asked of them.

It was very dark and quiet in the house as the girls held each other's hands and followed their father down the staircase to the first floor. As they moved closer to the front door, they became aware of the noise outside.

Papa turned to the girls and squatted down in front of them, taking their small hands in his and said gently, "Girls, you must listen to me. Something is happening outside. We are going to go out, but I need you to stay on the stoop and be as quiet as possible. Can you do that?" He didn't wait for an answer as he handed them their shoes. "Dora put on yours and help Sister with hers."

"Yes, Papa," Dora said as she sat down to handle their shoes. As they sat waiting for Papa to take them outside, Dora just couldn't stop herself from asking, "Papa, what's happening?" She looked around the foyer, feeling something or someone was missing, and suddenly realized Mama was not there. "Papa, where is Mama?" Sister continued to let Dora speak for her as she sat there holding onto Dora's hand.

Papa, not wanting to answer a question he did not know the answer to, went silent for a long moment. He stood without saying anything and went to the door. He just couldn't make himself open it; he felt somehow that the motion of opening the door would force him to admit something he didn't want to happen, had happened. Reaching out hesitantly toward the brass doorknob, he finally opened it. He turned back to the girls, took their hands in his, and led them out onto the stoop. They stayed together, holding hands, with Dora leaning against Papa's leg.

Chaos greeted them. Their senses were overwhelmed with the sounds of distress coming from neighbors, friends, and family scattered throughout the street. The smell of smoke lingered in the air and the general disorder lent an almost surreal look to the night. It appeared that all the neighbors had come outside in a hurry and most were still in their night-clothes. If it wasn't scary, it would be funny. Even Mr. Smith, the local preacher, normally very dignified with nary a hair out of place, was in the streets in a long dressing gown and a stocking cap that barely contained his wiry black hair.

People continued flooding into the streets from the surrounding houses. "Fire!" shouted someone, and a constant cry of "The fire will get us all!" came from the crowds that had formed. The spectators could smell the smoke and see the flames as the fire spread through the city and above the buildings. The blaze was actually at a greater distance from their neighborhood than it appeared, but the panic-stricken people couldn't process that fact.

Dora, not sure what would happen next, sat down on the top step of the stoop and started to cry in response to all the confusion, saying quietly, "I want Mama." Sister continued to stand next to her, quietly patting her head and silently taking in the confusion.

Papa, who had not moved from the stoop since exiting the house, seemed to visibly shake off the feeling of unease that gripped him. He gathered up his thoughts and spoke loudly and directly to the crowd. "Friends, neighbors, and family," he nodded to each group, "please be aware the wind direction doesn't appear to be driving the fire this way," he said in a calm but stern voice. "We must stay calm and keep watch on any changes in wind patterns. Those with small children, please return to your homes. Those who can help, we will need to start forming groups to organize shelter and food for survivors. If you can help, please join me over by my stoop."

That statement and his apparent leadership calmed the people down; it gave them purpose and direction. The groups started to disperse and families with small children returned to their homes. As volunteers approached the stoop to help, Papa assigned group leads and started them working on compiling lists of available food, resources, and shelter locations.

Papa went to where his girls still sat quietly. He settled between them, pulling each close to him, and said softly, "It will make me happy if you would go to Uncle Hans' house to get some rest."

Dora looked up from Papa's chest with tear-drenched eyes and asked one last time, "Papa, where is Mama?"

Papa could never lie to his girls, and this time he did not evade the question. "I think she might have gotten trapped by the fire at or around the bakery. We do not know more than that," he said honestly, trying to hold things together for his girls.

Sister watched his face and seemed satisfied. Dora's eyes threatened to overflow with tears, but she held them back. "Yes, Papa, we will go to Uncle Hans' house."

Papa motioned to Frederick to retrieve the girls. Frederick was the oldest son of Hans and the oldest cousin in the family. He was a very nice looking, slim young man with thick brown hair and a lovely smile. Papa was happy to see that he was already teasing smiles out of his younger cousins as he moved them to his house to get some rest.

Mama's brothers, Hans, Paul, Ernst, and Otto approached Papa about sending a small group of two into the area where Mama's bakery was located. Papa agreed and started to shrug into his jacket in preparation to leave with them. Otto stopped him, placing a hand on his arm, and said in a rumbling German voice, "Ellis, it is best for Sister and Dora that you remain here."

Hans agreed and added, "Also, the neighborhood will be looking to you for direction."

Papa wanted to argue, but he looked around at the people still in the streets, and then his gaze went to Hans' house. He knew they were right, and he reluctantly agreed to wait. They decided Paul and Otto would head out toward the business district and hopefully to Mama.

It was hours later when the brothers came back. They were sweaty and covered in soot. The two who had stayed behind ran up to them with water and wet rags. The four brothers hugged each other; glad they were back together.

Paul and Otto took the water and wet rags gladly; the night was hot and the fire had made it almost unbearable. Otto sighed, knowing he could not delay any longer, and said, "Let's find Ellis." The brothers nodded at each other and looked for Papa.

Papa was directing survivors into the established shelters when he spotted the four brothers coming toward him. He went quickly over to meet them.

The first to speak was Otto. He looked Ellis directly in the eyes as he spoke. "Ellis, the area is flooded with people evacuating. Paul and I could not get through, and we were advised by the Pinkerton detectives that the area will continue to burn overnight."

This statement seemed to affect the brothers and Papa at the same time. The men all appeared defeated, their heads hung low.

"There is still a chance," Papa whispered brokenly, "a chance she is among the evacuated or the injured." As Papa spoke, he glanced down the shadowed street.

The brothers looked at one another and shook their heads. Paul and Otto had gotten close enough to the area to determine it was badly damaged by the fire and very few people would have survived.

Papa wasn't ready to accept that Mama might have been taken from them. Looking searchingly in the direction of the bakery, he squinted his eyes, trying to see a greater distance. A familiar figure was coming toward him, he shook his head to clear it. "No, he said. Again, he looked and she was still there. He started smiling and broke away from them at a run. Hans started to go after him, but Otto said, "No, let him be." The brothers watched Papa but did not interfere.

He kept running toward her image, but the closer he got the more transparent she became. Finally, as he slowed down, he saw that she was smiling a sad smile and waving. Her image faded into the night before he could reach her. At that moment, he knew it had been Mama saying a last goodbye. The grief washed over him as he sank to his knees, crying.

Mama's brothers came to him, pulled him up off of his knees, and hugged him close. Papa let his emotions take over for a few moments and he cried into Otto's shoulder. The brothers watched with tears streaming down their faces.

When Papa was calmer, he looked back at Hans' house. "The girls," he said. He straightened and pulled away from Otto. "I must be here for them." The brothers nodded in agreement as they patted him on the shoulder and rubbed their own eyes.

Mama would still be unaccounted for as the hours went by and the fire was slowly extinguished. Her normal working hours started at 3am, but she had gone in early to prepare a special order that was to be picked up the next morning. The German pastry she was famous for—Chocolate Leaves with Asbach Uralt-Poached Pears and Grapefruit-Lemon Quark Mousse—required hours of preparation and baking time.

Papa kept muttering, "That dessert, if she hadn't needed to be in extra early, she would still be alive." Dora and Sister heard his comments that night. They would both revisit that memory one day.

The date was 1871, and the time was close to midnight. The news would filter in slowly through the rest of the night with details about what and who had been lost. The fire spread quickly through the business area of Chicago where the bakery was located. It was fast and destructive, the building materials mostly wood topped with highly flammable tar or shingle roofs. The recent drought also contributed to the city burning for three long days. Flying embers scared residents into believing they were at risk of losing everything.

The fire would eventually destroy approximately 2.2 square miles, killing 300 and displacing 100,000 people. Many people without homes took shelter in parts of the city where the fire had not taken hold.

Their fears had been realized; Mama was one of the 300 who had perished in the fire. The girls stayed with their aunts, uncles, and cousins while Papa and Mama's four brothers made their way through the barricades set up by the Pinkerton Detectives to protect residents from the still burning city.

They wetted blankets in horse troughs and draped them over their shoulders. They were able to make their way through the smoldering buildings to reach Mama's bakery. The men did not see the absolute destruction of the business district; they had a purpose—to find Mama.

As they entered the structure that used to be the bakery, they saw that the front area, where customers would buy from the display cases, had not survived the fire. The walls were gone, the cabinets were reduced to black rubble. They entered the kitchen and were surprised to find it largely intact due to the stone walls and cement floor Papa had insisted upon. *Still not enough to protect her,* he thought. *Not enough, I'll have to do better.*

Mama's blonde hair was seen first by Hans. "Here! She is here!" he called out. Her appearance was a surprise; she had not been burnt at all. For a moment, it gave the brothers hope that she still might be alive. Papa knew she was not.

In later visits, Papa would notice the structural concerns that led to Mama's death. For now, though, his only thoughts were to retrieve her. She was lodged under a large support beam that had fallen from the ceiling of the kitchen. He pushed the emotion back and helped Mama's brother's work throughout the morning to dig her body out.

None of them spoke while trying to free her. The men burned their hands, paying little attention as they removed the beam. Once her body was uncovered, they stood in silent prayer before moving her. They placed a white sheet over her, crossed themselves, whispered their final prayers, and carried her back to her home.

Notifications were made to the police, but there was no investigation. The cause of death was listed as accidental due to the fire.

Additionally, they reported one staff member was missing. He was a kitchen helper who was always by Mama's side. The police presumed him dead when a body could not be located.

There wasn't time to grieve, due to all the cleanup and work of rebuilding. Papa sat down and spoke honestly to Sister and Dora about what had happened to Mama. While they moved forward and stayed busy, Dora seemed the most affected by the tragic event and Papa could hear her crying at night. He did what he could to help the girls, all the while thinking that if Mary hadn't had that special order, she would have been safe with them.

Sister, Dora, and Papa were surrounded by Mama's family, friends, and customers at the funeral. Everyone wore black, mourning the dead and questioning how they might move forward. It was a dark and grim period of Chicago's history.

Time would start to heal wounds and life would move forward again quickly. The family agreed that Frederick, also known as Cousin, had the drive and talent to run the bakery. The family pitched in with labor, materials, and time to get it going again. They renamed the bakery "Cousin's Bakery with Ellis' approval.

Until the bakery was functional again, Cousin and other

family members worked out of the kitchen in Dora and Sister's house. There, they could watch the girls, keep the family together, and the bakery in business. Dora and Sister's Mama had already started training both of them, so they were helpful to Cousin and would continue learning at the same time.

As the cleanup began, so did plans for the reconstruction of the great city. Chicago would rebuild while the bricks were still smoking; nothing would hold the people back.

Papa, a structural engineer by trade, would also lead investigations into the fire. He would help determine that building codes were among the root causes, along with the lack of firewater available. He would be at the forefront of new codes and building standards for Chicago and would be in demand from other cities to help update their structures.

Chicago would rise out of the ashes, moving forward at a fast pace, but safe design.

CHICAGO 1881 – PRESENT DAY

*H*e was watching her window, located on the third story of the house, waiting for the lamp to illuminate and tell him that Emma had started her day. He stayed in the shadows, anticipating that light.

Emma woke early that morning, long before the sun could start its morning trek across the sky. She stretched her arms and yawned broadly before throwing off the covers. She laid there for a bit before she sat up and moved to the side of the bed. She stood and winced as her feet touched the wood floor. It was early spring in Chicago, and the early mornings could still be cold. She lit the gas lamp above her sidetable, the illumination allowing her to see around the room. Her nightdress was warm but did not protect her feet from the cold. Sitting on the bed, she pulled on heavy wool socks she kept on her nightstand. She ran across the room to stoke the wood in the fireplace. Once it was going, she stood there for a moment, enjoying the radiant heat, rubbing her hands, and thinking about her day ahead.

When she felt warmer, she went about her morning ablutions, using the washbasin and pitcher located in her room. She quickly used the lavatory, located down the hall, and returned to change into her bakery uniform. Trading her wool socks for long black stockings, she stayed as close to the fireplace as she could while dressing.

Finally dressed, she took a moment to look at herself in the tall standing mirror. She had made some revisions to the basic white uniform required by Cousin. Most of the bakery girls wore long white skirts that covered their boots. Emma had fashioned her full skirt into a split skirt and shortened it so that the hem just touched the top of her high black boots. The uniform top consisted of a white button-up shirt with puffed-up sleeves and included additional buttons to attach an apron. She would carry her apron and baker's hat with her to the bakery. Emma generally shocked people with her fashion-forward approach, but she didn't let anyone else's attitudes affect or change how she presented herself. She considered herself an advanced and independent woman of sixteen who did not follow the rules of fashion to the letter.

As she finished getting ready, she piled her light blonde hair onto her head in a high ponytail and perched her red hat on top. She carefully inserted her hat pin, grabbed her bag, and quietly headed downstairs through the dark house. *It's always odd,* she thought to herself, *how much a house can change when the voices that normally shake the rafters are quiet.* She paused for a moment. *I think I prefer the noise.* She smiled and continued to the kitchen.

She pushed open the swinging door to the kitchen and found her breakfast on the large round oak table. A note accompanied it. *Sister, do not forget your lunch and be sure to eat breakfast. Love you.* The family always alternated between calling her Emma and Sister.

She always made sure Emma had some fruit, bread, and a bag of treats waiting. Grabbing the butter from the icebox, she added it to her bread, already gobbling it down as she put on her red-lined coat and exited the house. She had a couple of miles to walk to get to the bakery to help with the early shift.

As she walked, she finished her breakfast and pulled out her omnipresent black notebook and pen. She took down her observations as she walked. *It's cold, the city streets are dark, and families are not yet stirring.*

Her white figure glowed in the night as she moved through the streets. The moon was full and illuminated the path. Emma didn't notice the shadow that would accompany her to the bakery.

Her watcher, lingering in the shadows, had long learned that Emma's skills at observation made his task difficult. He had to keep a long-distance between them, so she would not detect him following her. He started for a moment when he saw someone approaching her. He sank back as he realized it was Tony, the same boy who was always around her. He was her constant companion, especially in the mornings.

As usual, she felt more than saw Tony take her right arm and rest it on his elbow. She glanced over, smiled up at him, and teased, "You have nothing better to do than walk me to the bakery on my workdays?"

"Nope, I need to be there anyway, and you are on my way," he said cheerfully.

Emma knew this to be untrue. Tony lived close to the bakery and had to walk extra steps to be with her in the mornings. She didn't remind him of this. Instead, she absently handed him an apple and a sweet roll from the bag Dora had sent.

He took the offered food and covered his grin with a bite. *Slowly but surely, she's getting used to me. My next step is to ask her to the dance. I have long term ideas about my and Emma's future. She just doesn't know it yet*, he thought wryly.

They went along companionably, enjoying the quiet of the early morning and each other's company.

"So, what's on your schedule today? Though I think I know at least one of the items," Emma teased.

"Deliveries. Bakery in the morning and the afternoon, different courier jobs."

"And. . ." she said, encouraging him.

"And the museum," he filled in. "They have some amazing exhibits this week. Did I tell you the curator asked me for my opinion on some of the new paintings?"

"Really, Tony? That is wonderful." Emma knew Tony loved the museum and could either be found there or at the library looking at art books. His goal was to eventually work there.

"What about your plans?" asked Tony.

"Well, not as exciting as yours. I'm sure that my bakery list will have rye rolls, pies, and maybe some special desserts." She sighed, resigned to her current job.

Emma worked several mornings a week at the family bakery. It was the same bakery her mama first started when she emigrated from Germany, located in the business district. *Though, if Cousin has his way, they'll have locations all over Chicago*, Emma thought.

Mama's bakery had been heavily damaged during the fire of '71 and had to be rebuilt. When Mama's brothers were inspecting the damaged bakery with Papa, they realized many of the businesses around their shop would not open again. The family pooled their resources to buy the extra space and expanded into one of the largest bakeries in the area.

Papa was not involved in the day to day running of the bakery but was present every moment of the rebuild. He was there to ensure they kept to a high building standard so that not just the kitchen would survive the next fire, but the whole building. He also took a special interest in the anchoring of the support beams and the types of materials used. He wanted to be sure another preventable loss like the one that killed Mama never happened again.

On the day of the new bakery opening, a plaque was put into place that read: *Mary Evan's Bakery, first established in 1861.* Papa vowed that this bakery would stand and Mama would be remembered for it. The family was all in attendance when the plaque was unveiled. Emma and Dora were very proud of what their Mama had started.

The family believed the bakery would hold them together and be an extension of them. All members were involved in the running of it, from the baking to the cleaning and the accounting. All of the children were required to put in the time to help out and learn the trade. Not all of them would be bakers, but they would have an appreciation for hard work and family-led businesses.

As Emma and Tony approached the door, Tony stopped to chat with the other delivery drivers and Emma headed inside to start her workday.

❧

The watcher stayed in the shadows until she left his line of sight. He knew her schedule and would be back about the time she left.

❧

She loved the smell of the baking bread and other pastries as she opened the back door and stepped into the kitchen. At, that moment, memories of Mama would flood her senses. She hesitated only briefly because everyone started to yell about the draft coming into the room. Pushing the heavy door shut with her shoulder, she went to her workstation. The task list was waiting for her, she picked it up and saw the first item. *Rye bread, of course,* she thought, rolling her eyes as she continued to review the list.

The kitchen was busy with everyone arriving and setting up their stations for the day. It was a large room that contained a row of seven ovens against the back wall and individual work tables lined up in 3x2 rows. The room was already full of bakers, and working ovens made the room nice and warm.

Hellos sounded from all corners, and she waved to the other bakers. She slipped off her coat and hat and buttoned on her apron, tying it at the back. As she slipped on her baker's hat, she noticed it was just 4:15am—time to start her day. After she hung up her hat and coat, she glanced at her list again, then gathered the ingredients for the dough to make the pastries, pie shells, and rye bread. She placed them in a jumble on her workstation and started separating them for her first order of the day.

She began with the rye bread and began rolling out bread for buns and loaves, making small talk with the other bakers. The action of working the dough made her think of a quote she read in Early American Cookery, The Good Housekeeper, 1841. The author said, "There are three things which must be exactly right in order to have good bread: the quality of the yeast, the lightness or fermentation of the dough, and the heat of the oven. No precise rules can be given to ascertain these points. It requires observation, reflection, and a quick, nice judgment to decide when all are right. The woman who always has good home-baked bread on the table shows herself to have good sense and good management."

What Emma always took from that quote was the "observation, reflection, and a quick, nice judgment." That defined how Emma looked at all things in life.

It had become easier to make bread. *Yeast, what a marvel*, she thought to herself. It was invented in 1868 by the Fleischmann brothers and baking powder invented in 1869; this allowed the dough to rise without starters. In 1873, flour was improved with a flour mill that efficiently separated wheat germ and bran from the white endosperm, making cakes and pies so much easier to construct.

Rye rolls were made each day and sold out by lunch. As more and more households contained two working parents, bread had to be bought rather than made.

Rye Rolls
Ingredients:

- 1 tablespoon active dry yeast
- 2 cups warm water
- 4 eggs
- 1/2 cup nonfat dry milk powder
- 1/4 cup butter, softened
- 1/4 cup packed brown sugar
- 2 tablespoons dark molasses
- 2 teaspoons salt
- 1/2 teaspoon baking soda
- 3 to 4 cups all-purpose flour
- 3 cups rye flour
- 1 tablespoon cold water
- Maraway seeds and/or kosher salt

Directions:

1. In a large bowl, dissolve yeast in warm water. Add 3 eggs, milk powder, butter, brown sugar, molasses, salt, baking soda, and 2 cups all-purpose flour. Beat until smooth. Add rye flour and enough remaining all-purpose flour to form a soft dough (dough will be sticky).
2. Turn onto a well-floured surface; knead until smooth and elastic, about 6-8 minutes. Place in a greased bowl, turning once to grease top. Cover and let rise in a warm place until doubled, about 1 hour.
3. Divide dough into 30 pieces; shape each into a ball. Place 2 in. apart on greased baking sheets.
4. In a small bowl, whisk cold water and remaining egg; brush over dough. Sprinkle with Maraway seeds and/or kosher salt. Cover and let rise until doubled, about 45 minutes.
5. Bake at 350F for 14-16 minutes or until golden brown. Remove to wire racks.

"How are you today, Emma?" asked Chloe, one of the few employees who was not a cousin or family member. Chloe was getting to an age where she would be deciding to either continue working at the bakery or to be married. She had long-term ideas that might allow both and sent a long sideways glance toward Cousin.

"I'm good," Emma answered. As she continued to work on her rolls, she noticed Chloe's eyes drifting time and time again to Cousin. Emma smiled to herself and kept working.

The bakery was a happy place, full of gossip about the neighborhood, family, and all sorts of things. Emma knew she would have to remember what was being said and share it with Dora later.

Cousin worked the bread and chattered on about his weekend. "...she is a pretty girl and we had a good time. I may have to ask her out again." Cousin stood tall with broad shoulders, thick brown hair, and gray eyes. Both of his parents had come over from Germany.

Two of Emma's female cousins, working at stations near him, smiled, knowing he liked to play the field and thought of nothing permanent but the bakery. He would eventually marry, but it would be a while before he chose to mix time in the bakery with a family. He had plans to make this business grow and he didn't want anything or anyone to slow him down.

As the conversation continued, so did the baking. The bread and pies were being pulled out of the ovens and the shelves were filled for the morning deliveries and the breakfast rush.

Emma was especially interested in the delivery boys who arrived each morning. She watched as they piled in through the back door. They showed up in the early hours, as the sun was rising, to pick up orders consisting of bread, cakes, pies, and other assorted desserts, ready to be delivered that day. Tony got to the bakery earlier than other delivery drivers because he accompanied Emma. He usually waited for his friend Tim before coming into the kitchen.

As they entered the bakery together, Tony's dark brown eyes searched until he found her. He shot her a wide grin and tipped his bowler hat toward her. She nodded back and sent back a similar grin. Tim sent an absent wave her way and trudged to the boxed cakes, pies, and bread.

The delivery boys were typically dressed in long pants, shirts, and slouchy jackets. The hats they wore were different types, some of soft felt pulled over their eyes and others in dressier bowlers. They would slump in and grumble as they picked up their deliveries. Cousin would slip each a Berliner and a grin to get them moving.

Emma knew many of them but had grown up with Tony and

Tim. Tony Marella was Italian and had straight light brown hair, dark brown eyes, and a lanky build. He was sure he would be a businessman one day and make his family proud. Tony had a lovely family with a mom, dad, and three brothers. His dad owned a plumbing business with two of the brothers. Their business consisted mainly of new construction for gas and water lines.

Tim Flannigan was the quieter soul, big as a mighty oak tree. He was a good foot taller than Tony, and his arms were busting out of his sleeves. He had thick red hair and blue eyes, a true Irishman. Tim lived with his aunt and uncle; his parents had perished in the fire of '71. His life had been saved because he was staying with friends the night of the fire. A few years older than Tony and Emma, he was already attending night school to get his accounting degree.

Before his aunt and uncle moved to Chicago to take care of him, Tim lived at the boarding house for a time after the fire. Tony came over to Emma and Dora's house to visit him each day. They became very close friends during that time. The boys also started taking mathematics and engineering classes with Papa and Emma. Each excelled academically.

Emma gazed wistfully toward the wagons parked outside the bakery. She envied the boys' ability to leave the shop and run around the Chicago streets making deliveries, having adventures. They always seemed to be having much more fun than her.

Tim caught the look and gazed at her thoughtfully. He shook his head as if to clear it. *I'll have to think about how*, he muttered thoughtfully.

"Emma," said Cousin brusquely, but with a slight smile. "Stop daydreaming and get those pies in the oven." That snapped Emma and Tim out of their thoughts.

"Yes, Cousin," said Emma and immediately did as she was told. She completed the rolls and moved to the final preparation for the pies. Trimming the remaining dough on the edge of it, she added an intricate decorative twist. She finished them with an egg wash to make them shine before putting them into the oven. Next on her list was Almond-Cherry Soufflés with warm chocolate sauce.

Almond-Cherry Soufflés with Warm German Chocolate Sauce

Ingredients:

- Butter and sugar for preparing ramekins
- 1 and 1/2 cups German pitted preserved Marella cherries Sauerkirschen
- 3 tablespoons lemon juice
- 1/2 teaspoon German almond extract
- 5 large egg whites, room temperature
- 1/4 cup sugar
- 5 ounces German milk chocolate, coarsely chopped
- 3 tablespoons butter
- 1/4 cup heavy cream

Directions:

1. Preheat oven to 350F. Butter and sugar 6 8-ounce ramekins, place on a baking sheet, and set aside.
2. Combine cherries, lemon juice, and almond extract cutting up very small, pounding, and stirring until very smooth and almost fluffy. Transfer to a medium bowl and set aside.
3. In a large, clean metal bowl, beat egg whites with a large whisk until very soft peaks form. Continue to

beat while slowly adding sugar in a steady stream.
Beat until peaks are stiff but not dry. Use a flat
wooden spoon to fold 1/3 of egg whites into cherry
purée. Gently fold purée into remaining egg whites.
Divide this mixture among ramekins and smooth the
tops. Bake just until well-risen and beginning to
brown, 12-14 minutes.

4. For the sauce, heat 2 or 3 inches of water in a small
saucepan to a low simmer. Combine coarsely
chopped chocolate with butter in a heatproof bowl
that fits over the saucepan; the bowl should not touch
the water. Stir until chocolate melts. Remove from
heat and stir well until smooth; serve immediately.
(Sauce may be reheated by setting it over simmering
water.)

5. Split each soufflé in the middle and spoon in sauce.

"Emma," called out Cousin. "I have a change to your list this
morning."

"A change?" she asked as she paused, holding the additional
ingredients she had gathered for the next dessert on her list.

"Yes," said Cousin, "we have a request for your Mama's
specialty, Chocolate Leaves with Asbach Uralt-Poached Pears
and Grapefruit Lemmon Quark Mousse. They want it this
week, so we will add it to your schedule next time you are here.
Leave me a list of items you will need."

"I will," she said to him. She thought to herself, *That's odd.
Mama was known for this dessert, but it hasn't been ordered outside
the family since the fire.* She was the only person on staff that had
the experience to make it properly. She compiled her list of
needed ingredients and set it on Cousin's desk.

While Emma continued to work, she took careful notice of

the time the delivery drivers left. She pulled out her black leather notebook and wrote down as many notes about the boys as she could remember, cataloging the information for later review. How they were dressed in trousers, un-pressed jackets, and button-up shirts. How they wore their caps and hats. They were a bit disreputable, but that made them even more interesting

As Tony walked back and forth to the wagons, he saw her scribbling and smiled. "Getting it all down?" he teased Emma in a low voice.

She glanced up and returned the smile. "Trying to," she whispered, glancing around again for Cousin.

The delivery drivers would pick up cakes, pies, and different types of loaves of bread for early morning orders and bring back the additional orders for that evening or the next day. Once deliveries were completed, they moved on to other types of deliveries, such as papers, lumber, etc. They had free reign of the city and could go anywhere on their own. Cousin allowed the boys to keep the wagons and horses for their afternoon deliveries and in return, they fed them and kept the stables clean.

Emma wanted to have adventures; she wanted to see more than the bakery and the boarding house. There was no way that would happen if she did not find a way to get out. She would always have her love of baking, but she knew her future involved activities outside of the bakery.

I have to find a way to go on deliveries with the boys and see more of the city, she thought. Emma had seen quite a bit of Chicago already but wanted to see more. There was a time after the fire that Papa would not let her or Dora out of his sight, so that meant the girls were taken on many of his structural engineering jobs and could navigate the city at an early age.

She finished out her morning and headed home for lunch and afternoon studies.

Her watcher had stayed nearby and was there when she exited the bakery to head home. He knew her path; he stayed back so as not to be detected. He was ever vigilant about knowing where she was and what she was doing.

Brushing off her white skirt and shirt as she went, Emma continued her walk home, her red hat was perched jauntily on her head and her coat laid over her arm. She moved it to her shoulder, pulling out her notebook and pen to make observations as she walked.

A voice called, "Emma!" She turned toward it.

Her watcher took a step toward Emma until he saw her reaction to the person calling her name. He immediately recognized the delivery driver Tim and he stepped back into the shadows.

Tim pulled his delivery wagon next to the curb near Emma.

"Hey, Tim. Did you finish early today?" she asked.

"Nah, not yet. Want a ride home? I'm headed in that direction," Tim indicated with a nod.

"That would be nice," Emma said and took his hand to climb up on the wagon. "Anything interesting on the route today?" she inquired as they started onward.

Tim shook his head. "No, not unusual, but we did see several Stubing department store deliveries come in today. We also had some orders for the train station."

Emma liked to hear about people traveling. "Did you see the passengers?" she asked eagerly, inching up in the wagon seat.

"Yes, some. Mostly, we enter the back of the station, but this time they let us deliver Berliners to the train engineers. We also got to see inside the train," he said lightly.

Tim thought Emma was going to pull herself off of the seat with excitement. She had a million questions about the train. "How did the train run? Did you see the engine? Was it loud? Did you get to ride on it?" And on she went. They talked more about the train and what Tim had seen as they made their way to her house. He pulled the horses to a stop and hopped down to assist her off of the wagon.

"Is Dora home?" he asked innocently as he swung her down, looking everywhere but at her.

Emma hid a smile by placing a hand over her lips as if to wipe something off. "Why, yes, you might check with her to see if she would like any deliveries this week."

Emma knew Dora didn't usually order, but Tim obviously wanted to see her. She accompanied him up the stoop into the house. They entered the kitchen by cutting through the dining room off of the foyer.

Dora had the house opened up, sun streaming in all of the windows, the afternoon light adding highlights to her brown hair. She sat at the kitchen table making notes in her journal. She had the same head for detail as Emma but applied it to the household accounts. The break between breakfast and lunch was utilized to update her journal. Looking up, when she heard the door open, she expected to see her helper Amy, Emma, or one of the boarders. She was startled to see both Tim and Emma in her doorway.

Emma spoke first since both Tim and Dora were red-faced, busy trying to not look at each other.

"Dora, Tim wanted to check in with you about an order you might need." She looked encouragingly between them.

When neither would talk, she continued, chatting about anything she could think of. As the conversation veered to seeing tigers in the streets that morning, prompting no reaction from her companions, she realized they were not listening.

Emma got exasperated when it looked like Tim was turning to leave without saying a word to Dora. She stopped him, placing a hand on his arm. "Oh, for heaven's sake. Dora, Tim says there is a dance this weekend and would like you to go."

Tim looked astonished at this, since he had said no such thing, but went along anyway. "There is a church social this weekend. Would you like to go, Dora," Tim gulped, "with me?"

Dora had no way out and she didn't want one. She looked directly at him for the first time, smiled slowly, and said, "Tim, I would love to go with you."

He grinned so widely, it threatened to split his face. He started backing up and hit the wall, which caused the picture next to him to bounce. Mumbling on his way out that he would be by at 8pm on Saturday to pick her up, he barely missed hitting the doorway on his way out. Emma and Dora heard a loud "wahoo" from the front of the house.

When they heard the front door opened and closed, both girls dissolved into giggles. "I thought he would never get it out," said Emma.

"No," said Dora, "it would have taken twenty years." She sobered abruptly and asked Emma in a worried tone, "What will I wear?"

Emma pulled out her notebook and was reading over it when she heard Dora's concerned comment. "Weren't you planning on your pink dress?" she inquired.

"Well, that was before I was going with someone," said Dora wryly.

"We can put something together," she reassured her. She started drumming her fingers on her lips and said, "I have a lace overlay that might work. Leave your chosen dress on my bed and we can make some alterations this evening."

"Okay, but nothing too daring," she said with a wink, "and thanks."

"No problem. Well, I'll leave you to your work," Emma said. "I told Papa I would be in class this afternoon." With that last comment, she headed to her father's study, leaving Dora with her thoughts of Tim.

Both Emma and Dora were homeschooled by their father. Dora had moved away from engineering into mathematics. She was eighteen now and had decided mathematics was the skill she would need for working on her accounting books and expenditures. Emma continued to work on civil and structural engineering. Papa used her as his assistant for real-life application of code enforcement on buildings.

As lessons wrapped up with Papa, Emma applied herself to the lacework drape for Dora's dress. Dora had selected her blue dress for the dance. *It will look lovely with her blue eyes,* thought Emma.

Dinner that night was another noisy affair that Dora and Amy ran with quiet precision. As the meal came to a close, the groups separated. The kids worked on homework at the dining room table and the adults sat quietly talking in the family room. Papa would share his time between helping with homework and contributing to conversations.

Dora worked at a little table near the sofa, updating her books for the week, while Emma worked with Miss May, adding details to the lacework for Dora's dress. The other adults in the room were either reading or speaking in quiet exchanges.

Papa had heard about Dora's invitation from Tim. "As I understand it, Dora, Tim was so excited he got three blocks away before he remembered he had a wagon with him," Papa teased her.

Dora took the ribbing good-naturedly, pleased that Tim was

as excited as she was about the dance. She looked over her books and daydreamed a bit about Tim and their possible future.

Emma saw she was embarrassed and did not join in with Papa's teasing. She kept herself busy with the lace pattern for Dora's dress. Emma used her skill in engineering to start drawings and patterns for the intricate lacework that she and Miss May designed. She would have to apply herself to the project to have it completed by Saturday evening. Miss May would help her with the final attachment of the lace to the dress.

Miss May and Miss Marjorie chatted next to Emma while she worked the lace. The evening came to a quiet close with the gas lights being turned out and families heading up to their rooms.

CHAPTER 3

*T*he next morning at the boarding house, Emma woke with a start and then realized it was not her early day. She sank back slowly on the bed, stretched out with her hands above her head, and curled her toes. She was off for the day and she could already hear other boarders on the stairs, getting ready to start their days.

She took some time getting dressed that morning in a divided skirt similar to the style of the ones she wore at the bakery, but this one was a vibrant red. It also had a black band at the waist and a layer of lace showing just at the bottom. Her outfit was completed with a high-necked white lace shirt and a longish red jacket. Red was her favorite color, and she wore it whenever she could.

Standing in front of her mirror, she pulled her hair into a ponytail and grabbed her rounded modified bowler hat. It was black and had a similar red band to that of her skirt. Sitting on the bed, she slid on and laced up her black boots before heading downstairs.

"Sister," called Dora, hearing Emma's boots on the stairs, "kitchen first."

"All right," said Emma with a good-natured groan. She headed to the kitchen, slipping off her hat and placing it out of the way in a closet off the foyer. She had been hoping to sneak out, to practice her knives in the backyard before breakfast, but that was impossible in this house.

Breakfast first. She knew the drill and off to the kitchen she went. She knew what Dora expected her to do, so she breezed through the dining room, grabbing plates from the pantry, and twirled around the large brown table as she set it for breakfast. She entered the kitchen in her usual dramatic fashion.

Dora had whipped up a jelly cake early that morning. She was busy cutting it into the thin slices for the breakfast table when Emma entered the kitchen.

Jelly Cake

Ingredients:

- 1 cup butter, softened
- 2 cups sugar
- 4 eggs
- 3 cups flour
- 1 cup whole milk
- 1tsp vanilla extract
- 2 cups jelly—use your preference

Directions:

1. Preheat the oven to 350 degrees F. Grease and flour a 9x13pan.
2. In a large bowl, cream together the butter and sugar until light and fluffy.

3. Beat in eggs one at a time, mixing well after each one.
4. Stir in the flour and milk, alternating so the dough does not become too stiff or loose.
5. Mix in Vanilla.
6. Pour into the prepared pan.
7. Bake for 35 to 40 minutes, until the center springs back or the fork, comes out clean.
8. Spread jelly over the cake while it is warm but not hot. You want it to soak in slowly.

"Good morning, Dora, Amy," said Emma, fairly singing the greeting. Both Dora and Amy looked toward the door and smiled.

"Good morning, Sister," said Dora. "Did you sleep well?"

Emma nodded and said, "Very," as she grabbed a biscuit.

Dora glanced at the clock and asked, "Sleep in a bit?" Dora and Amy had been up early to start breakfast preparations.

"Yeah," Emma answered, her mouth already full of biscuit and jam.

Dora glanced down at Emma's divided skirt. "Lose the bottom of your skirt?" she teased.

Emma gave Dora an exaggerated frown and then they both smiled at each other. Dora and Amy continued their preparations for breakfast. Emma pitched in to help as they piled up the food on platters and placed them on the kitchen table, ready to be moved into the dining room.

The kitchen and the rest of the house were Dora's domain. Emma knew who was boss and did as she was told.

Dora and Emma were two years apart but closer than most sisters due to the loss of their Mama at such young ages. The sisters were ½ German (from Mama's side) and ½ Welsh/English (from Papa's side). Dora had more of the German build, with a very pretty full figure. Emma favored her father's family and was slight in build. Both girls had lovely hair, Dora's thick and light brown, Emma's thick and light blonde; Dora, too, had blue eyes while Emma had brown. Both of the girls favored their mother in looks.

Mama and Papa met when she first immigrated to America. She had been looking for a good solid building to start her business and had been told Papa was the best person to help with inspections. They hit it off from the start and the story went that Papa proposed in the first two weeks of their meeting. Mama evidently felt the same way, because she said "Yes."

Before the fire of '71, Papa, Mama, Emma, and Dora were the only people to live in the big house. Papa was a successful structural engineer and had saved his money to help his family have a comfortable life. The house had many unused bedrooms and was four stories high. Mama had teased Papa about wanting to fill all of the rooms with children. Sadly, that wouldn't be the case now.

On the first floor was a large entryway leading to the stairs. Additionally, on the first floor, there was a large kitchen, dining room, study, and sitting room. The second floor contained five bedrooms, and the third floor held an additional five bedrooms. The fourth-floor attic was the highest space in the house and had been mostly used when Mama was alive for projects and sewing.

After the fire, so many people were homeless and needed help. Papa opened their home to those needing a place to stay while their homes were rebuilt. What had started as a haven for friends and family would eventually lead to their house being turned into a boarding house business run by the family. These were a popular trend for many visitors and people moving to help rebuild Chicago. They provided lodging and meals for a price.

Papa always had a long view of the future for his girls. He was aware that, before 1860, any money made by a woman through a wage, or investment by gift, or through inheritance automatically became the property of her husband once she was married. The current laws also made the identity of the wife effectively legally absorbed into that of the husband. This would make the couple one person under the law.

Papa and Mama had never wanted that for their daughters; they wanted free-thinking women who could make their way in the world. They had always kept their money from their respective businesses separate in case something was to happen to one or both of them. The legislatures were working on the Married Women's Property Act to help protect women's rights, but that was years away.

The boarding house provided an income for the girls' future as well as the added benefit of helping them stay busy and not have time to dwell on the loss of their mama.

Once it moved toward being a permanent business, Dora's talent for business and organization became apparent. She talked Papa into letting her take over running the boarding house. He had the same thought in mind and it didn't take much convincing.

They had been worried about Dora since Mama had passed away. She had not been excited about anything until she took over the running of the boarding house. Dora liked the people around and the energy that came with it. Having children in the house and the kitchen made her happy.

Initially, Dora did both cooking and managed the house with help from Emma. Though she was young, she proved she could run it as a successful business. As it became more successful, Dora was able to hire Amy to help with cooking, serving, and general housework. Larger events, such as Christmas, required additional help to be brought in.

Dora assumed her new role with ease; her demeanor changed from quiet to one where she enjoyed being in charge. *Looking back, she would have been a great general of troops*, Emma thought with a smile.

~

As usual, Emma pulled out her small black notebook and was scribbling in it. "What are you writing this time?" asked Amy.

Amy Brown was a small woman but had a core of lead under her skin. Her size and general appearance made her look much younger than she was. She was in her mid-20s with a light frame, small bones, and curly red hair. She did not live at the boarding house, but rather she lived with her brother and his family nearby. Her unmarried state didn't seem to bother her. Work was something she enjoyed and was ready to help with whatever task was offered.

Emma replied with a shrug. "Observations of this or that. What I'm going to do today and things I need to work on." She didn't want to overshare before she was sure what her observations could mean.

Dora loaded up trays and said directly to both Amy and Emma, "Well, Emma, put that down for now. Both of you help load the table with breakfast."

Emma closed the notebook with a clap and stowed it in her skirt pocket. The trays were loaded with Berliners, eggs, sausages, bacon, fresh-baked bread, assorted jams, and jellies. As they moved the food to the dining room table, the fragrant smells wafted upstairs. Boarders started appearing before Dora could ring the breakfast bell.

The current boarders included two older ladies, Miss

Marjorie and Miss May, as well as two families with small children. In the general confusion of the table, Emma sat in her favorite spot between Miss Marjorie and Miss May.

Miss Marjorie gave the appearance of a fragile elderly woman of 80, but she was actually a criminal of the first degree with a spine of steel. She and her husband were professional bank robbers. They had gotten caught on their last job and were sent to prison. Miss Marjorie was the only one to make it out the last time. She was philosophical about what had happened to her husband and said they had a grand, adventurous life together.

Papa had been friends with Marjorie and her husband in the past. Emma wasn't sure how long Papa had known them, but she knew their friendship went far back.

Miss Marjorie was among the first of many "specialists" Papa had brought into the boarding house after Emma's "incident" occurred. The specialty Papa wanted Emma to learn from Miss Marjorie was not safe cracking, but throwing knives. They had been working together, developing Emma's skills for the past few years. Emma was as good as or better than Miss Marjorie.

Miss Marjorie looked over at Emma and asked, "Will we be practicing today?"

Emma nodded, her mouth full of pastry and sausage. She swallowed and wiped her mouth with her napkin before saying, "Let's meet outside after breakfast."

Marjorie agreed with a nod. Emma didn't see her, but Miss Marjorie looked over at Miss May and winked. Miss May nodded discretely.

Dora cleared her throat at Emma after hearing her plans for the morning.

"Oh, and after I help in the kitchen," Emma said hurriedly.

Dora smiled approvingly.

Miss May jumped in, not wanting to be left out. "We also need to work on that lace this evening. We have a deadline next week for some lace overlays."

Emma smiled warmly at her and covered her hand with hers. She said, "I'm looking forward to it." Her cheeks reddened and she smiled back warmly.

Miss May could work lace in the most beautiful styles and was much in demand. She didn't have any children of her own and wanted to pass on the craft to Emma, who was already selling her designs to local shops to give dresses a finishing touch. Miss May was another one of Papa's specialist; her specialty was as an escape artist. She could get out of any type of bindings: cuffs, ropes, chains, and locks. She said her lacework kept her fingers nimble just in case.

As Emma cleared the table, everyone went off·to start their day. Dora gave her a sideways look and nodded toward the kitchen. She and Emma finished clearing the table while Amy started washing the dishes. After they finished, Dora sat down and, resigned, said, "Okay, I don't like gossip, but if everyone else knows what is going on, then so will I."

Emma shared the gossip she had picked up the previous morning at Cousin's—Cousin's new lady friend, Chloe's longing looks, and all of the other information floating around the bakery.

After breakfast cleanup was completed, Emma met Miss Marjorie outside in the backyard. It was fenced in and had a well-cared-for grassy area, as well as garden plots full of flowers and vegetables. The area was used for many activities. Emma worked with her knives there, as well as training with her specialist in self-defense.

She carried the targets—plywood sheeting marked in the rough shapes of the human body—out to the far fence. Miss Marjorie and Emma had deliberately chosen an early time, after breakfast, so the boarding house kids would be at school and no harm could come to them.

"It is important to practice and know where the knife is going at all times. You want to wound your aggressor, but you need to know how to throw it lethally also," Miss Marjorie said each time they worked together.

Emma had two separate knives, one balanced and one unbalanced. Her preference was the balanced knife, one that could be thrown by the blade or handle.

"It is also important," Miss Marjorie said, "to know how to throw both types in case you get into a situation where you must use an unfamiliar weapon."

She went on to explain that the throwing knife was commonly made out of a single piece of steel or other material, without handles, unlike most knives. The knife had two sections, the blade, and the grip. The purpose of the grip was to allow the knife to be safely handled by the user and also to balance the weight of the blade.

Emma worked at it until she could throw over- and under-handed. She had a natural talent and knew the skill would prove useful.

"Emma, we need to work on concealed knives and how to access one without hurting yourself," stated Miss Marjorie.

The Narrator is interrupted by Dear-one as he reads over her shoulder. "You should mention the scars."

"Oh, yes," said the Narrator.

To continue with the story...

Emma learned to work with the knives through daily practice sessions with Miss Marjorie. During those sessions, a couple of accidental cuts occurred, one on her upper arm and one across the back of her hand. Both healed, but they left scars; the one on the back of her hand would be a constant reminder to keep her mind on the task at hand.

"Emma," Miss Marjorie said, "I have something for you."

"You do?" inquired Emma with a tilt of her head.

"You have learned so much about knives, but I need to share some secrets with you. One, you must always carry two knives with you. Those knives could one day save your life. Two, you must not let anyone, even close friends, know where you keep them," Miss Marjorie lectured.

Emma listened very closely. She had led an adventurous life and knew she was following in her path.

Miss Marjorie continued, "May and I have talked about where the second knife could be hidden." She pulled a small box from under her shawl and opened it; inside lay a small knife, about 6 inches long, with a leather sheath and a tie. "This will fit best around your upper thigh. We will cut a slit in your skirt pockets that will allow easy access. Let me show you how to put it on." Emma pulled up her skirt so Miss Marjorie could place the sheath on her leg. Emma let the skirt drop and Miss Marjorie reached over and quickly tore a hole in Emma's skirt pocket to show her how to access it.

"Should we place it on the inside of my leg, in case I am checked for knives?" asked Emma, worried someone might confiscate the second knife.

Miss Marjorie thought for a moment before saying, "Since you are a woman, I don't expect they will think you clever enough to have a clutch piece on you." She continued with a warning. "You will need to practice pulling it out and not cutting yourself."

"May?" she called gently, looking over Emma's shoulder.

"Yes," Miss May said breathlessly, "I have it right here." Emma turned at the other woman's voice.

"You startled me!" she said with a laugh.

"This is for you," Miss May said before handing Emma a hatbox.

Emma let out an excited squeak as she pulled off the box top and saw the beautiful black felt bowler hat with a dashing red lace ribbon and a red feather. She slowly took it out of the box, careful not to crush the delicate piece.

Miss Marjorie said sharply, "Emma, hand that to me. You must be careful. This is a special hat." Emma gingerly handed it to her.

Miss Marjorie pulled the "hatpin" out of the hat. The "pin" was a very lethal-looking knife with a black handle. Miss Marjorie threw it and hit the center of the target.

"That is no simple hat pin," Emma said as she went to retrieve it.

"No," Miss Marjorie agreed. Emma returned and handed her the knife. She continued, "I had Mark, my smith, balance it for you. I also asked May to put a compartment where the hatpin should go, so you can have this with you always. You must treat it carefully." The feather was attached directly to the hat and the knife had a special holder to protect Emma from being cut.

Emma nodded. "I'll be careful."

She noticed the intricate red lacework that accented the base of the hat, immediately recognizing Miss May's work, and gave her a long hug. Miss May teared up as she hugged her back.

Miss Marjorie cleared her throat; she wanted to get back to business. "Now," she said, "we need to work on removing the knife from the hat and throwing it in one smooth motion."

Emma nodded, serious and intent on the instructions she was given. She put the hat on her head and started practicing pulling the knife out and throwing it. The act took a bit of practice, but she managed to hit her targets.

Miss Marjorie commented, "You will have to continue to practice with both knives, but remember their location should stay a secret until they need to be used."

"Thank you, Miss Marjorie," said Emma and hugged her.

"Well," she said, patting Emma's shoulder, "we would do anything for you, dear."

After knife throwing, Emma spent the rest of the morning working with Papa on math equations and engineering designs for his company. She worked on Papa's draft table in the study, updating changes to the current building project drawings.

After the sketches were updated, there were clean-up duties and lunch to help with. Boarders were usually already off to work and school, so lunch was often just family, Miss May, and Miss Marjorie.

Papa noticed Emma's new hat perched on a nearby table. She saw the direction of his considering gaze and said in a rushed tone, "Papa, Miss May, and Miss Marjorie made that for me."

Papa looked to the ladies at the table. "That is a lovely hat, ladies, and a very thoughtful gift," he said. Both ladies blushed at the compliment.

"Emma," said Miss Marjorie, "you must not leave it out." She squinted her eyes as she issued the warning.

"That's right," said Emma. "I don't want it to get damaged." She picked it up carefully, took it to her bedroom, and placed it in a box under her bed. She had shown Dora the hat and the secret. Dora would be the only person to know about the knife, but no one would know where she hid her second one.

Emma's afternoon included reading and working on several lace designs. The day slowly wound down with the familiar routine of getting dinner on the table. Boarders filed in and conversation flowed about the day's events.

Miss May looked over at Emma. "We need to work on those new designs tonight and complete Dora's overlay."

Emma nodded and smiled. She enjoyed the lacework and wanted to show her some of the ideas she had drawn up earlier that day. The evening wrapped up with her working patterns and lace with Miss May. The intricate patterns were laced together and prepared to be delivered to the seamstress.

CHAPTER 4

The next morning, Emma wanted to discuss something with Papa. She went down to his basement lab and work area. "Papa," she called, watching as he sat at his work table, analyzing several types of concrete for defects.

When Papa was working on a project, he did not hear anything around him.

Emma tried again, this time tapping his arm.

"What!" Papa said, startled. He almost fell off his chair trying to see who was behind him.

"Nothing, Papa," Emma said with a grin and brushed the hair off his forehead. "You got tied up in your work again."

He grabbed her in a bear hug. "Don't do that again," he said with a chuckle. "What is it I can do for you? Is it time for lessons already?" he asked as he continued to look absently down at the concrete and other papers on his workbench.

"Well," Emma said, "I have a favor to ask."

"A favor, you say?" asked Papa and looked at her thoughtfully. Though she was a gifted student who could look at a building and calculate the angles without the aid of an instrument to measure, Papa knew she preferred being outside where things were happening. He had an idea of where this conversation was going. When Tim dropped Emma off yesterday, he had stopped by and brought up the idea of Emma going on deliveries with him. They worked out a plan that would allow Emma to join him when she felt ready. He had not expected the request to be so sudden. He took a deep breath as she began.

"Papa," Emma started nervously, "I would like to work with the delivery boys when I'm not at the bakery or helping out around here."

He took a moment to explain what this might mean. "Sister. . . After the incident." His eyes welled up with tears.

"I know, Papa, but you also know that I have worked with the specialists you brought in and I know how to protect myself," she said as she looked him steadily in the eyes. She did not show any emotion and refused to let the past affect her plans.

The event Papa was referencing was when Emma was about ten years old. She had started working the morning shift at the bakery and usually walked home alone before having lunch at the boarding house. The walk was normally uneventful, but that day she had taken a slightly different path to see some new neighborhoods. When she tried to remember details from that day, it only came in flashes. She remembered her notebook, something hard-hitting her head, and a man who was on the smallish side, but very strong.

She did not know how to defend herself and was almost beaten to death that morning. She was saved by someone who had interrupted the beating, forcing the attacker to run off. He got her back to the boarding house, left her on the doorstep, and knocked on the door before leaving. Tony and Tim were there for lessons with Papa and had answered the door to discover Emma lying on the stoop. As they moved her into the house, they heard her continually asking for her notebook. She was nearly unconscious, but she still wanted that book.

They never found out who saved her that day, and the notebook was never found. Papa had looked and put out feelers but was unable to learn who had beaten her up or who had rescued her.

Emma woke asking for her notebook, but she didn't know why she felt such urgency about it. Her memory continued to be a concern; the doctor indicated this was normal and she may never recover her memory of that day.

Papa had let Emma take time to recover. Dora, Tony, and Papa kept her company, reading to her and making her laugh again. They knew when they found her attempting to walk around by herself that there would be no holding her back.

Papa then set plans into motion to start protecting Emma as soon as possible, knowing her sense of adventure was so much a part of who she was.

His plan involved building a group of specialists who would teach Emma and Dora how to protect themselves. The first of these specialists—Papa's friend Danny Madden—moved in soon after the event occurred. Danny's particular specialty was self-defense methods. He believed in the importance of physical fitness and self-defense. They worked on kickboxing, parasol defense, shin-kicking, and jump kicking.

Emma had excelled at kickboxing and had started wearing special pointed boots in her training. She learned that her elbows and knees could deter most would-be villains. For the more serious attacks, her split skirt would help her utilize her kickboxing skills. Dora participated in the self-defense with Danny, but over time decided that her plans would not require Papa's other specialist training.

～

"Papa, you know I can take care of myself," said Emma, bringing them both out of the past.

"I know, Sister. I would not want to come up against you in a fight," he teased lightly, but still looked concerned. *It has been six years, and still, we have not found the man who attacked her,* he thought.

"Papa," she tried again, "you know Tim and Tony will look out for me." They were as close as brothers and let her tag around with them. Nobody messed with them and they kept out of trouble. Papa knew both boys well; he could trust them.

Papa said, "Ja, this is good." Though Papa was English, he had picked up the German expressions from their extended family. "If you get them to agree, you stay with them and you give me a hug." He smiled at Emma and she grinned back, hugging him.

"Emma," he said, "you must always wear the pointed boots."

"I will, Papa," she said and turned to go back upstairs. Before she got very far, Papa grabbed her lightly by her ponytail, gave it a quick tug, and let her go on her way.

Papa called after her as she ascended the stairs. "Oh, by the way, we will be doing some math tonight." She groaned but knew there would be a compromise. "One more thing, you must have breakfast first."

"On my way now," she said, racing up the stairs.

Papa smiled as he watched her leave the basement. He had some lingering fears, but he knew she had the training to take care of herself and Tim and Tony would keep an eye on her. He went back to his work, settled on his decision.

The breakfast ritual had started again, and the families were filling in chairs around the laden table. No one missed breakfast at the boarding house.

Emma entered the kitchen and asked, "Dora, what can I take to the table?"

Dora and Amy started handing her dishes of eggs and

sausages. They followed her in with trays of pastry, toast, and biscuits.

As they made one more trip to the kitchen to retrieve pitchers of milk and orange juice. Emma stopped Dora before she picked them up. "I don't have time to sit to eat. I'm going to help with the deliveries for Cousin's today."

Dora looked up at this news, concerned, but she knew there would be no holding her back. "Papa agreed?" she asked casually

Emma groaned a bit. "Yes, Mama," she teased. "Papa approves. Do you?"

Dora looked at Emma and said with a serious expression, "You are not my daughter, but you are my sister and best friend. Take care of yourself out there. Will you be with Tim and Tony?"

"Yes. Want me to take a note to Tim?" she asked cheekily.

"Oh, you," she said and swatted Emma on her behind. "Take something with you to eat." They both picked up the pitcher and moved them to the dining room.

Emma followed her and made a quick bacon and egg sandwich before dashing up the stairs. She finished eating it before reaching the second floor. Making her way to the small spare room to the left, off of the main hallway, she was looking for the items previous boarders had left behind.

Emma opened the door and entered the room. Moving the piled-up boxes out of her way, she sought a dresser located on the far side of the small room. She searched through the drawers until she found a pair of men's pants, a white shirt, and a well-worn newsboy cap. Undressing quickly, she pulled on the found clothes and pulled her long blonde hair into a tight braid, coiling it inside of the cap.

Emma wanted to see if the disguise worked on people who knew her. She remembered Miss Marjorie's advice and slipped out of the pants to look closely at the pockets. She slit the seam in the right one to allow access to the knife she had secured to her thigh. Practicing, she pulled it in and out of its hiding place. Her pointed boots were visible, her pants covering only the tops of the shoes. *Not exactly boyish*, she thought, *but they would have to do. I wonder if a knife could be added to my shoes, no one would expect that.* She would have to talk to Miss Marjorie about that.

She walked into the kitchen and saw Dora there, kneading dough for rolls at the table. Barely sparing Emma a glance when she asked quizzically, "Sister, what is that you're wearing?"

"You recognized me?"

Dora raised an eyebrow at the question. Emma was disappointed she hadn't fooled her.

"Yes, now what are you planning?" asked Dora. Emma told her the plan and how she would ask Tony and Tim to look out for her. She nodded and said, "If Papa is good, then I am also, but be careful. Tell Tim I'll have his hide if anything happens to you."

"His hide, huh? Is that all you want?" Emma teased, bringing a blush to Dora's face.

Dora made a dash for her around the table, but Emma was too fast.

The two sisters squared off across the table, and Dora was the first to stop. "Sister, don't stay out too late. Here, take a lunch with you since you won't be at Cousin's today." She handed her a bag packed with roast beef on a hard roll. "Also, there's a Berliner in there for a morning snack."

"Can I have one for Tim and Tony?" Emma wheedled.

Dora held out her hand to retrieve the bag and graciously gave in to the request, adding extra Berliners.

Berliner Pfannkuchen
  Ingredients:

  - 4 cups all-purpose flour

- 1 and 1/2 ounce of fresh yeast
- 1/4 cup sugar
- 3/4 cup lukewarm milk
- 5 egg yolks
- 2 and 1/2 ounces of butter at room temperature
- Salt
- Vegetable oil for frying
- German jellies such as raspberry, cherry, plum, or apricot

Description:

- Place the flour in a bowl; make a well in the center. Crumble the yeast into it with 1 tablespoon of sugar and 3 tablespoons of lukewarm milk. Mix and allow to stand in a warm place for about 15 minutes.
- Add the remaining milk, sugar, egg yolks, room temperature butter, and a pinch of salt to the dough and knead into a smooth dough with hands. Mix until the dough appears to detach easily from the sides of the bowl.
- Allow the dough to rise in a warm place until it doubles in size (approx. 30-60 minutes).
- Roll out the dough into 3/4-inch thickness on a floured surface and cut out circles approximately 3 inches in diameter using a glass or cup. Allow the cut-out dough circles to stand for a further 10 minutes, covered with a dishtowel.
- Pour 2-3 inches of canola oil into a large saucepan, heat to 370F. Lower the donuts into the hot oil 2 to 3 at a time and fry until they puff up and turn golden brown.

- Remove the fried donuts from the oil with a slotted spoon and allow to drain on paper towels.
- Allow the donuts to cool, then fill them with jam. Sprinkle with confectioners' sugar and enjoy!

Dora walked around the table and handed Emma the full bag. As Emma absently took it, her mind already on other things, Dora took the opportunity to pop her on the behind.

"Hey!" yelped Emma, jumping a bit. The boy's pants provided little to no padding between Dora's hand and her behind.

"You deserved it." She wagged her finger at Emma but had a sparkle in her eyes.

"Yes," said Emma with a cheeky grin, "and I'll continue to do so." She headed out at a jog and waved to the boarders still sitting in the dining room talking. Bounding down the front stoop, she took the steps two at a time. Stopping abruptly, she remembered that the delivery boys rarely had clean faces. She bent down at the base of the stoop where some flowers were planted and rubbed dirt on her face and hands. *No reason to go further with putting dirt on my arms and legs since they won't be seen,* she told herself.

How to approach Tim? She thought for a moment and started to drum her fingers against her lips until she remembered that her hands were dirty. *Well,* she thought, *the best way is to be me and be direct.* He was around the bakery off and on during the day, so she headed that way on foot.

Her watcher had a habit of sleeping at times when Emma was supposed to be home. *What a contrary girl,* he thought, just as he nodded off. The sound of her boots scraping on the concrete woke him with a start. He shook his head to clear it. *Okay,* he mumbled to himself, *we are on the move.* He noticed something different about Emma. *Boy clothes today? Interesting.*

~

She headed toward the bakery and was about halfway there when she saw Tim on his wagon.

"Hey, Tim!" she called, but he kept on without stopping. He did raise a hand and waved her way absently, but didn't direct his gaze toward her. She knew he did not recognize her, so she ran up to the side of the wagon. "Tim, I have a favor to ask of you," she said hurriedly as she jogged beside him.

That voice made him pull the wagon over to a stop and he turned. Quick as a whip, he grabbed Emma's hat off of her head. "Well, well, playing a bit of dress-up?" he mocked and bounced back into the wagon seat, still holding her hat. He tilted his head and gave her a wide grin, the type that takes up the whole face and crinkles up the skin around his eyes.

He had expected to see Emma at some point today. Her papa had sent a note to let him know she had his permission to ask about being a delivery driver. He had not expected her to be dressed as a boy. *Though,* he thought, *it makes things much safer and a lot less trouble.*

"What's up, Little Bit?" he asked.

Emma had thought about how to ask him but spoiled the plan by rushing into the question. "I need a favor. Can I hang out with the delivery drivers and help on the routes?"

He pretended he needed a moment to think about her question. "I'm not sure, Emma. We go into some rough neighborhoods," he said cautiously.

"I could stay with you or Tony," she coaxed. "I just want some adventure, to not be stuck inside all day."

He understood. He wouldn't want that either. "Okay," he said, knowing her papa trusted him and that she could handle herself. Tim and Tony were aware that Emma's papa had made sure Dora and Emma practiced self-defense and both knew some nasty tricks to get out of tight spots. "Just don't give yourself away to the other guys. Well, except for Tony. And stick close," he said with a serious expression on his face. Tim and Tony could be overprotective since the incident.

"Also," he continued, "we have an opening. Rudy's family moved and we could use the help. You'll make the lowest pay since you're the new guy."

She nodded and exclaimed, "That's great." And since she hadn't expected to get paid, any amount would be nice.

"Though you might want to try walking a bit differently. You walk like a girl," he remarked, tossing her hat back at her.

Emma nabbed the hat in midair and replied smartly, "Well, that's what I am."

"If you want to be taken for a boy, just keep your hips from swaying and keep the talking to a minimum," he suggested.

As she attempted to climb into the wagon, he dashed her dreams of working deliveries.

"Not today. Meet me at the bakery first thing Monday morning and practice walking like a boy," he said.

"Can't I come on your afternoon deliveries today?" she asked, disappointed. "I have Berliners and I can give you one if you let me go." She shook the bag at him as a bribe.

He had already spotted it and deftly snapped it from her hand.

"Well, I have the bag now, and you definitely can't start today. Once I finish my morning deliveries, my afternoon ones involve heavy lifting," he said. He also wanted to tell Tony what Emma was up to. Tony was his best friend and he knew the boy had special feelings for Emma, even though she chose to ignore those feelings.

"Okay, but can I have my sandwich?" asked Emma.

"Yes, I can do that," said Tim as he reached into the bag, retrieved her sandwich, and tossed it to her.

"Thanks," she said, turning to head back home, feeling both parts excited at the job and a bit sad she couldn't start right away.

As Emma walked off, Tim made a clicking sound to move the horse and wagon on to their next delivery.

CHAPTER 5

*T*ony came to the boarding house for dinner that night. She noticed he looked more serious than she had ever seen him. He sat by her at dinner and didn't say much, but did eat his fill of Dora's cooking. Papa had a good idea of why he was there and let the matter stay between Emma and Tony.

Just as dinner was being cleared from the table by Amy, Emma, and Dora, Tony placed his hand on Emma's. "I'd like to talk with you," he said quietly.

Emma glanced at Dora questioningly, who only nodded.

Emma and Tony were best friends and occasional partners in crime. She looked up at him and said, "Okay." It wasn't a surprise that he wanted to talk; she figured Tim had informed him about her plans. "Walk around the block?" she suggested.

"Yes," he said. He was much quieter than usual with her. His head hung a bit forward, his silky brown hair falling into his eyes as they exited the boarding house.

Once they were outside, they began the walk silently, side by side, not touching. "Emma," Tony started, looking down the street and, for once in her life, Emma did not interrupt him.

Tony was surprised she had not already spoken over him and had paused, expecting it. He took a deep breath to start again. "Emma, I know your Papa, Dora, and Tim have all said it's okay for you to start working deliveries with us, but will it be safe for you?"

Because she did know Tony, she let him talk. She kept her gaze averted toward the houses down the block. She could see more than just the street ahead of her; she could see her future starting to form. "Tony, it's time. Time for me to have an adventure and see all of Chicago and then, eventually, the world. You know that." She paused a moment, continuing to look down the street. "Tell me something. If I hadn't been hurt, would you still be so protective of me?"

He stopped her, put his hand on her arm, and turned her toward him. He reached out and tilted her chin to look him in the eye. "I honestly don't know. I think not. I want your every dream to come true but, Emma, I can't forget that day and carrying your broken body into your house." His voice broke for a moment.

"I know," she said earnestly, "and you were amazing, coming every day to sit with me; reading and talking to me when I was going out of my head from boredom. Tony," she paused and grabbed his hand, "you know I can handle myself." That event changed how she saw herself and how she wanted to be seen. She saw her previous self as weak. She was a much stronger person now and wanted him to see her that way.

"Yes," Tony said, having participated in some training exercises with her. He was aware of how well she could fight. He thought to himself, *she changed so much after that event. The adventurer is still there, but there is a new strength as well.*

"Emma," he said passionately, "I want you to enjoy your life and become the person you are meant to be. You are sixteen now, but I want to know you at eighteen, twenty-five, forty-five, sixty-five. . ."

This made her laugh. That was Tony, planning, and planning. At sixteen, she wasn't ready to know if she was in his plans, but for now, she wanted him as her friend, her best friend.

"You will be careful." It was more of a statement than a question.

"Yes," said Emma.

As they turned back toward her home, they continued walking side by side. Tony threw an arm around her shoulder and squeezed.

"Besides," teased Emma, "won't I see you first thing Monday morning, prior to my first delivery day?" She bumped against him with her hip. He had always acted like it was just chance, running into her and walking with her to the bakery.

"I'll be there as usual to walk you that morning," Tony said, admitting for the first time that he did plan to join her. "To be clear, it's not to protect you, but to keep me safe." With that statement, they laughed until they reached her stoop.

"See you," he said and watched her enter the boarding house. He thought about Emma all the way home.

"See you," Emma said softly and then closed the door. Her thoughts were on Tony and next week.

CHAPTER 6

*S*aturday came around faster than Emma had expected. She had laid her yellow and white dress with green trim on the bed. Dora walked into Emma's bedroom twirling around, showing off her bright blue gown with a beautiful lace overlay. Emma clapped and smiled, delighted her sister was so happy.

"Oh, Emma, the dress looks brand new. Thank you so much for adding the lace for me. What do you think? How do I look?" Dora asked excitedly, turning toward the mirror and patting her upswept hair.

"I think Tim will love it," Emma teased, answering the unspoken question. Dora turned a delightful shade of red but did not contradict the statement.

"Sister, Dora, your ride has arrived," called Amy from downstairs.

Dora opened the door and turned back to Emma. "Sister, are you ready to go?" she asked, distracted, thinking about Tim.

Emma looked at her a bit puzzled. She had not put on her dress as yet. Deciding to give Dora a break, she said gently,

"Almost, I'll meet you downstairs." She knew how important the dance was to both Tim and Dora.

Dora patted her hair again then headed downstairs.

Tim heard something and looked up; everything seemed frozen in place for a moment. As Dora stepped into the foyer, he said, "Dora, you look beautiful." It was the most personal statement he had ever offered her.

"Thank you," she said, glowing with the compliment, "and you look very handsome."

"Great," he said. "Let's go." He grabbed her by the hand and started pulling her toward the door. He had completely forgotten about everything except her.

She dug in her heels as he tried to pull her along. "Tim, we have to wait for Sister," she reminded him.

He shook his head as if to clear it. "Oh, that's right," he said as he glanced down and realized he still had her hand. Instead of dropping it, he tugged her toward him and gave her their first kiss. It was sweet and strong, just like Tim.

Dora's world tilted and her eyes closed as she enjoyed the moment.

Emma was coming down the stairs in her standard rush and realized she might be interrupting something. She stopped and leaned against the banister. "Hi, Tim. Do I get one of those also?" she teased.

Tim turned red but did snag her arm for a kiss on the cheek once she reached the landing.

The three smiled at each other. "Is Papa coming with us?" asked Emma.

"No," Dora said. "He has a late meeting. Tim's family will meet us there."

"Emma," Tim said innocently, "Tony asked if he could ride over with us tonight. I told him it was okay."

Emma nodded and said with a smile, "That will be nice."

Tim turned around and smiled to himself. *Tony would be happy with that response.*

He helped Dora up on the buggy seat of the wagon, using a box on the sidewalk to help with the difficult dress. He went around and swung Emma into the back of the wagon. He had cleaned it out and laid a blanket down for comfort. As they started toward the dance, Tony came running up behind them. Tim didn't stop and Tony ran to jump into the back with Emma.

"Hey," he said, nodding to Tim and Dora. "Hey, Emma." He bounced a bit as he sat down next to her.

"Hey yourself, Tony. What's up? Did you work today?" she asked, always interested in what the boys were up to.

"Yes, I got some extra deliveries for the curator at the museum," he answered.

"Anything interesting in the delivery package?" she continued.

He nodded. "It was some new sketches from a local artist. The curator was there and let me watch while he unpackaged them." They continued to discuss the museum until they arrived at the dance.

It was the End of Spring Dance at their church. It was colorful and lively, with a band and lots of people. As they entered the crowded room, Emma glanced around, seeing refreshment tables stretching along the walls, chairs set up for people to rest between dances, and finally a dance floor and a band.

Emma and Dora had dropped off the German chocolate cake for the dessert table earlier in the day. As Tim and Tony helped them with their coats, Emma was already eyeing the other refreshments.

German Chocolate Cake
Ingredients:

- 5 eggs
- 8 ounces carrots
- 10.5 ounces of sugar
- Zest from 1 lemon and 2 tablespoons of lemon juice
- 2.64 ounces of flour
- 1 tablespoon of baking powder
- 1 tablespoon of breadcrumbs
- 1 tablespoon of butter
- 5 ounces of ground hazelnuts
- 5 ounces of ground walnuts

Glaze

- 7 ounces of powdered sugar
- 3 tablespoons of hot water

Directions:

1. Grate carrots finely; separate eggs; beat yolk with sugar until foamy; add lemon zest and juice; add flour and baking powder.
2. Mix dough very well; add carrots and nuts.
3. Beat egg white until firm and mix it with the dough.
4. Grease a 10-inch diameter spring form with butter and breadcrumbs and fill in the dough; spread the surface evenly.
5. Bake it in preheated oven at 390F for about 55 minutes (lowest level).
6. Take out the cake and let it cool off.

7. Mix powdered sugar with hot water and spread it
   evenly over the cake.

Emma danced with Tony and Tim—when Tim could be pried away from Dora. She looked around and noticed Chloe was watching Cousin dance with multiple partners. She went over to her and asked in a whisper, "What are you doing? Go dance with him."

"Nope," she said, "that's not the way I'll get him to notice me. I have another idea." She approached the band and asked to set in for the next song. She had never done this before and Emma noticed that Cousin's eyes followed her graceful figure to the bandstand. He was talking to another girl but waved her off as he continued to watch Chloe.

Cousin was curious when Chloe pointed to a small case she carried. The band leader nodded his head and invited her up on the bandstand. She climbed the stairs quickly joining them. She opened her case and pulled out a violin and bow. Cousin watched her test the bow and tighten the strings. She raised the violin to her chin and nodded to the bandleader. She drew the bow across the strings and began a lively jig, the other players joining in.

It was entertaining and had Cousin's full attention. He started clapping his hands, realizing he was enjoying himself for the first time that night. *Hmm, I might have an interest in violins,* he thought and took a harder look at Chloe.

Emma watched Chloe in amazement and shook her head. She went on with her night, mostly watching the other dancers, walking around with Tony, listening as he described various things at the museum while they ate many of the delicious desserts. They both gave a small wave as they spotted Tim and Dora with Tim's aunt and uncle.

After the dance ended, the four gathered back together and located the wagon to head home. It was a quiet night and all four just let the comfortable silence linger. They stopped at the boarding house and Tony helped Emma down from the back of the wagon. They said their goodbyes and she headed up the stoop. Tony watched until she went in and turned to say good-night to Tim and Dora. He raised his hand but realized they couldn't see anything but each other. Slowly he let his arm drop and turned toward home with a spring in his step.

Tim and Dora sat a bit longer before getting out of the wagon. They continued looking into each other's eyes. Dora was the first to speak. "Well, I should go in," she said.

That got Tim moving, and he jumped down from the wagon and walked around to her side. "Let me help you down." He twirled her around to the sidewalk.

"Tim, I had a wonderful time," murmured Dora, still locked in his arms.

"Me too," he agreed, not letting her go. "Dora, would you like to go to church with me tomorrow?" he asked. As she was about to nod, he continued, "And to the park for a picnic next Saturday and then. . ."

He would have kept going, but Dora touched his hand with hers. "Tim, I would love to go anywhere you would like to go."

Grinning, Tim squeezed his arms around her and kissed her until her knees shook. He walked her to the door and kissed her again. Stepping back from her, he smashed his hat back onto his head and started down the steps of the stoop two at a time.

He had turned to the right of the steps and was on his way home when Dora called, "Tim?"

He looked up at her, still grinning, and asked, "Yes?"

"Tim, you live that way," she said gently, indicating to the left with her hand.

He glanced both left and right and realized she was right. He turned left and started toward home again.

"Tim?" she called again.

He looked up at her again and inquired, "Yes, Dora?"

"You forgot your wagon," she commented with a small giggle.

His face turned a bit red. He looked around and was able to locate the wagon. He made his way to it and climbed up on the seat, picked up the reigns, and turned to say to Dora, "All good now?" He waited for her nod and then headed home.

Dora continued to laugh softly at his antics as she went inside.

As she closed the door, she leaned on it and looked dreamily up toward the landing on the staircase where Emma waited patiently for her. She hurried upstairs to talk to her, ready to share secrets late into the night.

CHAPTER 7

*F*irst thing Monday morning, before the day broke, Emma started toward the bakery. The only difference was, this time, she was dressed like a delivery boy. Tony met her on the walk as usual with a casual greeting.

Her watcher saw the two boys and realized one was Tony. He couldn't hear them, but he saw that, when Tony pulled off the other boy's hat, a bright blonde braid came flowing down her back. It was Emma. *So, off on an adventure*, he thought. It would make his job harder but he would follow.

She practiced walking like a boy on the way to the bakery. Tony swatted Emma on the butt with her hat and gave it back to her to put on before the other boys saw her.

"Emma," he said, "stay in the back entrance near the wagons. I'm sure the cousins will recognize you faster than I did."

She nodded, thinking she should let Cousin know that she would be working deliveries for a while. She would go see him later that day.

The other boys started arriving. Emma didn't make eye contact and pulled her hat lower over her eyes. She stood next to Tim's wagon and waited for him.

Dear-one commented, "They knew from the beginning."

"Who knew what?" the Narrator asked, distracted when she realized he was reading over her shoulder.

"They knew Emma was a girl. They just didn't let on," he said.

"Hmm," she said, "that puts a few things into perspective." She grinned at Dear-one.

Dear-one just raised an eyebrow at her and said, "You will have to tell me what you mean."

"Maybe later," she said, getting back to her writing.

Back at the bakery...

As the other boys arrived, they parked their wagons and headed in for their deliveries. They normally contained pies, cakes, assorted loaves of bread, and other small pastries. These were brought out and carefully placed into the wagons. The bakery had several horse-drawn wagons with special lockboxes for the baked goods. Other local deliveries would be made via pull wagons or bags.

Tim and Tony were part of the group of drivers. Emma wanted to go on one of those because they journeyed deeper into the city and she wanted to see as much as possible.

Tim exited the bakery with the first load of bread, cakes, and pies. He motioned for Emma to help load them into the lockbox on the wagon. She climbed up on the back and he handed over the items. It took several trips before they could be on their way. After the final items were placed in the box and it was locked, she jumped down to the ground. She moved to the front to climb up to the buggy seat when Tony walked over.

He playfully pulled Emma's hat over her eyes and gave her a crooked grin. "Tim, you and. . .?" he asked.

"EJ," Emma filled in. EJ being short for Emma Jane.

"Okay, you and EJ have a good day," he said, emphasizing EJ. He looked to Tim with narrowed eyes.

Tim nodded at the silent question.

Tony nodded and headed back to his wagon; it was time to get the teams moving. Emma pulled out her notebook to document the day and the movement of people in the early morning.

Tim looked over at Emma and her ever-present black notebook. He couldn't remember when he first saw her using it; it had always been a part of her. The presence of that book did remind him of a bad day six years ago when he and Tony found her hurt on the stoop and all she could ask for was that notebook. She would continue to ask for it as she convalesced. They had never found it.

Tim had a list of the morning deliveries; most were routine, but there might be an addition to the schedule. "Emma, mark off each delivery as we make them," he said and handed her the list. Emma followed his directions as they started their deliveries, Tim instructed her to jump down and take them to the appropriate door.

When they pulled into a nicer area where all the homes were made of stone, Tim said, "Remember, you must go to the back door of these homes. The help will take the deliveries from you."

"I will," she said, familiar with the neighborhood. She had actually been in the front doors of many of these homes when Papa worked as an engineering consultant, updating the design requirements after the fire.

Tim handed down their orders of bread, pies, and a cake. She would have to make two trips. Making her way around the back of the building, she used her elbow to knock on the door. It opened quickly, revealing a tall, imposing housekeeper.

"Well, do you have something for Mr. Black?" she asked briskly. She was a woman who had things to get done and this little slip of a girl, dressed as a boy, was slowing her down.

"Yes, of course, your pies and cakes and assorted loaves of bread," Emma said as she was allowed into the kitchen to place the order on a large rectangular table. She inhaled the wonderful smells and noted the colors of the kitchen—black and white checked floors, white counters, and cabinets, and silver trays being prepared for the family's breakfast.

Emma quickly set the items down and made a second trip for the rest of the order. She placed it with the other baked goods on the kitchen table. "Well, on your way now, scoot," the housekeeper said, nudging her toward the door. The house-keeper's mind was on her schedule for the day.

"You there," Emma could hear her tell the maids and footmen in the kitchen, "get these pies, cakes, and loaves of bread put away." They went scurrying to carry out their task.

Emma headed out, trying to keep all of the details in her head to write down later. She jumped back into the wagon seat next to Tim without any help. She was already adopting more boyish mannerisms.

Tim noticed and the right side of his mouth quirked up, but he didn't say anything. The more boy-like she behaved, the safer she would be.

Emma didn't mind the work. She was so excited to be out and about. *There are so many people moving around, even in the early hours of the day. People on horses and trolley cars, on their way to work or just starting their days at home. Milk trucks trudging along slowly but surely on their routes.*

She took everything in on that first day: how the day changed, how the quiet streets filled with people, horses, buggies, and wagons. The noise started when the construction

NOTEBOOK MYSTERIES ~ EMMA

workers arrived for work. In Chicago, the rebuilding had been continuous since the fire. The buildings were going higher than anywhere else in the country. She could not wait to see the city from the new high views.

She was documenting the people she saw on the street corners. *It was interesting that the neighborhoods seemed to dictate the types of clothes people wore.* She observed that people living in the nicer neighborhoods had quieter, classy clothes, while the working areas had more rough clothes and the gaming areas were a bit flashier and more disreputable.

Tim interrupted her observation. "Emma, where are we on the list?"

She had it in her hand and read off the next two delivery locations.

"Got to keep our priories straight, Emma. We need to keep on schedule, and it's your responsibility to not let me miss a delivery," he reminded her.

"Oh, I won't miss one, I promise," she said and applied herself industriously, making sure the list stayed up-to-date. As she handled it, she kept looking around, making observations, and writing as fast as she could. She also added some notes to the delivery pages to help with identifying locations so she could be more helpful on the next trip.

As Emma continued her studies, she noticed the maids in the nicer neighborhoods had milk delivered to their doors and, in poorer ones, families carried pitchers to be filled by the driver on the trucks. A few hours into their deliveries, they started seeing businesses opening their doors and children being sent on their way to school.

Tim had indicated their routes had added more deliveries into working-class areas as women began working outside the home.

"Why is that?" asked Emma.

Tim answered, "The ladies no longer have time for baking

days, so the families' weekly bread and desserts are coming from us now."

As the morning wound down, Emma wanted to talk about everything she had seen.

Tim cautioned, "Emma, I love that you are happy to be working with me, but remember you will only be on the wagon a few days a week."

"I know," she muttered. "I just like being out and seeing so many things and people." She continued to talk about her day; a smile lit up her face, and Tim couldn't help but smile back.

Curiosity finally got the best of him. "What are you writing so often?" he asked, waving his hand toward the black notebook.

"Just what's happening around us," she said. Her face took on a more serious look as she continued, "I just don't want to miss something that might be important."

Over the next few weeks, Emma's schedule changed to allow her to spend more time with Tim on the delivery wagon. During those hours, she got to know the neighborhoods and the businesses on their route. She continued documenting her observations, looking for patterns in the people and their days.

In the evenings, she went over her notes and started grouping any that stood out. The first was around Stubbings, the large department store located on their route. There was something strange about Stubbing's daily large wagon deliveries, but she couldn't determine what it was. She transferred her observations from her general notebook to one that would focus just on that location.

She kept the two notebooks with her during the next week's deliveries. Emma also spent several afternoons after her shift at the bakery hanging around Stubbings, making notes on schedules and deliveries. The Stubbings' case book is filled with drawings and comments. There was something odd with the wheel height on the wagons being used for deliveries and returns at the Stubbings' dock.

Initially, she started making sketches of the different wheel heights to illustrate the difference based on the weight load of the truck. This allowed her to approximate the weights that would impact wheel height—how high or low the wagon sat on the wheels. By monitoring and documenting which types of trucks were delivered to the store, she was able to show that trucks leaving Stubbings were heavier than when they went in.

Patterns were also forming about the times of the deliveries. She kept separate notes and drawings on what the delivery drivers wore and their behavior.

She evaluated her notes after completing a few weeks' worth of observations. Organizing her findings, she felt she was ready to run the information by Tim to get his input before taking the next step. She waited until they were on the way to their first delivery before she broached the subject.

"Tim," she said determinedly, looking directly at him.

"Yes," he answered absently as he drove the wagon. He appeared to be looking ahead, concentrating on his driving, but his mind was actually on the next time he would see Dora.

"You asked about my observations and if anything comes from them?" she stated, keeping her voice flat, not wanting to sound too excited about her findings.

"Yes," he said again, this time slowing the wagon to a stop as he turned to look at her.

"The location we are at right now, this is where we usually are this time of day?" she asked, indicating Stubbings Department Store with her hand.

He nodded in confirmation.

"That truck has been here every day this week." She moved her head to indicate the large truck parked at the dock. "Correct?"

"Is there a point to this?" asked Tim, getting a bit exasperated. "We do have work, you know."

"I have a point, just a second," she said and continued sharing her findings. "In this area of town, delivery trucks come in and out to the various department stores, nice men's clothes shops and restaurants. I started thinking something was off about the Stubing trucks and personnel."

He waited more patiently for the rest, becoming interested. He did have one question, though. "What made you suspicious of these particular trucks?"

"Well, they all appear to be from the same company, but there are no insignias on the uniforms; the clothes the men wear doesn't match. And they are smoking. When I noticed those differences, I started monitoring the trucks," she said simply. "I also noticed something odd with the height of the wagon wheels when coming and going." She pulled out her notebook and showed him the drawings. "The wheels on the truck sit lower when the wagons are full. I compared the wheels on their trucks when they arrived and when they left. The trucks leaving should have more wheels showing; the truck here today routinely has a heavier load when leaving."

They were sitting with a clear view of the alley where the deliveries were completed for the store when Tim commented thoughtfully, "Well, that could be because they had returns to send back to the manufacturers."

"I don't think the difference would be that extreme, and the truck wouldn't be empty coming into the store," she commented.

"Anything else?" he asked, thinking through what she had shown him and rubbing his forehead with his right hand, keeping his left on the reins.

"That is it," she said as she snapped her notebook closed.

Tim looked up at the sky and appeared to be talking to a higher power when he said, "I just wanted to give her a chance to get out of the house and help with deliveries, but no, instead we are in the middle of an adventure." He shook his head in an exasperated manner.

He seemed to come to a decision and looked at her with narrowed eyes. "So, if you're right, it could be a long-term robbery."

"I think it might be," she said nonchalantly. And then she asked, "What should we do?"

"No cops," they both said at the same time. They knew that Mayor Harrison was in office and he was corrupt. The local gangsters in the area knew they could get away with anything.

"I have an idea," Tim said and parked the wagon at a nearby café. They jumped down and crossed the street, heading toward the Stubbings front entrance.

The store was not opened as yet, but they could see movement inside. Emma tapped lightly on the windows. At first, the personnel inside ignored them, but one figure came to the door when they recognized Emma and Tim from the bakery delivery cart. A woman in a black dress, ginger curls piled high on her head, unlatched the door but did not open it more than a crack. "What's up kids? Do you have some pastry for us this morning?" she asked and smiled at them.

"Is your manager here?" Tim asked, ignoring her question.

"Why? Need a job?" she joked. When they did not respond to her questions, she continued, "I am Miss Woods. Our offices will be open later today if you want to apply, though you are a bit young."

"No," Emma said, "we have some important information that your manager might want to know."

Her tone conveyed a seriousness that made Miss Woods cock her head. She seemed to come to a decision when she said, "Just a moment." She closed the door and latched the lock. They could see her hurrying through the store.

A few moments later, a tall, distinguished man dressed in a

dark blue suit with a crisp white shirt and matching tie, walked toward the door in an unhurried stride, followed by Miss Woods. He opened the door wide and asked them to come in.

"I'm Mark Jones, Head Manager of Stubbings. Miss Woods indicated you need to speak with me about something important. How can I help you?" he asked sincerely, looking them in the eyes as he spoke.

Tim nodded to Emma to begin. "Mr. Jones, we believe the delivery men on your dock are not delivering anything but are taking merchandise from your store."

He asked a simple question, without any inflection. "Why do you say that?"

Emma took out her black notebook to reference her notes. "Well, for one thing, the uniforms on the delivery drivers do not match the ones normally worn by your delivery drivers; secondly, they are smoking; finally, the wagons are fuller now than when they came in."

"How did you notice the wagons were fuller when leaving the store?" asked Mr. Jones curiously.

Emma referenced the engineering drawings within her notebook. "The truck is sitting lower." She pointed out the measurements.

"Hmm," Mr. Jones murmured, "the drawings remind me of someone. Are you, by chance, related to Mr. Evans, the structural engineer?"

"My papa," said Emma softly.

Mr. Jones seemed to come to a conclusion and turned to Miss Woods, saying in a commanding voice, "Can you get Mr. Taylor?" He turned back to the kids. "He is our Head of Security."

Miss Woods immediately went to find him.

She and a gentleman Emma assumed was Mr. Taylor arrived with about ten burly men. The men were looking to him for direction. *They must be the security staff*, thought Emma.

As she watched Mr. Jones interact with Mr. Taylor, she noticed there was something odd about his jacket. It seemed a bit larger than he needed in the chest area. She continued to study him when she realized the larger jacket must be covering a gun. She jotted down her observation of the people and their activities.

Mr. Jones looked at both kids and said, "You best be on your way. I will be in contact soon."

Emma and Tim headed out the way they entered. They were crossing the street when they saw Mr. Taylor and his men swarm out of the back-loading docks. They grabbed the delivery team loading the trucks and took the loading manager by the neck, pulling him into the store.

Emma and Tim got a front-row view. She shot Tim a wide-eyed look. "What will happen next?"

He shrugged. "I'm not sure. I think it depends on if the store wants to keep it quiet or involve the police."

"Should we wait?" she asked.

"No, I don't think so," he said. "Better to do the right thing and just be about our business."

"But didn't Mr. Jones say we would see him later?" she pointed out, still looking at the store.

"Yeah, but I think he's a bit busy at this point," Tim said wryly. "Come on." He and Emma climbed back into the wagon to continue with their day.

As they were leaving, Tim glanced at Emma, smirked, and said, "So, already stirring things up?" He continued with a warning. "I wouldn't mention our involvement in this to anyone." He made a clicking sound at the horses to be on their way.

They pulled the wagon out and began making deliveries on the road as if nothing had occurred. They had about an hour's worth of deliveries near Stubbings. She had hoped they would hear about the outcome from her observations but understood that could be dangerous. If one of the gangs was behind the theft, it was best that they were not mentioned. They continued on their way with people taking little notice of them.

Emma went back to jotting down other observations of their route. They finished for the day, and Tim dropped her off at home on his way to his afternoon deliveries. As she entered the house, she was thinking about the morning's events and how exciting it was to see her first case have a successful conclusion. Her head was down as she glanced at her notebook when she smelled butter and chocolate. She knew what was cooking in the kitchen and immediately headed toward it.

Inside, she found Amy working hard on cleaning up after lunch and Dora in the middle of dessert preparations for that evening. Emma's mouth watered when she saw the ingredients laid out, everything needed for a German Butter Cake with Egg Liquor.

German Butter Cake with Egg Liquor
    Ingredients:
    Biscuit Base Cake

- 2.82 ounces of butter
- 2.82 ounces of sugar
- 5 eggs
- 7 ounces of almonds, ground
- 3.5 ounces of chocolate, grated
- 1 package of vanilla sugar, 0.5 ounces
- 1 tablespoon of baking powder

Filling

- 2 tablespoons of flour

- 1 tablespoon of rum
- 7 ounces of butter
- 1 package of vanilla sugar, 0.5 ounces

Vanilla pudding

- 16.9 ounces of milk
- 3.5 ounces of sugar
- 1.35 ounces of egg liquor
- 3.5 ounces of grated almonds
- 1.76 ounces of sugar
- .70 ounces of butter
- Cherries

Directions:

Biscuit Base Cake

1. Mix 7.5 ounces of almonds, chocolate, vanilla sugar, flour, and baking powder.
2. Mix butter very well with sugar until sugar is dissolved; add one egg after the other.
3. Add almond-flour mix and fill the dough in a greased springform (diameter 26 centimeters).
4. Bake it at 390F for 15 minutes.

Filling

- Make the vanilla pudding with 3.5 ounces of sugar; let the pudding cool off to room temperature. Bring butter to room temperature.
- Place .70 ounces of butter and 1.8 ounces of sugar in a pan and roast the grated almonds until they are golden brown; let them cool off.
- Make a butter créme out of butter and pudding; stir butter and add carefully the pudding; mix well.
- Let cake cool off.
- Cut cake horizontally in half. You have 2 pieces.
- Place some of the créme into a decorating bag for later.
- Fill the cake on one half; place the other half on top and spread the créme all around the cake.
- Decorate the outer edge of the cake with roasted almonds and all around the top.
- Use cherries as decoration.

Emma tried to snag some of the cake batter, but Dora was too fast and pulled the bowl away. Emma sent her a sorrowful look and she soon relented and let her have a spoon to lick. Taking the proffered spoon, she sat down at the table to enjoy it. When she finished, she took it to the sink to wash it off.

"Tell us about your day," said Amy. She was curious about the city, but not curious enough to want to experience it, although she did enjoy Emma's stories.

Emma was very quiet as she moved to the icebox to pull out the ingredients for her lunch. Ice was delivered every 2-3 days to keep the food preserved. She took out the cheese and started building her sandwich. Dora and Amy looked at one another when Emma didn't start regaling them with her day's adventures. Normally, she would talk them to death with the details of her day. *What happened to make today different?* Dora wondered to herself.

Emma set the items on the table and grabbed a plate to construct her sandwich. She put the items back in the refrigerator and started out of the room with her meal. "I'm taking my sandwich upstairs," she said, so distracted by her thoughts she forgot to answer Amy's question. She was already opening her black notebook as she went up the staircase.

Amy looked at Dora, and Dora shrugged. *I'll have to check in with her later*, thought Dora as she went back to her flavorful dessert.

Meanwhile, Emma was making her way to the desk in her room. She finished her sandwich and started adding closure notes on the case of the Stubbings store thieves. It was an exciting case, but she was a little disappointed not to be involved in the takedown. *Maybe in the future*, she thought. Closing the book on that case, she put it away.

She pulled out her general black notebook and started looking at her notes from the previous weeks to see if they could be moved into an individual case book.

Neighborhoods have a rhythm to them, she thought as she continued to think about the different areas of Chicago. The rich residential areas were quiet with the only early morning activity being deliveries of milk, papers, and bakery items. The quiet on the outside of the houses was not indicative of the actual work going on in the downstairs area. Personnel worked hard to ready themselves for the day. Many of these houses required baked goods to start their day.

The working-class neighborhoods were already familiar to Emma since her family lived in that area. Many living there owned businesses or were professional people. The families had help for their households; some lived in and some did not. The middle class both bought and made bakery items.

They didn't deliver as much to the people of lesser means;

most of these ladies made their bread and, if pastries or other treats were wanted, they were of the day-old variety. Cousin sent day-old pies and cakes for these neighborhoods and the money made from these was split between the delivery drivers.

They also had Gamblers Row on their route. These streets were as quiet as the other business areas. They weren't street gangs but had business establishments that kept their goings-on hidden from the police. They were also good bakery customers. Cousin figured business was business and, if they were paying, he would supply Berliners, cakes, and loaves of bread. They were nice enough, but Tim took no chances and had Emma stay with the wagon during these deliveries.

She completed her review and snapped her notebook closed. *It's time to work on homework and knife throwing*, she thought as she got changed and went downstairs.

That evening was quiet with the family and boarders scattered downstairs, talking, doing homework, and other things. A knock sounded at the door. "I'll get it," Emma said as she hopped up. She opened the door to a postal delivery man. He handed her two envelopes and asked her to sign for them. She signed for the letters and closed the door. Looking at both envelopes, she saw one for Tim and one for her. Opening the one with her name on it, she saw it was from the Stubbings store manager they had assisted that morning. It said simply, "Thank you" and enclosed in the envelope was fifty dollars. She was stunned for a moment and realized Tim's envelope most likely also contained fifty dollars.

"Emma, who was at the door?" Papa called.

"No one. It was nothing," she said absently. Carrying the cards and thinking about the money, she went slowly upstairs. Tomorrow was her workday at the bakery, she would give him his envelope then. Prying off her bedpost she hid her money and card in the slot. As she put it back on, she thought, *I kept my word and didn't tell anyone about the adventure, that also means the money has to stay a secret.* It was safer for everyone if they kept quiet.

She carried Tim's card to the bakery the next morning. She said goodbye to Tony as he left for his deliveries and headed inside. She turned back around and called, "Hey, Tony."

"Yes?" he responded.

"Could you tell Tim to find me when he gets here?" she asked.

"Sure," he said, curious about why, but since she talked to Tim most days, it didn't seem out of the ordinary.

Tim got the message and came in looking for Emma. He spotted her and went over to her workstation.

"You wanted to see me?" he asked with an easy grin.

She nodded her head toward the coat closet. Tim looked questioningly but shrugged and did as she asked.

After they stepped into the closet, she shut the door and handed him his envelope. She said, with little emotion, trying to keep the excitement out of her voice, "I got these last night. I opened mine and I think you're going to like it."

He slowly opened the envelope and paused when he saw it was money. He teared up for a moment and thought, *This will pay for the rest of my school and allow me to become an accountant.* He was shocked and just stood there, not moving. He looked directly at her but could see so much more than just that closet at that point.

"Tim," Emma said and touched his hand.

It seemed to wake him up. He shook his head. "Yes?" he asked.

"I can keep the card and you can come by and pick it up this evening at the house," she suggested with a smile.

He nodded and said, "Yes, I don't want to be carrying this around today on deliveries." He handed her back the card and money. She tucked it into her dress pocket.

He grabbed her and hugged her fiercely. He left to begin his day, whistling on his way out of the bakery.

Emma went to her workstation to continue her task list for that day.

Tony was curious about the meeting but knew that Tim's heart belonged to Dora. He made a mental note to ask about that meeting at a later date and headed on his way for his morning deliveries.

CHAPTER 8

A few weeks later, Tim and Emma were making their way to one of the social clubs, also commonly known as a gambling house, for a delivery. She sat in the wagon while Tim carried the pies and cakes to the back door located in the alley. She was making notes and glancing around when she noticed a slight man leaning against the alley wall, smoking. He looked very familiar and she realized why. He was one of the "delivery drivers" they had turned in for the theft at Stubbings. The clothes weren't the same, but she remembered his straight black hair and distinctive angular face; he was one of the robbers. The look about him bothered her, his dark narrow eyes and the perpetual sneer on his lips.

Emma pulled down her hat and buried her face in her little notebook, hoping she would not be recognized. He glanced over a few times, then flicked his cigarette in her direction before heading inside the club. He deliberately bumped Tim's shoulder as he passed him in the doorway. Tim didn't think much of it and headed back to the wagon.

As he climbed in the back for more pies, Emma leaned toward him and muttered under her breath, "Tim, let's go."

"What's your rush?" he asked, his hands full of pies.

"That man who you passed in the doorway," she said and nodded her head toward the alley, "is one of the men we got into trouble a few days ago at the department store."

Tim offered a small, imperceptible nod and said in a low voice, "This is my last delivery and we'll be on our way." He climbed down and casually carried the pies into the club, not showing his nerves.

It seemed to Emma that Tim was in the building for an eternity. He finally returned, climbed on the wagon, nonchalantly took the reins, and clicked at the horse to move on.

Her watcher was also in that alley. He tried to be in locations where Emma might be at risk. He saw the man in the alley take notice of her. *Well*, he thought, *I'll have to keep an eye on that one.*

"Did he say anything to you when you went back in?" Emma asked a bit worried as he pulled the wagon out of the alley.

"No, he just walked past me." Tim didn't mention the man deliberately bumped into him again when he was exiting. He said briskly, "I'll switch this part of the route with Tony."

Emma cocked her head and said, "No, I think that would call more attention to us. Let's just act as if nothing has occurred."

Tim thought about this and nodded his head slowly in agreement. "Maybe you're right."

They continued to their final stops for the morning. Emma made a note in her notebook to open back up the Stubbings Department Store case and add the latest observation.

"Emma," Tim's quiet voice drifted to her as she continued to write. "I know what kind of things you write, but why? Why do you continue to scribble in that notebook?"

Emma continued her musings and didn't look up. "Mama," she said simply.

"Your mama?" he asked quizzically.

"Yes," she said, "I remember sitting in the bakery early mornings and Mama would tell me that baking, like life, required a person to be hyper-observant. Whether it is the smell of yeast when it is ready to be kneaded or the smell of a cake just about to be done or to recognize what's going on around you that may need your attention."

She continued, "Mama gave me my first little black notebook to start adding my observations and recipes into. When I take stock of my notes, I can visualize details I may have missed. It helps me correct errors the next time the situation occurs. It also helps me with baking and other things. If you're not paying attention, you could miss something obvious. Small changes in your daily life could mean big things."

"Or," he commented dryly, "it could mean very little." He chuckled and continued, "So, it's the details of things that interest you."

I'm different than that, he thought. He could see the details but felt the future could be as important as or more important than the present. He had dreams that moved past the details of this job. He thought about those courses he had used the reward money to sign up for. It would allow him to move up his plans and complete his degree within a year.

As both dreamed, Tim and Emma listened to the clacking of the horse hooves on the road.

Tim mentioned, at the end of the morning, that their last stop would be the Hells. Cousin had sent day-old bakery goods to give out—pies, cakes, bread, and, of course, Berliners. Tim and Emma went to the outskirts of, but did not enter Chicago's "Little Hell". It was a ghetto and lived up to its reputation for violence and gangs. Initially, the Irish immigrants who lived there had a hard time getting jobs and fitting in. They preferred to live on their own, but as new immigrants started arriving from Italy, they did not mix well, and violence was often the result.

Tim knew better than to enter down the main street; he instead parked at one of the outreaching apartment buildings. The kids that lived in the area, knew to be around there in case there were some baked goods they could pick up. Some days, Tim wasn't able to come but, when he could, they were very appreciative. They knew him by name, each trying to jockey for first place in line. Kids and adults called, "Toss me some bread" and "got any pie left today?" They paid as much as they could, mostly in pennies.

As they finished their day, Emma expected to be dropped off at home or the bakery, depending on Tim's afternoon schedule. But today, he indicated it was time to let Emma see the delivery boy's hangout. She had heard about this before but was never allowed to go. This was a big step for her—to hang out with the other delivery boys.

Tim pulled over near the alleyway where the hangout was located. The neighbors hadn't minded the kids boarding up part of an alley as a hideout and shelter. They kept the area clean and the structure could be taken down quickly if needed.

Tim bumped the door open with his hip while balancing a bag of Berliners and a lunch bucket. Emma trailed in behind him, also carrying her lunch bucket. The other delivery drivers sat against the wall, on a scarred-up bench, or stools at a small wood table. The boys made a move for the Berliners, but Tim, being taller than the others, held the bag above their heads. Tony leaped onto the table and nabbed it, getting the first Berliner. This seemed to be a normal occurrence, and everyone laughed. Tony tossed the rest of the treats to the group and jumped back down. He nodded to Emma to join him at the table. She pulled up a stool and sat down.

As the other boys continued to eat, they didn't seem curious about a new face. Emma noticed they were watching her, but then she realized she was eating her food too neatly. She used her arm to wipe her face. With this act, they ignored her and went about their business.

As they finished up, everyone went on to their afternoon deliveries. Emma stood and dropped her notebook. She didn't think anything of it when one of the delivery boys picked it up and handed it to her.

Dear-one was reading through her book and looked up and said, "Didn't you think it odd at that point that someone was helping Emma with her notebook?"

"They weren't just being polite?" asked the Narrator.

"Boys around other boys are not polite. They knew who and what Emma was," said Dear-one.

"Hmm," said the Narrator.

Since Emma had been taken to the hideout, she thought she might as well ask about accompanying Tim and Tony on their afternoon jobs. "Tim," Emma inquired, "can I tag along?"

Tim hesitated and looked at Tony, who did a sharp shake of his head and narrowed his eyes. Tim answered, "Not today, Emma. We're making deliveries to someone who doesn't like surprises. Wait here for us? Then we will take you to the boarding house."

Though she was disappointed, she was okay with waiting before heading home. She hung out for about an hour, reading through her notes. Some of the boys came and went during that time and acknowledged her with a nod of their heads.

Tim returned to pick her up and dropped her off at the boarding house. Dora was out front sweeping the steps as they pulled up. Tim, grinning widely, left with a wave and a shout out to her.

Dora was smiling as she accompanied Emma back inside. They made their way to the kitchen to discuss Emma's day. She told Dora about the different accents she had heard in the Hells and how she was allowed into the boys' hangout place. Dora was appropriately impressed.

Emma finished her descriptions and went upstairs to take a bath to wash off the grime from being on the wagon all morning. It was a habit she enjoyed. She reached out for her towel to dry off and climbed out of the bathtub, her hair escaping the pins holding it out of the water. After she dried off and changed into her dressing gown, she laid on the bed and fell asleep. Dora came up to check on her and remind her of her lessons and work with Papa that afternoon. She dressed and headed downstairs to begin her late afternoon duties.

That evening, after dinner, Emma sat with Dora in the kitchen, reading through the day's notes. Dora looked at her and asked in a studied, casual voice, "Emma, you and Tim talk a lot?"

"Yes," Emma murmured, not paying attention.

When she didn't continue, Dora asked the question another way, in a more determined voice. "When you are talking to Tim, do I ever come up?"

"Yes. No. What?" Emma exclaimed when that one question permeated her thoughts. The question shook her out of her notebook and into the conversation.

Dora repeated her question, and that got Emma's attention. Emma frowned, not wanting to stop her reading. She first looked down at her notebook, then at Dora. "Dora, when I'm with Tim, what we talk about is between us. I can't share confidences." She softened her tone and reached over to touch Dora's hand. "Even for you."

Dora looked down at Emma's hand on hers and sighed. "I know, but I was just curious if he thinks about me as much as I think about him."

"That, I can answer. Yes, he talks about you all the time and it is all good."

"Is it?" She smiled and said again, coyly, "Is it?"

"Yes, now no more sharing. I need to concentrate on my notes," she scolded.

"I'll work on my books," said Dora as she gave in to Emma's request and opened them.

Emma focused on her scribbles. The man who may have recognized them at the social club was troubling. *I'll keep the case file open, just in case,* she thought.

She continued studying her general notebook and noticed something peculiar about the observations from the business district that day. The same men were turning up at the same corner each morning for the past few weeks. It was not odd to see people out early, but at this time of day, they normally had a purpose—delivering bread, milk, that sort of thing. But these men's purpose for being in that location was unclear.

She marked the note with a star, determined to look into these men and their motives.

CHAPTER 9

*O*ver the next few weeks, Emma kept a close eye on that area. She made note of anything that seemed out of the ordinary. She also continued to talk to Tim during deliveries.

He was whistling and enjoying the day when Emma broached the subject of Dora. "Tim?" she asked, hesitant to get involved in his romantic life.

"Yes?" he answered cheerfully, thinking she wanted to discuss deliveries, observations of the day, or both.

"Dora mentioned she hasn't seen you as much lately," she continued.

He frowned. "Emma, you know I added more classes to complete my degree faster."

"I know, Tim, but Dora needs some reassurance. You might want to talk to her about any plans that involve her future."

"You know I'm working on that and, once I'm set, I'm going to ask her to marry me."

"I know that," said Emma patiently, "but Dora doesn't. You haven't mentioned your plans to her yet?"

"Well, at first I thought it would be a longer process, but

with our reward money, I'm able to move up the timetable," he explained.

"I think it is time for you to have a conversation with her and take me out of the middle," she recommended.

Tim thought a moment and said, "Yes, it's time. Dora should have input in our future. I'll speak with her."

Emma nodded, satisfied, and returned to her observations. They had started deliveries in the business district that morning. She started to notice odd things, such as the men she had seen before (noted in her journals to keep an eye on) appearing and disappearing on that corner near the businesses on the first floor of a multistoried building. Emma was familiar with the businesses and who worked there. These men did not match the typical profile of a store worker. Noting the time and the fact the stores were not due to open for a few hours, she frowned. *Are they coming from the shops or another location?* she thought consideringly and put a star next to that note for later examination.

She started thinking that, if something nefarious was happening, they would probably not have used the front doors of the businesses. The individual stores and surrounding areas would need to be investigated for openings. Glancing over at Tim, she saw he was preoccupied with thoughts of Dora, she kept the discovery to herself.

Looking closer at the men, she realized with a start that one of them was the individual she had recognized from the department store robbery and in the alley at the social club. A low profile would be key, he could be real trouble.

Later that evening, Emma sat at the kitchen table, marking her observations, when she saw Tim knocking softly at the back door. Leaning over, she tapped Dora, who was sitting with her back to it, reading a book. She looked toward Emma questioningly, who indicated the door with her pencil. Dora turned toward it. She saw it was Tim and immediately stood, a smile on her face.

"I think I have another place to be," said Emma as she hurriedly vacated the room.

Tim nodded gratefully but kept his eyes on Dora. "Can we talk?"

Tim sounded so serious; Dora wrung her hands and asked, "Of course. Is everything all right? Your aunt or uncle, are they okay?"

"No, no they are fine. I just wanted to let you know why I haven't been around lately. I'm trying to get our future moving forward."

"Our future?" she asked, all at once teary and happy.

"Yes, evidently, I have been thinking about it so much, that I never realized I haven't talked to you about it," he said in a self-deprecating way.

Dora nodded to him encouragingly.

"Dora, I only see you in my future, and I want to marry you. Would you marry me, when I'm done with my accounting degree and I have a job?"

"Tim, I would marry you without a degree or a job. You're what's important. The rest isn't."

"Your answer is?" he asked, his eyes darkening with emotion.

"Is yes!" she shouted.

Tim grabbed her and spun her around, kissing her until they were both dizzy.

They didn't hear the kitchen door open, but they did hear a very loud clearing of someone's throat. They both looked toward the door and a group of people looked on expectantly for news.

"Well?" said Emma impatiently, already grinning.

"I said yes!" Dora exclaimed, turning her red face into Tim's chest.

The group cheered and filed into the room to offer their congratulations to the happy couple.

Papa got to Tim first and shook his hand. "What are we thinking for the timing of this activity?" he asked half teasingly.

"We haven't had time to discuss that yet, but I'm working on completing my degree and getting a job first. Maybe next year?" he said with an inquiring glance to Dora.

She nodded, wiping her eyes.

Papa embraced his daughter and smiled broadly at Tim. "Welcome to the family."

Emma broke out some sparkling cider to help celebrate the news of the evening. After a toast, everyone left the kitchen to give the couple some time to talk quietly.

Emma went up to her room, smiling at the good news and carrying her notebook. She wanted to continue working on marking her observations as immediate or delayed actions that would require more study. Some questions, she needed answers to—*why were the men in that location at that time of the morning? Waiting for something? Someone? Were they taking something in versus taking something out?*

She finished up her notes and got ready for bed, thinking it had been a nice day.

CHAPTER 10

*E*mma went downstairs the next morning to help set up breakfast. "I wonder if the newspaper has been delivered yet," she mused as she opened the front door and glanced down. "There it is." Scooping it up, she started reading on her way to the kitchen.

Taking a moment in the dining room, she read the paper front to back. Observations sometimes came out of ordinary articles and not just the crime section. She was reading through the current events section when she came upon something interesting.

She heard Dora's voice. "Emma!"

"Coming. I'm checking on something," she called back, still looking at the paper. There was a story that caught her interest. It involved a flower store and the history of the area around the business district where it was located. The article also included detailed information about the mostly abandoned tunnels connecting the basements of the various shops. The tunnels were in place originally to move coal for heating and to move supplies.

It was the kind of article that would have normally been

skimmed, but Emma took a moment to tear it out. Tucking it into her pocket, she placed the paper on the table at Papa's spot. She needed to think about the article and how it might relate to her observations. Entering the kitchen, she put it out of her mind and was ready to help.

"Good morning, what were you doing when I called you?" inquired Dora.

Emma saw that she and Amy had breakfast ready and waiting to be served. Dora had already started working on a dessert for tonight's dinner.

Without answering her question, she quickly ran around the table and hugged her. "Dora, I'm so happy for you."

"Me too. Now start taking these to the table," said Dora, forgetting her question and returned her hug.

Emma focused on Dora, not moving. She wanted a taste of that batter before anything else.

She was staring so intently that Dora finally relented. "If I give you a spoonful, will that get you moving?" she asked, shaking her spoon at Emma.

Nodding, she grabbed it, licked it clean, and started transferring food to the dining room.

Dora had been so excited about her engagement; she had gotten a head start on breakfast and filled the time left by making her German Apple Cake. She knew Tim would like it, so she would fix him one to take to the bakery later today.

German Apple Cake Recipe
Ingredients:

- 2 eggs
- 3⁄4 cup of vegetable oil
- 2 cups of sugar
- 1 teaspoon of vanilla

- 2 cups of flour
- 2 teaspoons of cinnamon
- 1 teaspoon of baking soda
- 1/2 teaspoon of salt
- 4 cups of peeled chopped apples

Directions

1. In a large bowl, beat eggs and oil until smooth.
2. Add next 6 ingredients and mix well.
3. Fold in apples.
4. Pour into greased 9x13 pan.
5. Bake at 350F for 50-55 minutes.

At breakfast, Papa opened the newspaper, noticing a hole where an article should have been. He knew who was responsible and looked through the hole at Emma. He folded the paper down onto the table and tilted his head forward to look at her over his glasses. "Emma?"

"Yes, Papa?" she responded vaguely; clearly, her mind was on other things.

"Emma," he prompted, waiting for her to raise her eyes to his.

When she finally did look his way, he asked, "You're doing, I suppose?" indicating the paper.

"Yes, Papa," she said with a guilty voice. She knew he enjoyed his paper at breakfast.

He clicked his tongue, shook out the paper, and then went back to reading the articles still in place.

Later in the kitchen, Emma was helping Dora and Amy clean

up. Dora looked over at her curiously. "All right," she said, "what's so important that you had to tear Papa's paper?"

"I'm not sure," Emma said slowly. "It's just something that caught my attention and might be connected to some observations I've made previously." When she didn't provide more answers and went quiet, Dora knew to leave her alone with her thoughts.

Emma wasn't scheduled to work on anything else that day and thought she could talk Papa into letting her start her afternoon work later in the evening. Closing her notebook, she went to find him. She was right; he was working on a project that would need some additional study, but she could take the day off if she promised to complete it later.

"Yes, Papa," she answered.

She returned to the empty dining room and was able to think more clearly about her observations. *The men,* she thought, tapping her pencil on her lips, *were always near the place where businesses are connected through tunnels in their basement and at times when those businesses are not opened. Were they utilizing the tunnels somehow? Is it connected to the local businesses? Is it possible? But why, what were they after?*

She thought more about the area. *The bank was a couple of blocks off and it seemed like a lot of tunnels to access it. The article said parts of the tunnel were collapsed, so whatever is happening has to be related to one of the shops or businesses on that road.*

She looked at her list of businesses—flowers, jewelry, café, millinery, department store, and a few closed businesses. Emma made a note to ask Tim about the area tomorrow.

Shoot, she thought, *I won't be working on the delivery wagon tomorrow. I'll be at the bakery. I'll need to go over today.* She had been in the tunnels and explored them with Papa when she was younger. She knew how to get in and out without being seen. The café in that area had an accessible tunnel and it was just off the kitchen through the basement. Additionally, the basement door was usually kept open because it was used for food storage and could be accessed without much notice.

She finished her notes, closed her notebook, and thought, *it might be dirty work.* She went to put on her delivery boy clothes and grabbed the portable gas lamp Papa had fashioned out of a pipe and a repository for kerosene. Carrying her shoes, she slipped out the front door and put them on outside. Her watcher slept as she moved quietly by, making her way uptown.

She scanned the area as she approached the cafe, looking for anything that might be suspicious. Nothing seemed out of the ordinary and the men were no longer visible. She didn't expect them at this time of day, though she had to be careful once she was in the tunnels.

She looked down at her clothes as she approached the café entrance. *I should probably use the back door,* she thought ruefully, shaking her head. Ducking around the corner into the alley behind the café, she stayed close to the wall and made her way to the back door. Trying to stay out of sight, she entered the kitchen hesitantly and stayed close to the back wall. It turned out that she needn't have worried.

The cook saw her lurking around the door and he yelled, "Hey, boy, make yourself useful and take those crates downstairs to the basement."

Emma kept her hat pulled down over her forehead, grabbed the crates, and headed toward the basement, happy to note they were empty and easy to carry. She nudged the basement door open with her foot. There was enough light from the kitchen to allow her to see the gas lamp on the wall about halfway down the stairs. She made her way carefully down and balanced the crates against her hip to reach the lamp and turn it up. This allowed her to see the steps and further down into the basement.

She continued down slowly, the bit of nerves she had chased

away by the excitement of an adventure. Her steps moved more quickly as she reached the bottom of the stairs.

The basement was dark and there were gas lights scattered throughout, but Emma chose not to use them. She set the crates down near the stairs, turning to the right to find the wall with her hands. Feeling her way around the room, she moved, looking for some type of opening to the tunnels. Getting frustrated and almost ready to give up when she pressed against the wall and found herself falling through a doorway.

Once she picked herself up from the floor and dusted off her pants, she pulled out her small pocket gas light and lit it. It had limited life, so she was careful to not go too far into the tunnels.

Moving forward, Emma was able to see the area had been cleaned up and appeared to have been used lately. She noted mentally, *they shouldn't be this clean*. During her exploration with Papa, she had seen piled debris blocking most of their path.

Working her way further into the space, she slowed, not wanting to go too far without a map or some directions. More supplies would be needed to investigate, now that she confirmed the café entrance was still accessible.

Male voices sounded from the direction in which she had come from. Stepping quickly into the shadows, she extinguished her small lamp and waited. Their conversation got clearer as they got closer to her. Her hand found her hidden knife, she pulled it out, ready to defend herself if needed. The men stopped advancing toward her, she breathed a small, silent sigh of relief and continued to watch them. *It is the same men I saw on the corner*, she thought.

"That door is opened," one of the men said in disbelief. "How did that happen? It is heavy. It won't just open by itself."

Emma sucked in her breath. *Careless*, she thought, *I should have known better*. Staying where she was, she listened to them complaining about the rats, their heavy boxes, and general life as they made their way down the tunnels.

"Must have been rats," said the other man laconically.

The first would not let the conversation go. "Rats, how big would one have to be to open a door that heavy?"

The other man, not really caring, said, "I've seen very big rats here in these tunnels. Why does it matter? Could we just drop it and get these items delivered?"

At that moment, Emma realized the voices turned faint and then loud. *The men must be going in and out of various businesses,* she thought. She crept closer to make note of the locations, taking care to not be seen.

The first man was talking again. "I'll be happy to unload this stuff. How many more trips? And why are we so late today?"

"We will have to make 2 to 3 more trips. Our contact couldn't get the goods off the ship until now. At least it isn't hot."

His companion grunted a reply as he set his box down and opened the door with a small prybar from his pocket. They got through the door and it slammed shut behind them. Emma stayed, waiting to see if they would return. She didn't have long to wait; they exited one door and entered another, carrying fewer items out than they had carried in.

Ships, Emma thought, *smuggling. It has to be.* She jotted down the locations the men entered: the mercantile, the specialty fabric store, and the jewelry store. Oddly, no boxes were being carried into the jewelry store.

Better to get moving now while they are in the jewelry store. She made her way back to the café entrance and up the basement stairs to the kitchen. The cook had his back to her, and she was able to make it out to the alley without being seen.

Before exiting the alley, she dusted herself off, took her hat, and pounded the dirt out of it on the wall. The now clean hat was placed back on her head and her braid tucked inside. As she was leaving, she pulled it down over her eyes, made her way back to the main street, and continued home.

She started to ascend her stoop when she absently noticed the man in the adjacent alley was the same man who slept in the alleyway near the bakery. Nodding to him in recognition, she made a mental note about the location she had seen him today.

Emma took the stoop steps two at a time, thinking about her adventure. She made her way to the kitchen and, without saying hello, immediately went to a pile of papers near the door. "Do we still have the newspaper from today?" she asked, flipping through them.

"Well," said Dora as she answered a question not aimed at her. "I might have saved it for some jar storage. What are you looking for?"

"Types of ships coming in and dates," Emma muttered. The pantry door opened easily; she spotted the stack of papers there. Bending down, she shuffled through them, looking for the ones she needed. Quickly finding them, she moved them to the kitchen table for a more thorough review. Flipping through them, she noted the dates the ships were in docked in port and compared them with the dates she recorded seeing the men on the corners. After she confirmed both sets of dates coincided, she tore out the schedule to add to her notebook.

Dora raised an eyebrow and said, "Going to tell me what is going on?"

"First, I'm going to tell Papa, then I'll give you all the details," she promised as she spun around and left the room in a hurry.

"Why so fast?" Dora called after her, catching the swinging door and holding it opened.

"No time to talk now," she said over her shoulder. "I need to talk to Papa."

"I think you've been in those boy's clothes far too long. You're getting too many boyish mannerisms," called Dora ruefully.

"Why thank you." Emma tilted her hat at her with an impish grin and made her way to the basement.

The stairs were well lit and she could hear Papa talking to himself at his bench.

"Papa?" she called softly, not wanting to disturb his work, but she needed his input.

Papa looked up and said, "Oh, hello, Sister. What can I do for you? I thought you were taking the day off. Did you decide to help with some deliveries?" He noticed she was in her delivery clothes.

"Papa, I wasn't working with Tim today. I had some follow-up to do on some observations I made during my deliveries." She paused for a moment and pulled out her notebook and clips of paper. "I found this in the paper this morning," she said as she handed him the folded-up articles.

Papa unfolded the crinkled paper. "Hmm..." he said and pulled down his glasses on his nose to read the article. He looked at her over them. "So, tell me more," he said, resigned to the fact this daughter would forever be involved in some adventure or another.

Emma fidgeted a bit, then laid the case out for him. "When I was making deliveries, I noticed several men were hanging out on the same corner. I've seen them at that same location on and off for weeks." She chose not to tell Papa one of the men was also identified in the department store robbery. "There's no reason for them to be in that area in the morning if they don't have a business to open. Then, this morning while I was reading the paper, I saw the articles about the tunnels."

"When you saw the article, you put that together with the men," he finished for her, remembering the many times he and Emma had explored the tunnels.

"Papa, I went there today. . ." She stopped when she saw his concern. The tunnels were a sixty-mile web that wound forty feet below this city's downtown streets and riverbed.

"Papa," she put her hand on his and started again, "I was safe.

I know the location I was in. I did not stray far from the area and I kept in the shadows."

"Emma, we've been through the tunnels together, but are you sure it's safe? Especially if something is going on? If you got too far, you might be caught in floodwater from the riverbed," Papa said, concerned about this new development.

She looked down at her notes and then up again at him. "Yes," she said, her voice firm now. "I'm not taking any foolish risk. I wouldn't go down during heavy rain."

Looking down at her notebook, she continued with her observations and descriptions of what she had seen. "I saw the men taking heavy boxes into the mercantile basement, long tubes that looked like fabric into the clothing store, and they didn't seem to be taking anything into the jewelry store."

"What about this other article, the one about the ships?" Papa inquired.

"My observations are that the men tend to appear when the ships are in port from Rio de Janeiro. I believe it's a smuggling operation. The dates for ships from there fit the schedule," she said, indicating the article with her finger, "and the tunnels would be a perfect way to move illegal merchandise."

Papa looked at the notes closely, nodded his head. "You have something here."

"What do we do with this information?" pondered Papa out loud.

"Should I go back to the tunnels to gather more data before we go to the police?" asked Emma, ready to move forward to the next part of the case.

He kept his head down, quietly gathering his thoughts. "Emma this is excellent work and you have connected the dots on this case." He paused, thinking the current police chief for Chicago did not have a good reputation; taking this to him would only stir up controversy. He continued, "I think what we do, Emma, is wait—"

"But, Papa!" Emma interrupted, thinking he did not trust her to continue with the case.

"Let me finish, Emma. I want to wait, but I also want to contact a friend at the Pinkerton Detective Agency. They're a private company who can keep an eye on the situation," he said calmly.

When Emma heard the Pinkerton name, she stopped breathing a moment and then, in a rush, said, "Can we go now?"

"No." Papa chuckled at her eagerness. "I'll need to make sure Cole is in the office and is willing to hear about your observations."

"Cole?"

"Cole Tilden. I've known him for a while," he said quietly, not sharing more.

"Okay," she said eagerly, "I'll head up to change and practice my knife throwing until dinner."

"That's fine, Sister," said Papa and shook his head a bit as he watched her run up the steps and exit the basement.

Later that night, Emma sat with Papa and Dora in the kitchen. Almost all the boarders had retired except for Miss May and Miss Marjorie, they continued to sit together in the lounge, talking quietly.

Papa and Emma filled Dora in on the current case. "Papa," inquired Dora, "how do you know an investigator at Pinkerton?"

He sat quietly for a moment. "Well, I know Cole from a long time ago. We grew up together."

Dora and Emma looked at each other. They had heard very little about Papa's life before Mama. It was like his life began when he met her.

He continued, "You know my mama died when I was born and my papa, your grandpapa, worked himself to death by the time I was twelve. I ended up on the streets, living in alleys. I met Cole there, also on his own. We formed a club, we protected each other, and we made sure the other was fed. We were some of the best pickpockets in the area."

"Papa!" both girls exclaimed, shocked.

"We had to survive, and that was the way we did it. We didn't want to live in the county poorhouse and the only other option was on the streets. At that time in Chicago, there were many street children committing mischief. We were so good people were starting to notice," Papa explained.

The girls were fascinated and when Papa paused in his story, Dora spoke for both of them. "What happened?"

"Well, Cole and I were working at the corner of Market and Smith," Papa said, catching Emma's eye and winking at her.

"Of all places," she said, catching the connection to her observations of mischief at the same location. "Papa, were you scared?" she asked, concerned. Even though it was a long time ago, the sisters felt for the little boy with no parents.

"I was," he admitted, "but getting caught was the best thing that could have happened to me."

"Did you get sent to jail?" Emma sat back in her chair, astonished at the information.

"No, no. I didn't know it at the time, but I was being set up to pick a certain person's pocket. It was Mr. Gibler, a local teacher, though I didn't know it at the time since Cole and I didn't attend school," he admitted. "He had me by the collar. I thought that was it, that I would be sent off to the workhouse or jail.

He stopped for a second and laughed. "Cole was very protective of me and he rushed over trying to rescue me. Instead, Mr. Gibler grabbed him, too. For a little guy, he was very strong. Instead of calling the police, he hailed a cab and took us to his home. We weren't punished, but we were fed and allowed to get cleaned up. Mr. and Mrs. Gibler made us a deal—if we followed their rules and attended school, we could stay with them. Cole and I lived with them until we both made the move to college.

He got us janitorial work at the local school and tutored us on the side."

"Papa, why don't we know the Giblers?" Dora asked, curious about the people who had helped him.

"They passed away," he said simply. "They were older when we met them, and I think we were their last chance to have a family."

Dora gazed into Papa's eyes. "Why don't we know this story and why haven't we met Cole?"

"As we got older and went off to school, our lives led in different directions. We still care very much for one another. Also, Cole only just moved back into the area to take over the Chicago Pinkerton operations."

That gave the sisters something to think about. "Bed now," Papa said. Both girls nodded and headed upstairs.

A little while later, as Papa sat reading in the sitting room, a knock sounded on the front door. He answered the door and a delivery person handed him a note. Papa thanked him, shut the door, and opened the note. After reading it, he turned and looked up the staircase, toward the landing where Dora and Emma now peered down at him. "Sister, want to come with me tomorrow after making deliveries and meet with Cole to discuss your case?"

Emma's eyes sparkled. "Definitely, yes. I'll have Tim drop me here when we finish in the morning."

Dora smiled at Emma, knowing she was getting something she had always wanted.

"Night, Papa," said the girls quietly. The family made their way to their rooms to get some sleep.

CHAPTER 11

The next day, Emma completed her deliveries and met Papa at the house. He was waiting in the foyer when she arrived. "Hi, Papa. Ready to go?" she asked as she jammed her hat on her head and started making her way back to the door.

Papa cleared his throat.

She looked back and asked, "Yes, Papa?"

"Maybe you want to go as a young lady and not a ruffian?" he said, indicating her delivery outfit.

"Oh, sure, Papa." Though not really reluctantly, she would like to look her best the first time she met with the Pinkerton detectives.

"Emma, ten minutes, no longer," Papa warned. "We have a cab coming."

Nodding quickly, she headed upstairs, taking them two at a time. She changed into her red skirt with the black trim, red jacket, and white shirt with a black tie. The outfit was topped off with her red-trimmed black bowler hat. Before putting it on, she checked to make sure her larger hidden knife was secure.

Reaching for her smaller knife, she strapped it to her upper thigh. She shook out her skirt and looked at herself in the long mirror, took a deep breath, and was ready to go. Papa gave her an approving nod when he saw how she was dressed. He offered her his elbow, and they exited the house.

Waiting in front of the house was the hansom cab Papa had called. He helped her in and climbed in next to her. It pulled away and they made good time to the Pinkerton offices. He had them dropped off a few blocks from there so they could talk ahead of the meeting. "Emma, when we go in, Cole will be there. Just tell him your story. Do you have your notebook?"

"Yes, Papa, right here," she said and patted her jacket pocket.

As they passed an alley, Emma hung back a few steps behind her papa; suddenly, a hand grabbed her and pulled her in. Her first reaction was to pull her knife from her hat. Her "assailant," who was at least a foot taller than she, did not expect to be defending against a knife. Before he knew what had happened, she had him pinned to the wall and was holding a long knife under his chin.

The "assailant" was a tall, skinny kid just a bit older than Emma.

"Why did you grab me? You villain!" she shouted.

He smiled crookedly and tried not to move his head as he answered, "You're a bit of a villain yourself." He nodded carefully at the knife being held to his neck.

"Why are you smiling?" Emma asked gruffly, not removing the knife, still ready to defend herself.

Papa realized Emma was not with him and doubled back. She had expected him to jump in angrily. Instead, he leaned one shoulder against the brick wall of the alley and directed a question at the "assailant", completely ignoring Emma's knife. "So, are you learning the business?" He didn't wait for an answer and said to Emma, "This is Cole's son, Jeremy Tilden."

Jeremy waved his fingers at Emma with a slight smile, keeping his head very still. Emma slowly backed off; she removed her knife from his neck and replaced it in her hat, allowing Jeremy to straighten up.

"I was just testing you to see if you could defend yourself," he said as he grinned at her and offered his elbow.

"Uh-huh," she said. She looked at him and then at her father and slipped her arm into Jeremy's.

The trio headed to the large gray stone building on the corner. They started up the stoop together. "Pops is waiting for you," Jeremy said as he shoved the large wooden double doors open with his shoulder. Within, men sat at desks in the entrance. The gentleman at the first desk rolled his eyes at Jeremy and indicated they could go into Cole's office.

They went through another set of doors, then down a long hallway. Jeremy jauntily tapped the door and pushed it open. "Pops," he called out, "found them in the streets and had to protect them from the lower elements."

"Protection?" Emma murmured and fingered the hat she had taken off upon entering the Offices.

Jeremy saw the move and jumped to the side of the door, his hands raised and a silly grin on his face. "I give, I give," he said.

"Well bring them in," called a voice from inside.

They entered and Papa immediately went toward the desk saying, "Cole."

Cole immediately came around the desk and gave Papa a bear hug. "Ellis, it's been too long," he said in a gravelly voice.

"Yes," said Papa, a tear in his eye.

Cole cleared his throat and asked, "And who is this lovely lady?"

Papa took over introductions from there. "Cole, this is my daughter Emma."

"Emma," Cole said while taking her hands in his. "I've heard about you."

He looked over to Ellis and said, "I take it, Ellis, this is not a social call?"

"Yes, we have a case you might be interested in," commented Papa. He paused for a moment and then continued, "Well, Emma does."

Cole was about Papa's age, with rusty red hair and a gray goatee; he was slender as a rail and wore the typical black Pinkerton suit. He looked like he didn't eat much but did appear to be a cheerful man. Papa trusted him; so would Emma.

Cole invited them to sit down in the brown leather chairs facing the desk. Jeremy was slouching against the wall, observing everyone.

"Emma," Cole prompted.

She pulled out her notebook with notes on the tunnels and started going over them out loud. Detailing how people were seen entering and exiting and the crates and tubes and other items she had found.

When she got to the part about entering the tunnels, Jeremy spoke up, "Do you think you should have been there? Was that a safe decision?"

The group glanced in his direction but mostly ignored the comment. Jeremy shrugged and leaned back against the wall.

Papa added, "The use of those tunnels to move anything other than coal is suspect."

Cole leaned back in his chair, contemplating the information. "Our informants have been making noises of merchandise moving through the area, illegally." He went quiet for a moment, then continued, "We thought initially it might be a small, limited operation but, with this information, I think we could be looking at a much larger, organized effort. We can put some people over there with the locals who might be involved. For now, we'll need more data."

"Do we need to go to the police?" inquired Papa. He would trust a decision from Cole.

"No," Cole said, "not now. Some issues are going on there as well."

He looked over at Papa and asked, "Ellis, have you heard more about the chief being on the take?"

Emma and Jeremy were startled by this statement and made eye contact across the room. Jeremy straightened and paid attention to the next words his father directed at Papa. "We're getting more and more information that criminals are being let go within hours of being taken in. For now, I'll have my people look into it." He glanced at Jeremy and nodded, indicating he would be involved.

Papa started to stand. "Wait," said Cole, "I can't let you get away without making sure we get the families together."

Papa smiled broadly. "I agree. You and Jeremy must come for dinner. Do you know when you might be available?"

Cole grinned and said, "We're good most nights, but what about Sunday, after church?"

Papa nodded. "I think we have enough to share. Lunch is about 2:00pm on Sunday, after church. We're looking forward to the visit." With that statement, they all started toward the door. Papa and Cole continued to reminisce as they exited. Jeremy and Emma followed at a slower pace.

On their way out, Jeremy grabbed Emma by the sleeve. She looked down at his hand and then up at him as she teased, "Grabbing again? Will I need my knife?"

"No," he said, quickly dropping her sleeve. "I just want to inquire if you'll be at St. Vincent's for the Saturday evening dance."

"Why are you asking?" she asked suspiciously.

"No reason," he said as he dusted off a nonexistent dust particle from his sleeve.

"I may be there," Emma said slowly, thinking about Tony.

"Well, I may be there also," he said. He followed up with a

rushed statement, "If you're there and I'm there, maybe we could dance or something."

"Or something," Emma said and smiled. "If I'm there and you're there, I'm sure we could work something out." She whirled away to follow her Papa down the stoop.

Jeremy yelled at her as they started their walk down the street. "Hey, Emma, don't forget your hat!" He tossed it to her, and she caught it deftly.

"Thank you!" she shouted back, waving at both Cole and Jeremy.

Papa motioned for a hansom cab to take them home. "Papa, do you think they can do something about what I found?"

He looked over at her. "I think they'll keep an eye out and, when the opportunity strikes, expose what's happening. Keep in mind what Cole said. The police are starting to notice you. You'll have to be cautious about your observations and who you go to. We'll make a list of trustworthy policemen. And let me know what's going on, in case I need to help."

She frowned at him and stated. "Papa, why do I have to be cautious, I only make observations that anyone could make."

"No, Emma, you see more than most people. Close your eyes and tell me who is on this road."

Emma liked this game. "A woman is walking a baby in a stroller with a large black hat and a large bag. A businessman with a satchel and a delivery truck being pulled by two gray horses."

"Now, open your eyes. Everything you listed is exactly right. Most people can't do that, especially if they're simply going through their day. They might notice a few things, but they would miss the details you pick up. Emma, keep making observations and investigating, just keep a lower profile," he warned.

"Yes, Papa."

A cab pulled up, Papa helped Emma in, and they headed home. Emma continued thinking about what had happened at the Pinkerton office. The case was in good hands; she knew they would keep her involved. She was interested in how they would handle the next steps.

My ultimate goal, she thought, *would be to work at Pinkerton as a detective*. She knew Pinkerton had never hired a woman as a detective, and she would have to prove she was the perfect first one for the job. For now, she would continue building her skills.

CHAPTER 12

*S*aturday began quietly. It was an off day for Emma, both at the bakery and the delivery job. She slept in, knowing breakfast on Saturdays was at your discretion. There was plenty of food in the kitchen for boarders and everyone ate at their own pace. She thought she could grab a picnic basket and see if Dora would like to go down to the river to take a respite.

That idea got her out of bed with a spring in her step. She got ready for the day and dressed in a brown split skirt, a brown jacket with red trim, and a redshirt. After she pulled on her boots, she brushed her hair and braided it so that it fell straight down her back. Leaving the hat, for now, she made her way downstairs.

She looked for Dora; she wasn't in her room or the kitchen. Emma waved at Miss May and Miss Marjorie, who were enjoying their morning tea in the backyard, sitting on handmade chairs and taking in the sun of the day.

Emma found Dora in Papa's study, reading. She jumped on the couch, startling her, and asked, "What are you reading?"

Dora turned the book to show the spine to Emma—*Alice's Adventures in Wonderland*. It was a literary nonsense genre, but Emma loved the adventures in it. "Do you like it?" she asked excitedly.

Dora looked at her, considering, and commented, "It's good but not really for me. I think I prefer romances or mysteries."

"Oh, but what about the Mad Hatter? He was so interesting, or the part in the story about—"

"Sister, what can I do for you?" she interrupted. She knew Emma usually had something on her mind.

"Oh, nothing, I just thought we might take a picnic basket to the river and hang out a bit."

Dora thought a moment and said, "That sounds like fun. What about window shopping on our way?"

"Sounds like a plan," said Emma. "Leave at 11:00am? I can put together the basket."

"No, I can handle it" Dora offered, smiling.

"Thanks, Dora," Emma said in a singsong voice. "Add something sweet, please?"

Dora nodded and watched as Emma raced out of the room. *Off to practice her knife skills*, thought Dora. She called after her, "Eat something, please."

Emma headed to the kitchen for fruit and buttered bread. When she finished, she retrieved her hat and an extra knife. Weekends were a good time to practice different methods of accessing the knife in her skirt and get smoother at pulling the blade from her hat. Target practice helped her improve, but she needed a moving target. *Tony*, she wondered if he was busy that morning. Retrieving her knives, she headed to his apartment.

She knocked on the door and the youngest Marella answered, "Hey, Emma."

She glanced down, "Hey back, Enzo."

"Here to see me?" he asked hopefully, standing on his tiptoes, trying to impress her. He knew full well that she was there to see Tony and that he would need ten years and at least six more inches before he could impress her.

"Enzo, move out of the way and let Emma in," called Tony from the living room. As she entered, she could see his two other brothers lying about the room, each reading a newspaper. They were casually dressed and had their shoes off. Tony had scrambled up when he heard her at the door. He ran his hand through his hair and tucked in his shirt, looking around for his shoes.

Tony's dad sat comfortably in a large chair, reading the paper when he looked up and said, "Emma, nice to see you." He gave her a smile, very similar to Tony's.

"Hello, Mr. Marella," she said with a large grin. Tony's dad had brown hair with grey sprinkled throughout and was extremely charming. It was like seeing Tony twenty years from now. "How is business?"

Tony's dad owned a plumbing and gas fitting firm.

The narrator commented, "During this time, running water, sewer connections, and gas for lighting and cooking had become more common in both residential and business buildings.

His demeanor changed at the question. "Busy," he said, not looking up to answer. His response was odd; he was normally very open about his projects. She sent him a searching glance and started to ask him more questions when Mrs. Marella appeared.

"Emma," Mrs. Marella called from the kitchen. "Come give me a hug. Do you want something to eat?"

"No, Mrs. Marella, but thank you." She hugged the woman

tightly as she exited the kitchen. Mrs. Marella was like a second mom and always had food to feed guests. "I'm just here to talk to Tony." He came up behind Emma and put an arm across her shoulder.

"What's up?" he asked as he looked down at her.

"I'm working on my knife throwing today. I'm hoping you have some time this morning because I need someone to help with some targets."

"So," he teased, "you automatically thought of me when you needed a target?"

"Well, yes." She laughed. "Actually, I did. You make the best moving target."

Mrs. Marella heard the banter but was not concerned. She knew Emma was good with knives and would not hurt him. Frowning she watched them together, she continued to worry Emma could break Tony's heart. "She is so very young and could change her mind about things." She felt that he listened. He had answered in a serious tone with, "I think I just met my forever person too soon. I'm trying to give her space to grow or make any changes."

Mrs. Marella remembered something then. "Emma, I hear congratulations are in order."

Emma knew exactly what she was talking about and grinned. "Yes, Tim and Dora surprised everyone. They're very happy."

"Have her come by and see me. I want to hear all about it," said Mrs. Marella.

Before Emma could respond, Tony said, a bit impatiently, "Mom, we have to go."

"Remember, we have an early dinner. The dance is tonight," his mother noted.

Tony glanced at Emma and said, "Yes, Mom, I remember." This was Tony's chance to have Emma to himself. He had looked forward to this all week.

Emma turned a bit red because she had also been looking forward to dancing with him.

Tony's dad threw his jacket and hat at him and said, "On your way." Emma again thought about how he had changed when she asked about his job. She would have to ask Tony about it later.

As they descended the stairs, they talked about the news of the day, current games being played, and families. There was never a shortage of conversation between the two. She thought about asking if something was up with his dad but decided to keep it light. "Did Tim tell you before he proposed to Dora?" she asked interestedly.

"No, I don't think he wanted to share that before he spoke to her. It's a big step."

"Yes, they're so steady in their feelings for each other and ready to take the next step." They both quiet and contemplative as they approached the boarding house.

Tony shook off any deep thoughts and asked, "Backyard?"

She nodded and said, "Yes."

As they went through the house, Tony said, "Just a minute," and ran into the kitchen. Emma heard a shriek and ran toward the sound. She opened the door and saw Dora scolding Tony for scaring her.

"What happened?" she asked, entering the kitchen.

"I just came in to give her my congratulations," Tony said innocently and winked at Dora. "Ready?"

Emma opened the door and waved Tony into the backyard.

"What do you want me to do?" he asked.

"Well, I would like you to walk around over by the target. I want to work on hitting your garments rather than you," she said rather innocently, looking out the corner of her eye at him.

Tony looked over at Emma and squinted his eyes in playful consternation. "Now, Emma, you know I trust you, but this is maybe taking things too far." He mulled over what she wanted to do and said, "I have an idea that should help you without injuring me. Go grab an old large jacket and some shirts and meet me back here." Emma headed in as Tony went about setting up two boards in a cross pattern.

She came out with a large man's jacket. Tony took it and placed it on the crossed wood he had nailed together. He stuffed the sleeves with older shirts. "Let's try this." He stood it up and put a large amount of space between him and the target.

She tried to throw the knife to hit a sleeve of the jacket.

Tony watched her and acknowledged to himself that he could not match her skill. Though he noticed that she hit a little close to the fake arm. "Ouch," he said.

"Oh, you can take it," Emma said as she threw her clutch knife.

"What's the reason for this activity?" he asked curiously.

"Well, I don't want to hurt everyone I throw a knife at, or at least not badly," she said thoughtfully, thinking of her current cases. They worked on throwing knives for a couple more hours that morning until she was hitting exactly what she was aiming at.

Dora stepped outside and called, "Sister, it's about time. Hey, Tony."

Tony smiled and waved back. He noticed the basket. "Something to eat in there?" he asked hopefully.

"Yes," she said. "And Tim," who stuck his head out the back door behind her "just happened to show up when I was putting the basket together. Emma, are you fine with the boys coming along?" She looked to Emma, ready to tell them no if she didn't agree.

Emma considered and saw Tim's hopeful expression. She grinned and said, "The more the merrier."

The group got organized with blankets, a picnic basket and exited the house together. They climbed into Tim's wagon, Dora in the front with Tim and Emma in the back with Tony.

Tim turned around so he could see both Dora and Emma and asked them, "Where to, ladies?"

"I believe there was window shopping, strolling along the boulevard, and a picnic by the river planned for today," said Dora.

Tim nodded, conscious of the fact that he and Tony were the interlopers into the sister's day. "I'll have to drop the wagon off before we get too far."

They left it at a safe location to begin their day together. Tim jumped down and went around to help Dora. Tony also jumped down and assisted Emma out of the back of the wagon. Tim called, "Tony!" and tossed the blankets to him. He grabbed them deftly and watched as Tim took the picnic basket.

While they were strolling, Emma glanced around, looking for anomalies while Tim, Tony, and Dora were enjoying the day.

Tony noticed where Emma's attention was leading. He tapped her hand, tucked in his elbow, and shook his head silently at her. She understood what he was referring to and tried to shut down her hyper observation.

Okay, she thought, but she kept an eye on the skinny kid who seemed to be walking too close to people in front of them. She could see him lifting wallets as he went through the crowd. He started to drift back and sidled up to Tony, so she grabbed his arm as he reached for the wallet and quickly had him face-planted against the wall.

"Hey, what are you doing?" shrieked the kid in surprise.

Tony knew Emma could handle the situation and just stayed close. He spotted a police officer walking his beat and called him over.

The police officer hustled over and said, "What's going on here?"

The pickpocket still flattened against the wall, decided to take the defensive route. "I wasn't doing nothing and she grabbed me."

Emma looked at him steadily and stated, "Really?" She had taken her small knife out without anyone noticing and cut the pickpocket's jacket pocket. He didn't realize what she was up to until multiple wallets fell to the ground.

The policeman looked on, astonished. Tony looked resigned.

The policeman grabbed the pickpocket by the collar and scooped up the wallets.

"Those are mine," the boy said indignantly.

"Yours? So, you're Blake Smith, Marty Hochberg, and Phil Mozier?" He didn't wait for a response. "Off to jail for you. Thanks, little girl. What's your name?"

Oops, thought Emma, *I'm supposed to keep a low profile*. She hesitated for a moment and then admitted, "Emma."

The officer nodded. "Emma, you did a good thing today. I'll remember this."

Great, she thought, *just what I need*, and nodded to the officer, who walked off with the defeated pickpocket.

Tony and Emma had to run to catch up with Dora and Tim. They were so taken with each other, they had not noticed what happened behind them. Emma squinted a bit at Tony as a warning; he understood that it might spoil the day and didn't say anything. He nodded and gave her a slight smile.

The two couples continued enjoying their sunny walk and easy conversation as they headed down to the boulevard and river on foot.

They found a grassy area overlooking the river and sat down for a nice lunch. After they had eaten, Dora and Tim wandered near the water for quiet conversation. Emma and Tony lay side by side on the blanket, looking at the sky. She glanced over at Tony with a hand shielding her eyes and said, "Will you be coming to the dance tonight?"

"Yes," he said, still looking up at the sky. He wondered why she had asked. Since Tim had started seeing Dora, they all rode to the dances together on Saturday night. "Why ask?"

Emma was looking up at the sky again and stayed silent.

He leaned over her and asked again, "Why?"

She finally slanted a look at him. "A son of one of Papa's oldest friends is planning on attending. I thought you could meet each other. I think you might have a lot in common."

"Meet me?" Tony was bewildered at the turn in the conversation and the introduction of a new character into their lives. *And what is he to Emma?* he thought to himself. He took a breath and fell back on the blanket; he wanted to reserve judgment until tonight.

They lay quietly until Dora and Tim returned. The other two put the leftover food into the basket while Tony and Emma folded the blanket. They headed back to the stable to retrieve the wagon and head home.

Tim said, "I'll see you this evening for the dance. Tony, let's go." He reluctantly dropped Dora's hand to leave.

Tony looked searchingly into Emma's eyes and said, "I'll see you tonight."

She didn't smile but nodded and stared back before breaking contact.

Dora and Emma watched as Tim and Tony departed in their wagon. Dora looked at her sister with a worried expression and said, "What did you say to Tony? He looked upset."

Emma shrugged and said a bit defiantly, "I told him Jeremy, Cole Tilden's son, would be at the dance. I've told him, prior to this, that I'm too young to make any decisions about my future. I can have other friends."

She touched Emma and stopped her before they entered the door. "Please don't hurt Tony. If you do, it could be a mistake with long-term repercussions."

"Dora, I don't have Tony's view of the future. I can see my path as an adventurer, but I don't want to get married or have kids."

"Emma, you're sixteen and you'll probably change your

mind later. I'm just letting you know that you should be careful with other people's feelings," Dora cautioned.

Emma shook her head to clear it. "First, I have trouble with one boy, and now I think adding another boy to the equation will help. I'm an idiot."

"No," said Dora, hugging her, "just very young."

CHAPTER 13

They went their separate ways until dinner. Emma had some lacework and went to find Miss May. While she worked on her patterns, she thought about Tony's dad. She should have taken the time to talk to Tony about her concerns; instead, she let herself get emotional about their relationship.

The afternoon wound down to dinner with Emma and Miss May working on lace commissions. Dinner was an independent affair. Dora didn't cook on Saturday nights. The family met in the kitchen for a casual meal of sandwiches before the dance.

Emma packed up the Snickerdoodle cookies she had made the previous night to bring with them.

Snickerdoodle Recipe

Ingredients:

- 1 cup of unsalted butter
- 1 and 1/2 cups of granulated sugar
- 2 eggs, room temperature
- 1 tablespoon of vanilla extract

- 1 and 3/4 cups of all-purpose flour
- 1 teaspoon of cream of tartar
- 1 teaspoon of baking soda
- 1/4 teaspoon of salt
- Cinnamon sugar
- 3 tablespoons of granulated sugar
- 3 tablespoons of ground cinnamon

Directions:

1. Preheat oven to 375F; prepare cookie sheets with parchment paper.
2. Hand mix; cream together butter and sugar.
3. Add one egg at a time, then vanilla.
4. Add flour, cream of tartar, soda, and salt.
5. Scoop into 1 tablespoon balls.
6. Roll into the sugar and cinnamon.
7. Place 2 inches apart and bake for about 6-8 minutes.

The evening was just beginning when the girls went up to change for the dance. Dora put on her green dress with yellow trim, while Emma wore a deep pink dress with a lace overskirt.

"Dora, have you seen Mama's scarf, the red one?" Emma called down the hall.

Dora entered Emma's room, brushing out her hair. "Of course, red," teased Dora, knowing Emma had to have something red on most of the time. "I think it's in Mama's trunk."

She nodded in agreement. "I'll check there."

"Try to hurry," Dora said. "We need to get going soon."

Emma ran quickly to Papa's bedroom to open the trunk

located at the end of the bed. She had been through the trunk before but had never gotten to the bottom. Kneeling, she opened it, pulling out blankets made from their baby clothes, a jewelry box, assorted dresses, and finally scarves. She found the scarf she wanted, but as she pulled it out, she found it had gotten caught on something. Gingerly she pulled on it and found it snagged on a 6"x6" wood box. Laying the box in her lap, she carefully unhooked the scarf, laying it at her side. Turning the box over in her hands, she examined all of its sides. It was plain, with no distinguishing marks, and appeared to be latched but not locked.

She wondered for a moment if she should ask Papa's permission to open it. Just before she made that decision, she heard Dora calling from downstairs to hurry up. Glancing back down at the box, she decided what was in it could wait until after the dance.

She went to her room, taking the scarf and box with her. The box was placed under her pillow and she put it out of her mind as she finished getting dressed.

A second shout came from downstairs. Tim and Dora were eager to get going.

As they exited the house, they saw Tony waiting in the wagon. He jumped down to help the girls. Emma sat on the lockbox in the back of the wagon and Tony sat on the wagon floor. Dora road up with Tim. Emma hummed a bit, looking at the sky and trying to not think about that box under her pillow.

They pulled up to the church and saw that many people had arrived. The musicians were already playing.

"Fun," said Emma, and she jumped down without help.

Dora commented, "Emma."

Emma glanced back at Dora's pointed look and realized that some of her boyish tendencies were still with her.

"I'll be more careful," she promised and waited for Tony to catch up. He offered his elbow and they walked into the dance together. As they entered, she glanced around for Jeremy. She found him quickly across the hall and her eyes made contact with his. It was a look she did not want to glance away from. She waited, wondering what he would do next.

Smiling crookedly, he slowly made his way over to her. She found herself returning that smile when he said, "Good evening."

She introduced a reluctant Tony to Jeremy. Jeremy reached out his hand to shake with him. Tony looked at it but did not shake it.

When Tony didn't respond, Jeremy withdrew his hand with a shrug of his shoulder.

"Well, we're all here. Emma, would you like to dance?" asked Jeremy. He was looking at Tony when he asked. Tony looked like he wasn't going to let her go but then finally relented.

Jeremy offered Emma his elbow and they proceeded to the dance floor.

Tim came up behind Tony and placed a hand on his shoulder. "Don't worry, it's only one dance. Remember, you always said you were in for a long wait with Emma."

"I know," he said a bit shortly.

He started thinking about what his mama said about Emma. "Tony, you might want to back off from her until she is older."

"But, Mama, I like to be around her."

"I know, but she isn't ready to see you as a suitor. It might be time to let her go her own way for a while."

"Mama, I just feel a connection with her that I don't feel with anyone else."

Mama smiled indulgently. "You're like your Papa. He took one look at me and told me I was for him. It also took me a while to see that same future. If you want her, the best way might be to separate for a time."

Tony had disregarded that conversation until now. He began thinking about what Mama mentioned about a separation.

Meanwhile, Emma and Jeremy danced a lively tune together. Tony waited patiently and claimed the next one. Jeremy and Tony monopolized her time until she was too tired to dance. She was just walking out for some air with Tony when Jeremy came up and greeted them cheerfully. Tony tried to get rid of him, but he didn't take the hint and said, "Oh, I could use some air also."

Tony looked annoyed by the additional third person on his walk but said nothing. The three strolled around the little park connected to the church.

Well, this is getting a bit tiresome, Emma thought to herself.

She ventured some conversation, trying to involve both boys. "Jeremy is working with his father at Pinkerton detectives."

This comment made Jeremy preen a bit, though he was curious about his competition. "Tony, what do you do?"

"I'm working deliveries, mostly around town," said Tony.

"Interesting," he said honestly. "You and Emma work together?"

They both nodded.

"What are your plans?" he inquired to Tony.

Tony took a moment to answer the question. "I have some ideas I'm working on. I'm not sure right now what form those will take."

Jeremy nodded, understanding about future choices. "I'm working with my dad at Pinkerton. I think that's where my future is."

Emma was quiet, thinking about the opportunities afforded to boys and not to girls. To be anything in this world, a girl would have to be two-to-three times as good as a boy. *That will just make me work harder,* she thought.

Emma looked at the timepiece attached to her dress. "I think if we're going to dance any more, we must get back into the church." They realized she was right and hurried back. When

Jeremy reached for her hand, she glanced back at Tony with a raised brow and he waved them on to the dance floor. Jeremy was a good dancer, and his funny nature kept her laughing throughout the dance.

The evening went on and Emma continued switching off between Tony and Jeremy. All three were getting along well together, but there was a bit of a struggle when the last dance was announced. Both boys had an arm and took off in opposite directions. At that moment, Emma felt like a wishbone about to be pulled in half. When Jeremy accidentally tore a lace drop on her dress, she said quietly, "Stop. Outside, both of you."

The three moved toward the door and she felt her exasperation boil over. "There are plenty of girls to dance with - in there. It doesn't have to be only me." She looked over at Jeremy and said, "We just met this week. I think you can find another partner for this dance." She smiled at him to dampen the negativity of her words.

Jeremy nodded and said, "Sure, I'll see you tomorrow," and headed back inside.

"Tomorrow?" Tony inquired.

"Yes. His father is a very close friend of Papa's and we're having them over for Sunday lunch after church." Emma could tell he wanted to be invited, but she knew she had to have a hard talk with him.

"Tony, don't you think we need some time apart? You can't be happy with just scraps of my time."

He took her hand and held it gently, looking into her eyes. "Emma, I'm happy with whatever time you give me. I get that you're young and I don't want to overwhelm you. You're my best friend," he said simply.

Emma used her free hand to cover their clasped ones. She looked up and said, "Tony, the time just isn't right for this. I treasure our friendship above all else and, when I'm ready, I'll let you know."

He nodded reluctantly. "Maybe it would be best for me to back off for a bit."

"But I don't want to see less of you," she said plaintively, realizing what she might lose.

"I think you're right," he said, pulling his hands out of hers, he turned away. Raising a hand, he wiped at his eyes. "I think it would be best if I found other friends to hang around for a while. It will give you space to grow and be yourself without me."

Tears also welled in her eyes; she hadn't foreseen losing her best friend tonight. She didn't think she could handle not seeing him. "Tony, please wait." She tried to take hold of his hand.

"No," he said, stepping back from her. "This is for the best. But know I'm here anytime you might need me."

That step he took from her felt like an ever-widening gulf. "Tony?"

"Yes, Emma?" he murmured, wishing to be anywhere but here.

"Can we dance the last dance together?"

He couldn't deny himself or her this last opportunity. He pulled her to him, closer than he had at any dance before this, and they swayed to the music drifting out into the garden. She looked up at him as the music was ending, and he looked down at her. He started to bend his head toward hers, and she held her breath in anticipation. He shook his head to clear it.

"Emma, what we need is space," he said in a low voice and turned to leave, exiting through the garden gate.

Emma just started to realize what she'd done, but could only stand miserably, watching him leave.

"Tell Tim I found a way home tonight," Tony called without turning around as he disappeared from her sight, leaving her alone in the garden.

Emma wandered slowly back into the room as the dance was breaking up. Dora waved at her from across the room and approached her quickly. She searched her face and saw that Emma was very pale. "Are you ill?" she asked, concerned Emma might be coming down with something.

Emma stood there, miserable and not wanting to talk about it. When Tim walked up to them, she ignored Dora's question and asked, "Tim?"

Tim glanced down questioningly.

Emma kept her voice devoid of emotion and her face blank as she continued, "Tony left early and he said to tell you not to wait for him."

Tim frowned. Tony wouldn't leave Emma for any reason. He would have to go see him after he got the girls home and get the full story. But for now, he had his Dora to be with. He squeezed her hand and she smiled up at him. It had been a fun night with everyone offering them congratulations on their engagement.

As they wandered out toward their wagon, Emma noticed Dora and Tim were preoccupied with each other, holding hands and staring into each other's eyes.

Emma cleared her throat. "Well, it looks like I'll be driving the wagon home."

Before they could contradict her, she got it ready for the trip home. Dora and Tim sat in the back, talking softly while she drove. Once they reached the boarding house, she waited a moment and then said rather loudly, "I'm going in now."

She jumped down without help and slowly walked up the stoop. Tim helped Dora from the back of the wagon and took the opportunity to give her a quick, intense kiss. There were more kisses, and he took a deep breath and allowed his head to clear. He said regretfully, "I'm going to check on Tony. You might want to talk to Emma."

Dora nodded. She had been thinking along the same lines.

Papa and Emma opened the front door for Dora. "Was the dance fun, girls?"

They both nodded.

"Papa, Emma, and I are going to set out some macaroons. Would you like some?" Dora asked.

Papa smiled a wide smile and followed them to the kitchen.

Macaroons

Ingredients:

- 14 ounces of sweetened shredded coconut
- 1/4 teaspoon of salt
- 14 ounces of sweetened condensed milk
- 1 teaspoon of pure vanilla extract
- 2 extra-large egg whites at room temperature

Directions:

1. Combine coconut, condensed milk, and vanilla extract in a bowl.
2. In a separate bowl, whisk egg whites and salt until they make medium-firm peaks.
3. Carefully add in the coconut, condensed milk, vanilla extract, and fold in evenly.
4. Preheat oven to 325F.
5. Use a spoon to drop the batter onto sheet pans lined with parchment paper.
6. Bake for 25-30 minutes or until golden brown.
7. Drizzle or dip in chocolate and let it cool.

Dora was still dreaming about her evening with Tim, but she knew she needed to talk to Emma before she went upstairs.

Papa finished his macaroons and, with a wave, departed to continue his work in his study.

"Sister," Dora said, reaching across the table to gather Emma's hands in hers. "What happened with Tony tonight?"

Emma felt an emotional response wash over her. Her eyes filled and she had to gulp to get air. "I don't know. I think we may not be friends anymore," she said in a halting tone.

"Oh, Sister," murmured Dora. She was sympathetic but had to be realistic with Emma. "Sister, when you talked about this with me earlier, you were clear that you weren't ready to be with Tony in a romantic way and you were ready to tell him."

"I didn't think that would affect our friendship!" she wailed, placing her head on her arms and started to cry harder.

Sister is so very young, thought Dora with a shake of her head. She scooted her chair closer to her and put her arm around her shoulders.

"Sister, in this situation you can't have it both ways. Tony cares a great deal for you and being around you as a friend is going to hurt him."

"It will? I didn't think about that," she said, slowly raising her head and showing her tear-drenched eyes to Dora.

"No, but you must think about it now. I would not be surprised if we don't see Tony for a while," Dora said firmly.

"So, no visiting him? No seeing his family?" she asked, completely stunned that one conversation had completely changed her life.

"Sister," Dora tried again, forcing Emma to look her in the eyes. "You asked for this space and you're going to have to let him have his as well. Do you understand?"

Emma understood that Dora cared deeply for Tony and did not want Emma to continue causing him pain. She took a deep, shuttering breath to clear her thoughts. "Okay," she said, "I'll give him some space."

"Good," said Dora, relieved. "I'm going up to bed." Her

thoughts shifted to Tim and she kept those with her as she went upstairs. Emma followed after her with thoughts of Tony on her mind.

Emma entered her room, still a bit down knowing she wouldn't be able to talk to her best friend. As she flopped back on the bed, her arms out-flung, her hand encountered a solid object. She looked toward it and noticed the box she had found in her mama's trunk peeking out from under her pillow.

Just what I need to keep me distracted.

Reaching out, she slid the box toward her and sat up with it in her lap. She didn't know why she thought this box might hold something important. It might just be a pair of old shears.

She unlatched it slowly. The lid creaked as it opened and revealed newspaper articles. *Articles,* she murmured to herself, taking them out carefully. *The dates,* she thought, *were when Mama was still alive.*

The articles documented different crimes that had gotten attention about ten years ago. Each seemed attributed to an unnamed source. *Curiouser and curiouser,* she thought. She stood, taking the box with her to the desk.

She laid the articles out on the desk in date order. Each article alluded to a local crime boss. There were murders, burglaries, gambling halls. The articles referred to information coming from an inside source, exposing the different crimes.

Who was the informant and why were these in Mama's chest? Emma wondered. *Was it something Mama was curious about? What makes these special enough to cut out and place in a box?* Most of them had occurred when Emma was little, in the time prior to the fire.

She moved the box to the side of the desk and opened her drawer to pull out a new black notebook. She opened it quickly and began to document what the articles might have in common:

- All were in Mama's chest.
- All were from the Tribune newspaper.
- All were within a two-year timeframe, before the fire.
- All had an unnamed source who implicated local crime boss (John Harden).
- Same byline, written by the same author.

First thing, Emma thought, *find the author and see if the source is still around.* She had a gut feeling Mama was somehow involved in these old articles. *But how?*

She carefully folded them back and placed them in the box and put them back in the chest. They hadn't been disturbed all this time. They would be safe until she wanted to evaluate them again.

With a final read of her new case book, she made a note to go to the paper's office on Monday. She wanted to see if the writer was still on staff and if he would agree to speak with her. It might be a stretch to think the writer was still there, but she would try.

Closing the notebook, slowly, she thought about the next day. *Tomorrow,* she was looking forward to lunch with Cole and Jeremy.

CHAPTER 14

"They are here!" said Emma, running into the kitchen. "Then you should be helping me get ready," Dora scolded her. Emma went immediately to the cabinet and pulled out the serving bowls to move the cooked vegetables into. Dora was stirring up her mashed potatoes and moved them to one of the bowls Emma put out.

Tim came in and said, "They are in the sitting room talking to Ellis. What can I do to help?"

"Take the chicken platter into the dining room," Dora directed. The table had been set earlier in preparation for the meal. As everything was settled on the table, Dora went to get Papa and the guest. "Papa," she called. "Lunch is ready."

He looked toward the doorway when he heard her voice. He nodded and said, "Dora come in for a moment, this is Cole Tilden."

"Nice to meet you," she said warmly, curious about Papa's oldest friend.

"You also," he said in the same tone.

"And this is Jeremy," Papa said waving his hand for him to walk over.

He came over and took Dora's hand in his.

"I have heard a lot about you," she said with laughter in her voice.

"You have?" he commented. "You will have to tell me all - later."

They all laughed at that reply.

"If you will follow me," Cole asked and graciously offered her his arm.

Ellis murmured, "You always had eyes for the ladies."

Cole chuckled, and said, "Only the prettiest ones."

Dora's face turned red, but she enjoyed the attention.

The group spread out around the table. After they sat, they said prayers and began to eat. Cole and Jeremy were full of compliments on the meal. Ellis leaned back and said, "The best is yet to come."

Cole and Jeremy frowned at him and he said, "Dessert."

"Ahh," Jeremy said as Dora brought out the macaroons, she had made the day before.

"You were right, my favorite part," said Cole, patting his stomach, after trying the macaroons.

Dora said to Papa, "Why don't you and Ellis go to the sitting room and relax, while we clean up." Papa nodded and walked out with Cole.

Dora said to the remaining group, "Everyone grab something and move to the kitchen."

Jeremy realized he was included with that command and did as she asked. He took a stack of plates and followed them into the kitchen.

"Emma you wash, Jeremy you dry. Tim will put up when you are done." Jeremy noticed everyone getting organized without question and went to pick up a towel. Emma grinned at him and whispered, "We follow her lead."

He nodded and waited for her to set up the wash water. As

she washed, she handed him the plates and asked unexpectantly, "Did you know about Papa and us?"

Jeremy juggled and almost dropped the plate he was holding. He also noticed that all motion had stopped in the kitchen. Dora commented, "I would like to know also."

The plate in his hands was dry and he handed it to Tim before stating simply, "I did."

Dora sat down heavily in a nearby chair and said, "How?"

"Ellis visited us in NYC."

"The trips," Emma said out loud, "for engineering jobs."

"Yes, he would stay with us when he was in town," confirmed Jeremy.

"How long?" asked Emma.

"At least since I was ten," he admitted.

"Why the secret? Why not share this part of his life with us?" asked Dora.

"I don't know, they have always been secretive, growing up the way they did. There are things about Pop's life I do not know."

"That's fair," said Emma. "If he wants to share more, we will always be here."

Dora would have liked to run in and demand answers, but in this situation, Emma was the more rational of the two.

They each went back to their jobs working companionably. Tim asked, "Is it ok if I leave? I have to work on some papers for my classes."

"Of course," said Dora, "I'll walk you out."

"I was hoping you would," he murmured. They started to leave and he said over his shoulder, "Bye Jeremy it was nice to meet you."

"You too," he called after him.

Dora held out her hand, he took it and they wandered out of the kitchen together.

Emma wiped up around the sink and looked over at Jeremy drying the final glasses.

"Jeremy," she asked, thinking of those articles she had found the night before.

"Yes?" he asked absentmindedly, wiping the last of the glasses in front of him.

"I need to question someone, that I haven't met before. How would you recommend I start?"

"Do you know anyone that knows that person or someone close to that person? That would give you a beginning," he suggested.

"I might," she said, thinking of Tim, *he worked the docks and delivered papers, he would have the contact I need. I will have to go see him tomorrow.*

"Is it something I can help with?" he asked, interested in spending more time with her.

"No," she smiled, "just something I am working on."

She started to dry her hands, he caught them and he pulled her over to him and said, "I enjoyed our dance last night. "

She turned red and said, "I did also." She let him hold her close, longer than she should have. She finally pulled back from him and said, "I don't think I want anything other than friendship right now."

He shrugged and said, "That sounds good to me also." They walked into the foyer and saw Ellis and Cole were standing in the sitting room doorway. Cole noticed him and asked, "Jeremy are you about ready to go?"

Jeremy wanted to say no, he would have liked to spend more time with Emma, but he said, "Sure, ready when you are."

Ellis and Emma walked them out. Dora passed them on the stoop and said her goodbyes.

Papa was quiet when they shut the door, he wondered toward his study. Emma and Dora watched him, Dora made a movement, like she wanted to go after him. Emma held her back and shook her head. Dora wanted to struggle but instead waited. The sisters didn't say much after that., Dora headed to the kitchen to set up the next day's preparations and Emma went upstairs thinking about what Jeremy said about interviews.

CHAPTER 15

*T*he next morning, the articles were still on her mind as she made her way downstairs. She was getting organized to head to the bakery, where she was scheduled to work that morning.

As she entered the kitchen, she grabbed her regular breakfast roll and her lunch bag. She also took the last two pieces of pie, she planned to give to the little man who always seemed to be nearby.

She had known for some time that she had company on her early morning walks. She didn't know why, but she felt there was no threat from him. The presence felt more protective than anything. As they walked, Emma and her shadow, she thought about how to get him the pie.

Do I hand it to him? No, she thought, *that might make him upset. I know, I'll sign the note 'From a friend.'* Pulling out her notebook as she walked, she jotted down the message. *How to get him that pie,* she would find a way to make sure he got it.

Someone was running near her and she could tell without looking, it wasn't Tony. "Hey, Tim," she said in a low voice without looking over.

"Hey, how did you know?" asked Tim, sounding disappointed.

"I just knew," she said, sad that Tony had continued with their agreement of seeing less of one another.

"Emma. did you want to talk about it?" asked Tim, concerned about her.

"No." She knew what he was referring to. Outside of Emma, Tim was Tony's closest friend. They continued to walk to the bakery, more quietly than normal.

Her watcher noticed the change also. *What happened?* he thought. Tony always watched out for her in the mornings.

"Tim, got a second to do something for me?" inquired Emma.

"Sure," he said, wondering if the favor involved Tony. "Working at the bakery today?"

Glancing down at her clothes and then up again, Emma said, "Yes, it's my day here." With a slight smile, she handed him the bag with the pie in it. "When we get to the bakery, could you take this and my note to the alley and give it to the man hanging out there?"

"Why would you want to do that?" he asked, bewildered.

"Papa told us a story, not long ago, about his childhood and how hungry he could be living on the streets. I just thought about that little man when I saw that pie this morning," she answered honestly.

Dora had told Tim what Papa had said about his childhood and he understood. He looked at her and then at the pie she held out to him, shrugged, and said, "Sure."

She went into the bakery while Tim delivered the pie to her

shadow. In the process of taking off her coat, she realized she didn't talk to Tim when she had a chance. *I will have to go to the clubhouse.*

She made her way to her station and her day went on as usual from there.

Today, she was working on Spitzbuben, a traditional dessert. She sandwiched two cookies together with a decorative cutout and a layer of jam running between the German cookie layers. She started by making a buttery cookie with a light lemon flavor.

Spitzbuben
Ingredients:

- 2/3 cup of butter
- 2/3 cup of confectioners' sugar
- 1 and 3/4 cups of all-purpose flour
- 1 egg yolk
- 1 pinch of salt
- 1 jar of raspberry jam

Directions:

1. In a large bowl, mix the butter in small pieces with confectioners' sugar, flour, egg yolk, and salt, and knead with your hands until you get a nice smooth dough.
2. Put the dough in a clean bowl and place a cloth over it. Place in a cool area for 30 minutes.
3. Preheat the oven to 350F on baking sheets.
4. Cut the dough in half and roll out on a floured surface

to a thickness of 0.08 inch. Use a round cookie cutter (or a glass) with a diameter of 2.4 inches and cut out cookies. Use a smaller cookie cutter to make a hole or heart in half of those cookies. Place the cookies on the baking sheets and knead the remaining dough again and cut out more cookies.

5. Place one baking sheet at a time in the oven and bake for about 10 minutes. Let the cookies cool down a bit on a wire rack.
6. Add the raspberry jam to a saucepan and bring to a boil. Force through a sieve and let cool down for about 5 minutes. Place a small amount of jam (about a teaspoon) on the cookies with no hole and place a cookie with the hole on top.
7. Dust with confectioners' sugar and let cool/dry for an hour on a wire rack.

The jam was jarred in the summer so the cookies could be made all year. Once the jars were opened and the cookies had come out of the oven, Emma started compiling the treats and placing them on parchment paper to be placed in the cases in the front and for special orders.

As she worked, she thought about how she could meet the writer, if he was still working at the newspaper office. *I'll just have to go there and ask*, she thought.

She finished up at the bakery and headed home to change. It had been a productive morning and she was feeling good. It was also coming up on lunch, so she stopped by the kitchen on the way in. Dora had a sandwich waiting for her. She sat down and started eating, tearing at the crusty bread and putting pieces into her mouth.

Dora said, "Chew please," and gave her a glass of milk.

Emma winked at her.

Dora handed her an apple to eat as she finished her sandwich.

"What are you doing today? Working with Papa?" asked Dora.

"Oh, shoot," Emma said out loud. "Well, I'm supposed to, but I need to run an errand."

"Papa is out at the new building. You have some time," Dora said helpfully.

"Great," Emma said, relieved. She didn't want to let him down. "I'll be back in about an hour." She didn't want to share information from the articles with Dora until she knew more about their possible meaning.

"All right," Dora said cautiously. This quieter Emma was a new thing.

Emma headed upstairs to change out of her bakery clothes and into her delivery clothes. She undressed and attached her sheath to her leg before pulling on her loose shirt and pants. She slid her knife into its sheath inside an opening in her pants pocket. She wrapped her braid on her head and covered it with her cabbie hat.

She hurried, trying to catch Tony and Tim before their afternoon deliveries started. Using her shoulder, she pushed the door of the clubhouse open and went in. The other delivery boys didn't take much notice of her, but Tim did. He immediately got up from the table where he was having lunch with Tony when she entered. Before coming over to her, Tim leaned down and said something to Tony in a low voice.

Emma noticed that Tony was not going to come over to speak with her. She tried to not let the hurt show, pulling her hat down to hide her eyes.

Tim came over and said casually, "Hey, what's up?"

She cleared her throat and leaned in a bit, speaking in a low voice. "Tim, I need a contact at the Tribune. I'm following up on a few things."

"What things?" he asked suspiciously. He had already been pulled into more than one adventure with her.

"Nothing really," she said evasively. "I'm just looking into something I saw in the paper." She smiled to distract him. A pretty girl could make a young man forget almost anything.

The smile did its job and Tim said, "Speak with Harry Morgan. He works on the dock and knows all of the goings-on at the paper."

Emma jotted the information in her notebook. "All right," she said and tipped her hat to him. "Off I go." She headed out. She noticed her shadow was with her, she shrugged and went on.

She found the location of the paper and headed to the dock at the back of the building. In the mornings and evenings, wagons would be parked in the area, waiting for papers to be loaded. There was little activity this time of day.

"Away with you, boy. We don't have any work and papers won't be available until this evening," called a man from the dock. He was a big man with dark longish hair, a mustache, and was heavy around the middle. He waved a hand dismissively toward her.

Emma ignored this direction and moved closer. "Are you Harry?"

Harry looked a bit surprised at the voice coming from the boyish figure and peered at her. "Well, it's a girl dressed like a boy." He chuckled and said rather loudly, "I am Harry. What can I help you with?"

"Tim Flannigan said you might know someone who used to write for the paper or might still."

"That big Irish kid who makes deliveries?" he asked.

"Yes," she said briefly.

Harry looked a bit impatient and then said briskly, "What's the name of the person you are looking for?"

She pulled out her notebook and glanced down at the page. "His name is Daniel Cooper. He would have been a writer here about ten years ago."

"Oh, Danny boy. Well, he's still here but he isn't writing much other than editorials these days. You want to meet him?" he offered.

"Yes," she said eagerly, nodding her head, almost dislodging her cap in the process.

He leaned down, reached out his hand, and pulled her up on the dock. She landed with a bounce. Harry said, "Follow me." Emma did so, through the large open warehouse doors to a back staircase. As they went past the second floor, she looked at him questioningly and he said, "Up we go." So, up they went.

They exited the narrow stairway into a busy room full of desks and cigarette smoke. She coughed a bit as she went by. The reporters did not glance up as the dockworker accompanied by a raggedy boy crossed the room. They headed to the opposite side where an office was closed off from the rest of the room by glass. Harry knocked twice and was able to get a response from inside to enter.

Emma glanced at the wording printed on the door and realized they were heading into the Editor's office. *It appears the reporter has moved up since the original articles were printed. I wonder if it was the articles that helped with his promotion,* she thought.

The door opened and Emma could see a gentleman at a large desk. He looked to be in his forties, with a trim waistline, a full head of brown hair, and a bit of gray in his sideburns. He looked impatient at the intrusion until he saw Emma. His eyes went wide and then he sat back in his chair to look at her consideringly.

"Thought I was seeing a ghost for a moment," he said with a

faint smile. "Emma, Mary's daughter, I presume?" He stood and came around his desk to greet her with his hand extended.

Emma shook hands and commented curiously, "You knew my mama?"

"Yes," he said, looking at her a little too intently. "You do look just like her, but a bit taller. Although," glancing down at her, "I don't think I remember ever seeing her in pants." He glanced up at Harry. "I have it from here." Daniel waved a hand at Harry to vacate the room. "Thanks for bringing her upstairs."

With a nod to Daniel, Harry left the room with the door swinging shut behind him.

"Well, Emma, what can I do for you?" asked Daniel.

Emma pulled the articles out of her pocket and said, "I was curious about these."

He frowned when he saw what she was holding.

She hurriedly continued, "Also, they have things in common; they're all of your articles during this time and about the same groups of criminals. Why would Mama have kept them and how did you know her?"

Daniel avoided the questions by starting a conversation about Mama. "I met your mama in the bakery. Her pastries made me fall a little in love with her."

Emma was startled by that remark.

Daniel raised his hand and held it up. "Not to worry, girl, it was all on my side. Your mama only had eyes for your papa. Though I did try to get her attention by hanging out too much at the bakery," he reminisced.

Emma let that information go by and instead started in on more questions about the articles. Daniel had no choice but to answer.

"Emma, those articles are old news. News that ended with the fire." He trailed off, looking very sad for a moment. "What's your interest in these after all this time?"

"I'm looking at what her role was in these. How was she involved? Was she a source?"

"Emma." He came around his desk and took her hands and pulled her up. "Emma," he began again, "I would rather not go into this now. Maybe sometime in the future. I would like you to keep in touch with me; here's my card. Let me know if you need anything." And with that, he escorted her back through the doorway.

Emma felt like she was being rushed out, with Daniel providing little to no information about Mama. The act of not sharing gave her new information to investigate:

1. Daniel did admit to knowing Mama.

2. Daniel said things that happened ten years ago didn't matter, leading Emma to believe Mama probably was involved in the cases and possibly provided information to Daniel for the articles.

She let herself be walked out of the building and to the docks where Harry was still working. As she passed him, he abruptly bumped into her. Daniel glared at him but didn't say anything. Daniel's attention seemed to be on getting rid of Emma as fast as possible.

There was nothing more to do, so she headed down the side stairs and off the dock. Casually placing her hand into her pockets, her fingers encountered a piece of folded paper. She didn't pull it out until she was out of sight of the docks.

As she was leaving, she heard Daniel speak in an angry tone to Harry. "What are you doing standing around? Get back to work!"

She waited until she was several blocks away before she pulled out the paper. It had an address and time on it—234 Smith Street at 8pm—and today's date. She knew it well. The location was the downtown library. Slipping the note back into her pocket, she patted it with her hand. She would be there.

CHAPTER 16

*S*he was thinking about the meeting that evening with Harry as she completed her assigned work from Papa later that day. She tried to concentrate on the work, but she was nervous. It would be nice to have more information about Mama and her involvement in those articles. She put the thoughts out of her mind and focused on her work and got it finished before the dinner hour.

Dinner was the normal noisy affair with Miss May and Miss Marjorie talking about the past and the kids talking all at once. Emma sat there thinking about her evening meeting. The person was a stranger and she thought it best to not go on her own, but Papa was called out of town on a consulting job so he wouldn't be available and Tim was in a night class that evening.

She would like to get Tony to come with her. *But, she thought, it is probably too soon to ask him for a favor. Though I might just wander by his apartment building on the way to the library and, if I accidentally run into him, that would be. . .* She shook her head. *No, I'm better than that, and I won't use Tony in that way.*

She wore her blue and red plaid skirt with red trim and a redshirt. She slipped on her jacket and grabbed her hat. She made sure both of her knives were in place. When Emma heard a tap on her door, she called "Come in." She saw it was Dora. "Hey, what's up?"

Dora watched Emma getting ready to go out. "Sister, where are you heading out to this time of night? Isn't it a bit late?"

"Just headed to the library." The path there was easy from the boarding house.

"Library?" she asked as she sat on the bed with a bounce. "Looking for a new book?" she asked curiously.

It was time to tell her what she had found. "No, I'm going to see if I can find some additional information on a case." She pulled out the articles she had found in Mama's chest. She handed them to Dora, explaining her suspicions and the similarities between them. She also explained where she had gone that day and the note placed in her pocket.

"This person who put this in your pocket. What's his name again?"

"Harry. Harry Morgan."

"Sure, but why all the secrecy? Does this involve Mama?" Dora was interested in anything that might involve her.

"I'm not sure," Emma said, "but I would like to know why she kept these and why Daniel doesn't want to talk to me about her. It's obvious she had something to do with these articles and maybe the outcomes."

"Sister, shouldn't you take someone with you? You don't know this person," said Dora worriedly.

"Well, I thought about Tim but he's in school, and Papa's out of town. I think it'll be fine, and I'll be out in the open at the library," she answered truthfully.

Begrudgingly, Dora nodded and sent her on her way.

Unbeknownst to Emma, Dora sent a note via one of the local boys to Tony and explained Emma's situation. She was hoping he would put aside his hurt feelings and show up at the library. *I did what I could,* she thought as she put the matter out of her mind and set to compiling her food list for the rest of the week.

In the meantime, Emma had started skipping down the stairs on the stoop, heading in the direction of the library.

Her watcher had settled into the alley for the night and had not expected to be running around. When he saw her, he sighed and got up to follow. They both caught the cable car to the library. She and her watcher jumped off and walked the final path toward the library. He stayed outside and kept an eye on people going in and out.

Her meeting was scheduled for the nonfiction stacks. She went to a table in the area and sat down. Waiting nervously, she held the articles tightly in her left hand and tapped her lips with the fingers of her right hand.

It had been about thirty minutes when she heard something behind her. "Don't turn around."

It was Tony. To say she was shocked was an understatement. She didn't turn but murmured, "Why are you here?"

"Dora was concerned about this meeting," he murmured.

"Oh, okay, thanks," she said but thought, *I think.*

"How long are we going to wait for this guy to show up?" Tony questioned.

Emma mumbled out the side of her mouth, "Another twenty minutes, then we're out of here."

"That's fine," he said, grabbing a book from the shelf, and moved to sit at a nearby table. He glanced at the title and laughed out loud; he had inadvertently picked up a book on true crimes. He just shook his head and started to read.

Twenty minutes later. . . "Time's up," murmured Tony, closing his book.

Emma nodded, resigned that there would be no additional answers tonight. She sighed and got up to leave.

Well, for now, she thought, *I'll put these back in the chest and revisit them at a later date.*

They took the long way home walking instead of taking the trolley. There wasn't a lot of talking, but there was a companionable silence.

∾

Her Watcher followed at a distance behind.

∾

Tony left her at her door without comment. As she watched him walk down her stoop, she said softly, "Thank you, Tony."

She didn't think he heard her, but he turned his head toward her with a nod.

She softly closed the door and headed upstairs, mulling over the day's learnings. Though she tried to keep her mind on the case, her thoughts kept drifting to Tony. She would have to remember to thank Dora for sending him to the library. She knew she could defend herself, but it was nice to know Tony would still look out for her. There might be some hope for them.

At this point in the case, she thought, *if Harry didn't consider it important enough to meet me, maybe I should put it away for a while.* She made some notes in her notebook and inserted the articles back inside.

She heard a soft knock on her door. Emma called softly, "Come in."

Dora entered, wearing her nightgown and her hair under a bonnet. "Did you meet him? Did he tell you about Mama?"

Emma shook her head regretfully and said, "No, he didn't show up."

"Oh, that's too bad. Will you keep looking into the articles?" she asked, disappointed.

"For now, I think I will hold off. I will let you know if something changes," promised Emma.

"Thank you, Sister. Get to bed," Dora said as she kissed her on the head.

She got ready for bed with thoughts of Tony and the case swirling in her head.

CHAPTER 17

A few days later, Emma opened the front door to retrieve the newspaper lying on the steps that Saturday morning. It was early and she had the day off. She picked it up and unrolled it.

The front page was pretty routine and contained mostly ongoing political events in the city. It was the article on the bottom of that page that got her attention. A body had washed up in the river and was found by several children. It had yet to be identified.

Hmm, thought Emma, *interesting*.

She looked at the description carefully. The body sounded familiar: dark, longish hair, a mustache, over 6'4". It matched her own written description in her case book. She tore out the article and folded the paper back up. *Was it Harry?"*

She needed to run by the paper office and quietly inquire if he was there today. It was still early enough for her to get there before breakfast. Running back upstairs, she dressed quickly in a black skirt and red blouse, got her hat, and checked her knives. Grabbing a toasted egg sandwich from the kitchen, she gave Dora a quick hug as she headed out. The information would be kept quiet for now, she didn't want to upset Dora.

She made her way to the docks. The wagons were getting back from their morning deliveries. A man she didn't recognize was at the dock where Emma had last seen Harry.

She recognized one of the boys unloading papers from the wagon and walked over to him. "Hey, Mike."

"Oh, hey, Emma." He looked surprised but happy to see her. His face flushed so much it matched his red hair. A pretty girl could really fluster a young boy.

"Mike," she said in a low voice. "Have you seen Harry for the last few days?"

He tilted his head and said, "Now that you mention it, no. I just figured he was on holiday."

Emma started to write that comment down when Mike put out a hand to stop her. "It is odd, though, Harry had said he would see me the next day." He shrugged and went on unloading his wagon.

Hmmm, murmured Emma thoughtfully. *It might be him. There is no guarantee, but the coincidences are piling up. Did this have to do with my questions? I need some real help on this.* The problem was, Papa had gone out again for a meeting in New York. Even taking the train, he would not be back for two weeks.

Jeremy, she thought. *He's training at Pinkerton. Either he or his dad can make the necessary inquiries.*

She knew Cole and Jeremy lived close to the Pinkerton's office in a very nice neighborhood. She had been by there many times on her route.

Instead of using the back door as she would have with deliveries, she went to the front and knocked. She had expected a member of the staff to answer the door but found herself face-to-face with Jeremy.

"Hey," he said, surprised but happy to see her. "Here to see me?" he teased. He knew she and Tony weren't talking and thought he might have a chance.

"Yes, but also to see Cole," she said in a firm voice and a set face.

Jeremy hid his disappointment and said in a more business-like voice, "Something we can help with? Find us an interesting case?" Emma was proving to be someone who would bring excitement wherever she went.

Without waiting for a response, he turned and called out, "Pops."

Cole walked out of the dining room into the open space of the living room. He had his shirt unbuttoned at the collar and a napkin tucked into the top. He was also carrying a cup of coffee. "You called?" he said to Jeremy a bit sarcastically.

"Yes, Emma is here on a visit. She wants to share some information."

"Oh!" said Cole and snatched off his napkin and tossed it on the table. "Emma, welcome. Come in, come in." He waved her toward a couple of chairs in the living room. "Would you like some breakfast?"

Emma took a seat but sat on the edge as she answered. "No, sir, I have something to cover with you."

He could see she was serious. Emma wasn't sure how much to share. She started with the article about the body. "I think the man listed here is Harry Morgan, the gentleman who runs the docks at the local paper." She handed him the article of the man found washed up on the beach.

"Yes, I saw this," Cole said, tapping a hand on the article. "How did you know him, Emma?"

"I was following up on some newspaper articles I found, and he volunteered to go over them with me." She took a deep breath and continued, "When he didn't show, I thought he changed his mind and just didn't want to meet me." She didn't mention her mama's connection to the articles. "I also went by the docks this morning and found out that Harry has not been around for a few days."

"Who did you speak with?" asked Cole formally.

"A friend, Mike Carmichael. He works delivering papers in the mornings," she answered in the same tone.

"You spoke to no one else?" he asked.

"No, I came straight here," she answered.

Cole knew something more was there but didn't pry further. "Okay," he said, "I'll notify my contacts at the morgue and see if we can confirm that it is Harry Morgan. Emma," he said looking directly into her eyes, "good job."

She smiled and looked over at Jeremy. He had been silent throughout the story. He sent her a crooked smile.

"Jeremy, could you see Emma home?" Cole asked, though he knew the answer.

Jeremy could tell it was not a question and did not hesitate to agree. Plus, he had the added benefit of more time alone with her. He liked having her to himself.

As she was leaving, she glanced around the home. It was a grand multistory house, but you could tell they actually lived there. There were books open upon tables, notebooks lying around. It was a house that made you feel comfortable.

"Thank you, Cole. I appreciate your help in this matter," Emma said in a heartfelt manner.

"No, Emma," he said taking her hands, "thanks for coming directly to me."

As they made their way to her home, Jeremy kept Emma entertained with detective stories. She was laughing at his antics but sobered suddenly when he asked casually, "Can I take you to the park this weekend and maybe the dance also?"

Another friend to let down, thought Emma, feeling a bit dejected on the topic of boys. "Jeremy," she started.

He stopped her when he saw her expression. "Okay, I give. Wrong moment?"

"For now," she said, relieved he understood without a long conversation. "Thank you, Jeremy."

"That's all right, I understand," he said, not feeling let down because she had not said no.

"We'll let you know if he is indeed Harry Morgan." And, with that, he tipped his hat and skipped down the stoop toward home.

A few days later, Emma received a note from Jeremy. *Confirmed to be Harry Morgan, will follow up when we get more details.*

He was murdered. Taking a moment to realize what that meant. Harry, a man she had met briefly, was not there anymore because of a brief conversation with her. Was she responsible for his demise? If she was even remotely responsible, she would continue to investigate. It was time to pull out each article and investigate them one at a time. Retrieving them, she laid the first on her bedroom desk. It detailed an investigation into illegal gambling operations found in a local flower shop.

She made notes on the name of the shop and the location. It was off her route but she did know it. The investigation would start tomorrow, she would head there after her shift at the bakery.

Should I tell Dora? she thought to herself. *No, I will wait.*

CHAPTER 18

*T*he next morning, she was surveying her list at the bakery. She also noticed that the Almond-Cherry Soufflés with Warm German Chocolate Sauce was again on her list. *Odd,* she thought, *that has not been ordered for years but now is being ordered once a week.* She made a mental note to add that observation to her notebook. She also made a mental note to ask Cousin who was ordering that particular dessert.

She then put it out of her mind and pulled the ingredients together for a German Red Wine Cake.

German Red Wine Cake

Ingredients:

- 6 ounces of butter, unsalted
- 8 ounces of flour
- 5 ounces of powdered sugar
- 1 teaspoon of baking powder
- 2 tablespoons of cocoa, unsweetened
- 1/2 teaspoon of ground cinnamon

- 1 tablespoon of vanilla sugar
- About 1 cup of chocolate flakes
- 1/2 cup of red wine
- 4 eggs, separated
- Confectioners' sugar or powdered sugar

Directions:

1. Separate eggs. Beat egg white until firm. Set aside.
2. Combine warm butter and egg yolks. Hand mix until creamy.
3. Mix flour with baking powder.
4. Add flour, cocoa, cinnamon, vanilla sugar, and powdered sugar (all dry ingredients) to the egg-butter mix, then add the red wine and firm egg whites.
5. Mix well with a wooden spoon.
6. Place batter into a greased pan.
7. Bake in a preheated oven at 300-350F for about 50 min.
8. After the cake has cooled off, dust with the confectioners' sugar or powdered sugar.

She finished up her list of baked goods, taking a bit longer to put together the special dessert. When her morning was complete, she cleaned up and changed into street clothes before leaving. These included a black and white checked dress with red trim at the bottom. She did a quick check for her knives and took her hat with her as she left the bakery.

She went directly to the flower shop listed in the article. Walking around the area, she could see it was a nice, clean location. As she approached the shop, she could see flowers in buckets and containers on the sidewalk. *This must be it,* she thought. She looked into the window and saw displays full of brightly colored flowers and greenery. Taking a deep breath to steady herself, she entered the shop. A bell jingled above her head, she glanced back at it and then forward toward the sales desk.

"Hello," she called to a man of about fifty. He had a round stomach and a cheerful expression as he came out of the back carrying flowers in one hand and a vase in the other.

"Oh, hi," he called back cheerfully. "Do you need some help?"

"No. . . Yes, I think so." She hesitated and then came to a decision and pulled out the article to show him.

He raised an eyebrow at her. "Okay, so maybe no flowers." He lowered the items he was carrying and placed them on a table. Reaching out, he took the article she was holding and sighed as he read it. He moved to a nearby stool and slumped down on it. "It's been a while since I thought about this event."

"Is that you in the article?" she asked tentatively.

He was silent for so long, she thought he didn't hear her question. He looked up at her but his eyes appeared to be looking through her. "Yes, this was a lifetime ago. Every day after they took over my business, it felt like parts of my soul were being cut away. Then, one day like today, a pretty blonde lady came into my shop and changed my life. Now another very similar pretty blonde lady comes in. . ." He focused on her and asked, "And you are?"

"I'm Emma Evans and my mama was Mary Evans."

He nodded slowly. "Yes, I thought so. I guess you have the right to know. The article is about me and this shop. I am Karl Murphy."

He stood and stepped to the shop door. He turned the opened sign to closed and pulled the shades. Emma wasn't threatened by his actions and felt comfortable staying and hearing more.

"Would you like some lemonade and maybe some cookies?" he asked.

"Yes," she said.

He indicated that she should follow him to the kitchen in the back of the shop. Once there she saw a small white table with four chairs in the cheerful bright yellow room.

"You did know my mama?" she asked, focusing back on him.

"Yes," he said, pouring the lemonade and waving her into a chair. He handed her a glass and a cookie, fixed one for himself, and sat down. "Yes," he said again. "I knew her. She had that lovely bakery. I believe it's gotten bigger and has a new name?"

She nodded in confirmation. "The bakery still belongs to the family and one of my cousins has taken over the day-to-day operations. He has lots of expansion plans." She waited a beat and then started again. "You have more information on Mama?" She was ready to get down to business.

"Yes," he said, sinking into his memories. "We would sometimes trade flowers for Berliners." He savored the thought of that pastry for a moment. "I don't suppose you have any with you?" he asked hopefully. When she shook her head, he sighed. "It was a weekly habit. She would come by when she was out making deliveries and stop by to share the news."

"What happened? How did you get involved in that?" Emma asked, indicating the article, really wanting to know why Mama had it. *Was it because they were friends?*

"Oh, that. . ." He grimaced. "A bad element had moved into the area. They started pressuring different businesses. They used threats and intimidation to get us to partner with them. I was struggling at that time; flowers weren't selling well and, when they offered a business deal to use my storage space, I agreed."

"At first, I didn't realize what I got myself into. The money seemed good and I tried to go along, but what started as a rental opportunity turned into something much worse. I was alone. I tried to contact my brother for help, but I couldn't reach him. It was just me and I didn't know how to get out of the situation."

"Mama was still coming around?" she said, trying to determine her mama's role.

"Mary knew something was wrong when she visited me. The men had started hanging out in the front of the store, bothering the customers and ruining the small amount of business I still had. They started using my back room to keep stolen goods and to run gambling operations. I just had no one to turn to, except for Mary. She took me to the side and asked if I had someone who could help. When I said no, she suggested she might know someone."

"Daniel Cooper, the reporter?" she asked, wanting to connect the dots on the case.

"Yes, but I didn't know his name until the articles started coming out."

"Why go to a reporter and not the police?"

"At that time, we didn't trust the police in Chicago. The department was even more corrupt than it is now."

She cut an eye to him on that one, knowing there still wasn't a lot of trust in the local police.

He continued. "Mary hoped that, if they stirred up enough trouble for the police, they would have to intervene and shut down the illegal activities. She was the main contact with Daniel."

"Mama was the source for the articles?" she asked.

"Yes," he confirmed and stopped for a moment to wipe his eyes, his thoughts steeped in memories of her. "She was so special and cared so much about us. She was able to talk to the different store owners and not arouse suspicion by pretending to make deliveries to their shops. They wanted the assistance and were willing to talk to her once they saw she could help.

Some people talked because they were already being infiltrated and being forced to do illegal things. Others talked to her because they were afraid they might also be drawn in."

"Going by the series of articles, it looks like Mama kept going after your shop was saved."

"Yes, the articles kept coming out. I worried about her but she assured me that Daniel could keep her name out of the paper. She counted on him to keep her and her family safe."

"Did she mention us?" she asked hopefully.

"Yes, she talked about your papa and her special girls all the time."

Emma would have loved to spend the day hearing about the past, but she needed to get moving. "So, what happened? How did it finish for you?"

"Finally, I was cleared of any wrongdoing, but the persons responsible for setting up the operations had not been arrested. They went away, but the threat was still around. I almost lost the shop during that time."

"How did you get through it?"

"Well, the articles kept coming out about other businesses nearby and eventually the area seemed to get too hot for the organization to stay alive. Mary took no credit for helping us. She loved the mystery of it all. She also deeply cared for the people whose lives were affected." He shrugged. "I do know that she made this Daniel Cooper famous. I remember him. I trusted Mary and she trusted him, so we shared our stories. I have to admit, if he had not written the stories, I don't know where we would have ended up." He trailed off, seeming to be lost in the past again. He looked down for a moment and then came abruptly back into the present.

"And you, girlie, what are you doing asking about the past?"

"Mama died when I was very young and this is a way for me to find out more about her," she said simply.

He nodded, understanding loss and trying to connect with those lost to the past.

Emma started to leave but turned back with a question. "The leader of the organization, you indicated that the police were able to shut down many businesses they determined were involved. Who was the main person?"

He shook his head. "It was probably John Harden, but we will never know for sure. The organization had so many layers, the main guy was never found. It was like a regenerating organism; cut off its head and another grows in its place."

"Did John Harden leave after the police got involved?"

"No, I don't think so. I think they just went underground."

A bell went off in Emma's head and she thought, *Underground—could it be the same organization or just a new variation of the same thing, this time more hidden and through the tunnels?*

"I have to go," she said abruptly.

She stopped herself and said in a kind voice, "Thank you for your time today. I appreciate it. I'll stop by again soon and maybe we can trade some flowers for Berliners."

He smiled and then laughed out loud, delighted at the way the day had turned out. "Yes, girlie, you have a deal. Stop by soon and we will have a trade."

He watched her leave and immediately grabbed his jacket. He needed to let certain people know that the smuggling operations were being looked into by outside people. Exiting out the back alley, he avoided areas where he might see Emma.

CHAPTER 19

*E*mma stepped up her investigations and started gathering information on which stores were involved in the current smuggling operation. It was fairly obvious if you knew what to look for. She continued sending her notes to Pinkerton for review. Meetings were held face-to-face every few weeks to communicate new observations. The lines from the stores to the tunnels and suspected businesses involved were becoming clearer. Cole asked her to step back some and keep a low profile while they used the new data to build a file.

As the weeks went by, Emma threw herself into her other cases and stayed out of the smuggling incident. Several of these cases panned out into arrests; such as the gambling establishments and pickpockets frequenting the streets during heavy traffic times. The last discovery had been more accidental, with her stumbling into a room full of gambling tables. When she notified Officer McGarity, he immediately shut down the operations and put more people on the streets to watch for pickpockets. Papa had provided McGarity's name as someone who could be trusted.

She was doing exactly what Cole asked her not to do; she was being too obvious and getting too much notice.

During that active time, a note was delivered to her at the boarding house. It was during the evening hours, so everyone was in the sitting room enjoying the conversation. Tim and Dora were on the small sofa with their books in front of them— Tim's for school and Dora's for house accounting.

There was a knock on the door and one of the older kids, Joe, had run to open it. A moment later he yelled, "Emma, there's a letter for you."

A letter? I wasn't expecting anything, she thought to herself as she went into the foyer to take it.

"Is it from Papa?" asked Dora in a worried voice, joining Emma.

That was also Emma's first thought, that something had happened to him. She opened it and read. "No, no. It's a note from the Chief of Police. He wants to see me in his office in the morning. Too bad Papa isn't here to scrutinize this with me."

Tim appeared at Dora's side as she said, "I think it would be all right. It is the police chief and it's not as if he's a crime boss or something."

Emma's mouth quirked up and she remembered the conversation Cole and Papa had about the current chief's character.

Dora continued, "The note also indicated that McGarity would be picking you up. Isn't he one of the officers you trust with your cases?"

"Yes," said Emma, tapping it, considering what she should do.

"Wait a minute," Tim said, feeling like he should step up. "Shouldn't I go with you?"

"No," Emma said slowly, shaking her head to emphasize it. "I can handle it on my own."

· · ·

Dear-one was reading over her shoulder and said, "I think you should include the rope story here. You're making it sound like it all just came to her when, in fact, she had to work to get those skills."

"Yes, I agree."

Back to the story.

"Emma, we need to talk," said Dora determinedly.

"I agree," said Tim firmly, placing a hand on Dora's shoulder.

"You have a say also?" scoffed Emma, bristling at people wanting to dictate her comings and goings.

Tim nodded and said in a strong voice, "In this case, with Ellis out of town, I think I do."

Dora nodded at him encouragingly. "I think we need to talk about your continued investigations when multiple people have told you to stop. You're attracting attention, such as this meeting with the police chief," he continued.

"Dora, let's move into the kitchen," said Emma, motioning toward the attentive boarders in the sitting room who were all but leaning toward their conversation.

They went into the kitchen.

"Sister," started Dora as they sat down at the table, "you know we love you, but you are fallible. You let your temper and stubbornness push you into decisions that may be questionable. You have to realize that these decisions could affect more than yourself."

Emma started to interrupt, but Dora cut her off. "Don't you remember when you thought you didn't need Miss May to show you how to get out of the ropes the first time?"

Emma turned bright red. "Not my best moment," she admitted.

"And what happened?" Dora prodded.

"I wouldn't ask for help and I sat tied up in that chair all morning and then ended up turning it upside down on myself."

Tim, finally finding humor in their conversation, laughed out loud. "I didn't know about that."

"I didn't think we needed to let anyone know. It would have embarrassed Emma," shared Dora, "but you are family now." She placed her hand into his.

She focused back on Emma. "I bring it up because the rope story proves you sometimes need help and you need to ask for it before you get into trouble."

Emma agreed and told her she would try to be more thoughtful. "I still think I should go alone."

Tim looked doubtful but knew he couldn't miss work at that hour and said, "Fine, just make sure you let us know if there's any trouble." He leaned over and kissed her on the cheek to apologize silently for his slightly overbearing manner.

She smiled, showing she understood and reassured them that she would take no chances.

She thought about the rope story on her way upstairs.

Miss May had tied her up and tried to give her direction on how to escape, but Emma thought she could do it alone. She couldn't and after she knocked herself down, she laid there for an hour struggling, Emma had apologized to Miss May and asked for her help. After she untied Emma, Miss May showed her the trick for getting out of the ropes.

"There are tricks to escaping ropes, many of them involve pretending to not understand what is happening to you." She started to demonstrate by having Emma tie the rope around Miss May's wrist.

"If I'm in a position where I'm being tied up, I sit putting my elbows here against my ribs." She demonstrated the position. "What I'm doing is creating a false space in my wrist. Under no circumstances put your arms straight out when your hands are being bound. Instead, appear submissive as your wrists are tied. Doing this creates a position in the curvature of the wrist, leaving enough space, so when the time for escape presents itself you can extend your arms, place your hands flat and slide them out." She demonstrated this quickly.

Emma asked, "Can you show me that again?"

Miss May smiled, happy Emma was paying attention. "Yes."

"Can I do it now?" she asked excitedly.

They worked on ropes for hours after and tied Emma up several times a week after that until she became proficient.

Jerking herself out of her memories, Emma started to get ready for bed and thought about her meeting tomorrow. She pulled out her notebooks to distract herself. She was making additional notes about fairly obvious crimes that were being overlooked by the local law enforcement. She would keep this to herself for now.

The next morning, after breakfast, Emma heard a knock on the front door. The kids were getting ready for school, so she ran to the window overlooking the stoop. Glancing out, she saw McGarity there in his dress blues.

Emma pulled open the door to greet him. "I didn't realize we were so formal today," she teased as she pulled a cloth from her hair. She had been using it to hold it back as she helped clean up after breakfast.

McGarity was a young officer, very serious about his job, wanting to show his best side for the chief. *Letting Emma see me in my suit wasn't bad either*, he thought.

"Let me change. I won't be a moment." She hurried upstairs, forgetting to ask McGarity to sit down or offer him something to drink.

Dora wandered out of the dining room at that time and

stumbled into the officer. "Oh, excuse me. Am I under arrest?" She grinned up at him in a teasing manner.

"No, miss," he stuttered, taken a bit off guard by a pretty girl. "I'm waiting to take Emma to meet the chief."

"Yes, yes," murmured Dora. "I did hear something about that."

Emma was tucking in her shirt and tightening her belt as she descended the stairs. Reaching into her pocket she found two pins, which she dashed into her hair before plopping on her dashing red hat. She grabbed her jacket from the coat rack before McGarity could offer to help and slipped it on.

"Ready," she said brightly.

McGarity looked a bit bemused at this very pretty girl, he had only seen her in her baggy, boyish delivery clothes. "Yes," he said and offered her his elbow. "Off we go. Nice to meet you," he said to Dora as they were leaving.

Emma took the offered elbow and the two headed out to McGarity's hired cab. Dora waved them off, still worried about the meeting, but knowing Emma could take care of herself.

The trip was quiet, with only Emma providing most of the conversation. The closer they got to the station, the quieter McGarity got. Emma was getting a bit nervous and had many questions.

"What should I expect when I see the chief?"

"I'm a bit confused as to why he wants to see you," McGarity wondered aloud. He continued, "Normally, no one sees him but the top brass. Funny thing is, I didn't even know he knew my name until we started working on these cases a few weeks ago."

They pulled to a halt in front of the precinct. "I'll be taking you in, but I'll not be allowed in the chief's office. Be polite," he advised. "He's a powerful man."

Emma nodded slowly, realizing this meeting may be more involved than a simple thank you. She didn't think and jumped out of the cab before McGarity could make it around to help her. McGarity was a bit startled when she didn't wait to be helped down, but she was too preoccupied to notice.

She made her way through the precinct. Each room filled with blue-coated police officers going quiet as she entered. As she started to ascend the stairs to the upper offices, McGarity was replaced by a higher-level officer. He escorted her to the third floor, where a pair of heavy double doors stood closed. The male secretary inside barely paused to glance at her, told her to take a seat in the chairs in the outer area.

The officer who had escorted her upstairs stayed with her. They sat in complete silence during their wait. Emma wasn't sure if there was someone in the office with the chief or if she was being kept in the waiting area to intimidate her.

The secretary stood, went to the chief's door, and entered the office. He came out and finally deigned to look straight at her. "You may go in now."

Emma and the officer rose. The secretary frowned at him and said, "You may stay seated." He sat.

Emma walked to the double doors, unsure how to open them.

"Oh, for goodness sake," the secretary said as he came around the desk to open the door. Once the door was opened, he gave Emma a good push into the room.

Emma stumbled a bit as she entered. It was a large office with a wood desk positioned on the far wall. The wall behind the chief was all windows. He sat at his desk and did not stand as she entered the room. *Evidently, I don't rate high enough to be allowed to sit. That's ok*ay. She had heard enough about him to know she didn't want to be in that room very long.

This man was purported to be corrupt, but his appearance was more like that of a kindly grandfather with a round body and soft white hair. Well, that was until she got a good look at his face. He had a set expression like granite. She continued to take his appearance in and saw that he did not appear to be in the best physical shape, his uniform covering a lot of fat around his middle.

Strange, she thought, *there is something familiar about him.*

Before she could process this, he spoke, his voice loud in the quiet room. "Girlie, I hear you are causing trouble."

"Trouble?" Emma parroted back to him.

"Yes," he thundered. "You need to keep your eyes and ears on your own business. Let the police handle things."

"But you aren't," she said without thinking.

That response changed his expression from granite to absolute fury. His face started to turn purple; he stood and leaned forward, planting his hands on his desk. The motion made Emma back up, but only a pace. She didn't want to show that she was intimidated.

He waggled his fingers her way. "I'm warning you that you will not like my response if you don't stay out of business that's not yours."

"Warning me?" She decided to just let her responses fly. "Really?"

The narrator commented, If Emma hadn't been only sixteen, she would have known to not poke the bear or not to aggravate or irritate anyone who can make you sorry.

"I'm just seeing what anyone would see if they looked," she said heatedly. The chief returned her glare as Emma continued. "What about the illegal gambling on Houston Street? What about that house of ill repute on 4th?"

The chief had heard enough and slammed his hands on the desk. "Listen here, girly, if you don't think I can bring down retribution on you and your family, then you better think twice."

That startled Emma and immediately shut her down. She didn't think her actions could hurt her family; she had only been thinking of herself. Dora had been right; the decisions she made could impact people other than herself.

The chief sat back down at his desk, feeling more in control of the situation, and picked up a pen. His voice went low and menacing. "I have been told your family owns several businesses. What if the permits for those got revoked?"

Emma realized she had gone too far and schooled her facial expression to look contrite. "I'll keep my observations to myself in the future."

That calmed him down. He averted his gaze. "Fine then. I think we have nothing more to talk about." He waved his hand, indicating she could leave.

She turned slowly and left the room.

The secretary, who seemed to be aware of what was said in the room, muttered to her as she passed close to him on her way out. "You'll want to listen to him on this and keep a low profile for a while." With that bit of advice, he turned her over to the waiting officer.

He escorted her back to McGarity. McGarity looked at her questioningly, but Emma was quiet during the ride home. He walked her to the door, tipped his hat, and left.

She didn't go in immediately; it was still early in the day. She took a long walk to clear her head. The threats to the business were worrying and she would do anything for her family. *What to do next?* she thought.

CHAPTER 20

*W*hat Emma did over the next few days was continue to work her schedules at the bakery and on the delivery wagon. She was committed to keeping the low profile the police chief had insisted upon. She would do anything to protect her family.

While riding in the delivery wagon with Tim, she started thinking about the last time she had seen Tony's dad. He seemed to freeze up when she asked about his job. Tony hadn't mentioned anything about the family having financial troubles. Coming to a decision she decided to check it out, in a low-key way. Laughing suddenly, she thought, *Well, at least I'll get to spend time with one of the Marella's, and this case has an added benefit of not involving the chief of police in any way.*

The next morning, she was off from the bakery and the delivery wagon, so she took the opportunity to go by Tony's apartment building. She probably wouldn't be welcomed inside, so she waited at the edge of the stoop for Mr. Marella to exit the building. She was dressed in her boy gear to blend in as she followed him to his job. As he descended, she ducked out of sight, behind the side of the stoop, pulling her cap lower over her eyes. Waiting a moment, she followed him, keeping her distance.

~

Her watcher was unsure what Emma was up to, but would accompany her in case she needed him.

~

This could be a waste of time, she thought. *I may just confirm that he was working at his normal job and didn't want to talk about it. People have good days and bad days. Maybe that was a bad day for him.*

She watched as he entered a building under construction. *That makes sense,* thought Emma. Holding back, so as not to be seen, she looked around and followed him in. Workmen walked by her on their way out, not giving her much notice. Continuing to the back, she thought, *I might as well say hello to Mr. Marella since the covert activity hadn't worked out.*

She made her way through the long hallway and heard voices toward the back. As she got closer, she realized they were arguing. Mr. Marella was saying to the unnamed man, "I can't continue to hide this. It's too much to ask." His voice sounded strained, not at all like his normal self.

"You agreed," the unidentified man said loudly.

"Yes, because I didn't want to ruin your son's life. But what about her parents, don't they have a right to know?" Mr. Marella asked in a quieter voice.

"I don't want to talk about that," the unidentified man said flatly.

"Well, you're going to have to talk about it. I can't lie anymore about what I found," said Mr. Marella in a more heated voice.

She could hear someone pacing. A loud sound, maybe equipment falling, and a scuffling caused her to make a quick decision. She drew her knife and entered the room. Mr. Marella saw her and dropped the older, rather rotund man he was holding against the wall. The man slid down to the floor and tried to crawl away. He noticed Emma's knife and said, holding his hands up, still on his knees, "No trouble here."

"Mr. Marella?" she asked, indicating the man on the floor with her knife.

"Let him go," he said in a defeated voice, pulling his fingers through his hair.

"We'll talk about this later," the man said, getting to his feet and shaking his fist in a threatening manner as he left the room. They heard him scurry down the hall and out the front door.

Mr. Marella continued to stare at the door. Finally, he turned his gaze toward Emma. "Emma, what are you doing here?" He was shocked at her appearance and he seemed stunned by the knife in her hand. She lowered her arm slowly down to her side, she had forgotten that she still had it out.

"Are you all right?" she asked, avoiding his question.

"What?" he asked, clearly having a hard time concentrating.

She repeated the question. "Are you all right? Who was that man?"

"Him?" She nodded, and he finally answered, "My boss on this job. This is his house."

"What were you arguing about?" she asked, trying to figure out what he was involved in.

He looked at her, ignoring her question, and repeated his own. "Emma, why are you here?"

"I was worried about you. You looked distracted last time I saw you," she said, feeling at a loss. She was trying to help but it wasn't working out.

"That was quite a long while ago," he stated, thinking of that last visit.

"I know," she said, feeling guilty. "I had planned to check in with you earlier."

"Well, you needn't worry. I'm just fine," he said brusquely, not wanting to involve her in this matter.

"But. . ."

"Emma, I said I was fine. Leave it at that," he said in a harder voice.

"Just one thing," she said. He looked at her in exasperation as she continued. "If you want to talk about this or need some help, please let me know. I do have resources that we might use if needed."

"I will," he said, feeling he couldn't involve her in this.

"Promise me," she pressed.

He looked at her silently for a long time and finally said, "I promise."

"Good," she said, relieved, knowing he would keep his promise.

"Don't you have somewhere to be?" he asked.

"Yes, yes I do," she said and turned around to leave.

"Emma." He reached out to touch her shoulder. "I appreciate your worrying about me. We miss you."

She just couldn't stand it. She whirled around and hugged him tightly. "I miss you all so much." She left the room in a hurry, but not before he could see her tears.

Mr. Marella stood there, wishing he could call her back and ask for help, but he was in a position where he could get someone hurt if they found out what he knew. Trying not to think about it, he started working on the gas lighting in the room he was in. He was glad he had his boys working another job, keeping them out of this mess.

A few days later, he wasn't sleeping and he was withdrawing more and more from his family. He made a difficult decision, thinking of his promise to Emma, and made his way to the bakery. She had the afternoon off and he hoped to catch her on her way home. Not wanting anyone to see him, he waited a few blocks down the street for her. Spotting her, he called out, "Emma, can I speak with you?"

She looked over and saw Mr. Marella. She was surprised to see him so soon after their last conversation. "Of course," she said.

"Is there somewhere private we can talk?" he asked, looking around.

"Papa is in New York this week. We can use the basement lab," she suggested, happy he had kept his promise and was coming to her.

He nodded and they walked together to the boarding house. He seemed so upset, she didn't want to ask him any questions until they got somewhere private. It was a silent walk.

Dora was in the dining room as they passed. Emma motioned to her to stay back; she nodded and stayed where she was. Emma and Mr. Marella made their way down the basement stairs. It housed Papa's lab, but there was a sitting area where they could have their conversation.

Mr. Marella slumped down into the chair and put his face in his hands. Emma sat across from him and waited patiently.

"Emma, I'm so scared and I need some help to get out of trouble," he said with a tremor in his voice.

"What kind of trouble?" she asked trying to keep the worry out of her voice.

"Bad. Really bad," he said.

She waited for him to continue.

"They're threatening my family and they tried to take Enzo yesterday," he said.

"Take him?" she asked incredulously.

"Yes," he said simply.

"But why?" she asked, not understanding what he could be involved in that might cause someone to take a child.

"I saw something they didn't want me to see. I was working

at the Barrett Street building, the one you followed me to," he said, looking at her. When she nodded, he continued. "The building I am working in made it through the fire of 1871 and now we're rehabbing and updating the gas and water lines."

She nodded again, encouraging him to continue.

"We were making good progress, and there was one room they had told me to limit the piping in. The layout they had in mind was going to cause lots of extra pipe by avoiding this one wall. I was the only one there at that point. I had sent everyone else home as I continued to work on that area. I just thought I could save us some time and check inside the wall to see if it could hold the piping." He took a deep breath and continued, "I started taking down the plaster wall, using smaller holes to check for clearance. Initially, there didn't seem to be any problems, so I increased the size of the upper hole. I saw this material inside. It was rough. I admit I was curious and pulled on the fabric. When I pulled on the cloth to remove it, I found it was caught on something.

She was thinking about that and asked, "Didn't you worry that they told you not to work there?"

"Not really," he said candidly. "Usually, if I can save the client money, they forgive any liberties I may take." He paused for a second, knowing what part of the story was coming up next.

Emma saw his hesitation and encouraged him by saying, "Keep going."

This part seemed to cause him pain. He frowned heavily and looked at his hands. "That was when I realized what the cloth was covering. I pulled it out. It was a girl of about twelve, such a little thing with black hair and brown eyes."

Emma was shocked. She didn't know what he had found, but she hadn't expected to hear about a body. She asked hesitantly, "Did you recognize her?"

"No, I haven't seen her before this. I don't think I could have kept quiet if I knew her. I keep thinking of her parents and what they're going through," he said as he looked up, tears streaming down his face.

"How long do you think she's been there?" she asked, thinking about how long bodies took to decompose.

"Not long. She still looked like she might wake up," he admitted, wiping his eyes with both hands.

"What did you do?" Emma wasn't sure what she would have done in his place.

"I didn't know what to do. I felt dizzy and couldn't catch my breath. I kept telling myself I had to go to the police and show them what I found but. . . I don't know how long I stood there; I just couldn't move. That was when the building owner Mr. Simpson and his son came into the room."

He seemed to be reliving the experience. "They were angry that I had started in that room. I realized the anger was because I had found her. I could tell from how they were acting that they knew she was in there."

He remembered that conversation so clearly. Mr. Simpson was shouting at him, "What are you doing? You had instructions to not enter this room, much less to start taking down the walls."

"There's a girl in there," he stated, still feeling fuzzy in the head.

Mr. Simpson turned to his son and said, "Kevin, check the house to see if anyone else is here. Now!" Kevin moved quickly through the house, opening and closing doors, checking for anyone who might still be there.

Mr. Simpson kept shouting questions at him. "Why did you enter a room you were told not to? You know this is a firing offense."

Odd, he thought, *they aren't mentioning the girl.* Michael tried to talk to Mr. Simpson. "Do you know who is in the wall?"

"That's none of your concern," Mr. Simpson stated.

"But shouldn't we go to the police?" Michael asked.

"For what?" Mr. Simpson asked belligerently.

"To tell them that we found her," he said lamely.

"No, you won't tell anyone anything. You'll keep working the job and forget what you found."

He was so confused, but something did get through the fuzziness that had taken him over and he straightened up. "Did you kill her Mr. Simpson or was it Kevin?"

Mr. Simpson looked nonplussed at that question. "That's my business, not yours."

Michael just shook his head and said more firmly, "No. I'm going to the police."

At that moment, Kevin came back into the room with a gun drawn, saying, "I don't think so." He looked over at Mr. Simpson and said, "We're going to have to do something with him."

"No. no. I think we can reach an agreement. Can't we, Michael?" Mr. Simpson inquired softly.

Michael just looked at the two without saying anything.

Kevin said, "How about, if you don't cooperate, we take your youngest from you?"

Whatever fuzziness was still affecting Michael cleared up with that one statement. "Enzo? Why would you want to bring him into this?"

"I didn't, you did. Now, if you just repair the holes and follow our instruction about the lamp placement and keep your mouth shut, we won't take Enzo."

"You can't be that evil," Michael said incredulously.

"If you don't follow our instructions, you'll find out how evil we can be."

Michael felt he had no choice. He covered up the holes and told his boys to work other jobs while he finished that one.

❧

He brought himself back into the present with Emma and said, "I can't live with what I've done."

"Where's Enzo now?" she asked.

"He's in school," he said.

"First thing is to pick him up and place him somewhere safe," she said, drumming her fingers on her lips.

"Yes, but where are you thinking?" Michael said, ready to have someone direct him in this mess.

"Not here at the boarding house. They've seen me now and they may check here. Let's put him with my uncle Otto. He has all those boys and he works early mornings, so he'll be there during the day to watch out for him."

"Will Otto be all right with that?" Michael asked. He was concerned about involving more people in this.

"Yes." She was sure he would help; he loved kids and would do anything to protect them. "Next, we need to get you to the Pinkerton office. We need to meet with Cole to decide the next steps. Are you in agreement with my plan?"

Michael was amazed at Emma's planning. "I'm in," he said. "Let's go."

First, they wanted to pick up Enzo at school. Michael told the principal that the boy was needed for a family emergency. It was the truth; there was an emergency in the family.

Enzo walked up to greet his father and said, "Emma, what are you doing here? Papa, is something wrong?"

Michael bent down in front of him, looked him in the eyes, and said, "I made a bad decision that I don't want you affected by. That person that tried to take you yesterday is part of this. In order to protect you, we'll need to put you with Emma's uncle until we straighten it out."

Enzo didn't argue. He could tell Papa was serious and understood that he needed to do as he was told. They took Michael's wagon to Otto's house and made sure Enzo got safely inside.

Otto was there and awake when they entered. "Emma, what's happening?"

"We have some trouble," she said simply, "and we need to keep Enzo from being taken." She explained that there were people angry at Michael and had threatened him.

"Of course, we'll help." He looked down at Enzo and said, "Go in the kitchen to see Freida." He called out, "Freida, Enzo is coming back to see you." Otto had known Tony's family for a long time.

She called back, "I'm in the kitchen and I have a pastry."

Otto puffed on his pipe and said to Michael and Emma as they watched Enzo run to the kitchen, "What now?"

Emma answered for them, "I'm taking Michael to Pinkerton to get some help."

"You can't tell me more?" he asked.

"I shouldn't involve you any more than I have," explained Michael.

Otto nodded and hugged Emma. "We will take care of him for you. Now, you best be off."

Michael and Emma took the wagon to the Pinkerton offices. Michael asked with worry in his voice, "Will they help? Should we go straight to the police?"

"I'm not sure the police can be trusted and I know we can trust Pinkerton. They'll involve the police when appropriate," she said reassuringly.

"Good," he said, trusting her. He already felt better, knowing Enzo was safe.

As they made their way to Pinkerton, Emma asked, "What do you want to accomplish here?"

"I want to get the girl back to her parents and I want Mr. Simpson and his son Kevin in police custody."

Emma nodded and said in a firm voice, "That sounds like a plan."

They entered the office and she went up to the main front

desk where the secretary sat and asked, "Is it possible for us to see Cole?"

"They're out on a big job just now and aren't available until later today," the secretary replied.

Emma looked at Michael and nodded. "Do you want to leave a message?" she asked him.

"Yes, tell him to come to 247 North Street as soon as he gets back. Tell him to bring more men with him."

"I'll tell him," the secretary promised. Mr. Tilden had instructed that, if Emma came in, she was to get an immediate audience with him. He thought, *I should send someone to let them know she needs them.*

They turned and were leaving as Michael asked, "What now?"

"We keep an eye on the house so they don't move her somewhere else," she said simply.

"Do you think that's necessary? Couldn't the police do that?" he asked, ready for this to be over.

She said quietly, "I have serious concerns about going to the police without Pinkertons' involvement. I'm afraid they may try to blame you. The men involved may try to say you killed her and you were threatening THEM."

"I hadn't thought of that," said Michael slowly.

"So, you go back to work as if nothing's happened," she said.

"What if they come in while I am there?" he asked, concerned for her safety.

"Tell them you just panicked and had a change of heart," she suggested.

"What will you be doing?" he asked.

"I'll be inside with you. I'm hoping the Pinkertons will show up soon," she said.

"What if things go wrong?"

"Then we react and defend. You use anything at your disposal to do that and I'll be there," she said.

"I understand what you're saying. We can do that," he said, liking the plan. He wouldn't abandon that child in the wall again.

They made their way back to the house and started working in the room nearest to where the girl was hidden. It wasn't long before Mr. Simpson and Kevin showed up. They entered the house with a slam to the front door. Michael motioned for her to move into another room.

Emma mouthed, "Stay calm."

He nodded and went back to his work. He heard them come up behind him.

Kevin shoved Michael's shoulder and said, "What are you still doing here? I thought you wanted out."

"No, I'm okay now. I was just nervous," he said, continuing to work on the wall, still not looking at them.

"Nervous?" Kevin laughed with a sneer. "You appeared angry, not nervous."

"Yes, well, I understand where you're coming from and I'm okay," he said.

"Yeah, somehow I don't believe that. And by the way, I went by your son's school and he was gone. Now, where could he have gotten to?" Kevin asked musingly.

Michael tensed but still didn't turn around.

Mr. Simpson was running out of patience and shouted, "You turn around and look at me!"

Michael turned slowly toward him, keeping his wrench hidden at his side. He remembered what Emma said about going on the attack. Mr. Simpson had the gun aimed at his chest. Kevin didn't have a gun and was waiting for instructions from his father, his gaze focused on Michael.

Michael saw Emma come up behind Mr. Simpson with a large piece of pipe. She raised it to swing at Mr. Simpson's head. There was a whoosh and he went down in a heap. Michael took the opportunity to take his heavy wrench and bring it down on his back. The gun slid across the room.

They could hear running steps coming into the building. Kevin looked confused and decided to take that opportunity to leave the house by diving out of an open window.

Jeremy led the charge inside. Emma and Michael were sitting on Mr. Simpson, holding him down.

"Is he. . ." started Jeremy.

Emma finished for him, "Alive? Yes."

Jeremy waved at two of his men, directing them. "Take care of him."

"Jeremy, another man got away, out the back," she said quickly as she got up.

"You two, after him." Jeremy pointed to two more of his men. They left at a run.

The other Pinkerton detectives got Mr. Simpson tied up and placed him in the corner.

Emma went up to Jeremy and whispered in his ear. He went pale but looked at Michael and said, "Can you show me what you found?"

He indicated the room next door. Emma followed them. He started opening the walls and immediately an odor permeated the room. Emma continued to watch as they fully revealed the body of the young girl. There was not a dry eye in the room as they viewed the little girl in a light blue dress, her dark hair covering part of her face.

Jeremy had sent for the police and said, "Emma and Michael, we can take care of the follow-up if you want to leave."

"Will you need our statements?" asked Michael.

"No," said Jeremy, "we can say we had a source who turned this in."

"Thank you," said Michael.

Emma said to Jeremy, "Thank you for coming."

"Anything for you," he said sincerely. "Now get, you know you don't want to be found here."

Emma looked at Jeremy and said quietly, "I took this case because I thought it would keep me out of the police chief's path."

Jeremy nodded and said, "We need to make sure he doesn't know your involvement. Get going NOW!"

Michael and Emma left in a hurry on foot and, as they turned the corner, they noticed the police arriving. They parked their wagon in an alley a few blocks down. They went to retrieve it and headed home.

Jeremy did not disclose their involvement in the case.

The girl's name turned out to be Meghan Walters; she was twelve years old and had been missing for about two months. The papers reported that she had been snatched on her way home from school. The parents were heartbroken; she was their only child.

Mr. Simpson went to prison for the murder, Kevin had not been found.

That case was harder emotionally than Emma was used to. She hoped future cases would have a less personal element.

CHAPTER 21

The case with Mr. Marella made Emma want to see Tony. Since they had their fight, she hadn't seen much of him outside of work. She had not known how much she would miss him. He had been her constant companion and life was empty without him.

Tim had kept her updated with Tony's latest activities. He had started working for the museum and was over the moon about it.

That evening, she went home with thoughts of Tony on her mind and baked him his favorite Strudel to celebrate.

Strudel
Ingredients:

- 3 cups of all-purpose flour
- 1/2 cup of canola oil, divided
- 3/4 cup of warm water (120F)
- 1 large egg, lightly beaten

Filling

- 1 and1/2 cups of fresh breadcrumbs
- 6 cups of chopped, peeled apples (about 6 medium)
- 1/2 cup of raisins
- 1 cup of sugar
- 1 and1/2 teaspoon of ground cinnamon
- 1/3 cup of butter, melted
- 3 tablespoons of sour cream

Directions:

1. Place flour in a bowl and stir in 1/4 cup of oil (mixture will be slightly crumbly). In a small bowl, slowly whisk warm water into beaten egg; add to flour mixture, mixing well. Beat in remaining oil until smooth. Transfer to a greased bowl, turning once to grease the top.
2. Cover with a kitchen towel and let rest in a warm place for about 30 minutes.
3. Preheat oven to 350F. Spread breadcrumbs into an ungreased baking pan. Bake 10-15 minutes or until golden brown, stirring occasionally. Cool completely.
4. Dust surface with flour.
5. Divide dough in half; place one portion on parchment and roll to a very thin 24x15 inch rectangle. (Keep remaining dough covered.)
6. Sprinkle 3/4 cup of breadcrumbs over rectangle to within 1 inch of edges. Starting 3 inches from a short side, sprinkle 3 cups of apples and 1/4 cup of raisins

over a 3-inch-wide section of dough. Mix sugar and cinnamon; sprinkle half of the mixture over fruit. Drizzle with half of the melted butter.

7. Roll up jelly-roll style, starting at the fruit-covered end and lifting with towels; fold in sides of dough as you roll to contain the filling. Transfer strudel to a baking pan.

8. Bake on lowest oven rack 45-55 minutes or until golden brown, brushing the top with sour cream two times while baking. Repeat with remaining ingredients.

9. Using parchment paper, transfer to a wire rack to cool. Serve warm or at room temperature.

She got the dessert organized at home, boxed it up, and started in the direction of Tony's apartment. Just outside of it, she ran into his mom. Mrs. Marella appeared to be upset to see Emma so near their house.

Emma tried to start a conversation, "Mrs. Marella, hello. How are you?"

"I'm good," she said, her face set in angry lines. "Are you just going through the neighborhood?" She hoped the answer was yes, wanting to protect her son beyond all else.

"No," Emma said quieter than before, sensing she was not wanted. "I just wanted to drop this off for Tony to congratulate him on his new job." She indicated the box she held.

"Emma, do you think that's appropriate now?" Mrs. Marella asked rather shortly.

She mumbled a bit, her head hung down. "Well, I just thought. . ."

"It would be best if you headed on your way," Mrs. Marella said with a glare.

She looked down at the box she carried and then back at Mrs. Marella. "Can you give this to Tony?" she asked in a rush and put the box in an unsuspecting Mrs. Marella's arms. She turned and slowly walked away.

Mrs. Marella looked at the box, shrugged, and balanced it with her other packages. She made her way upstairs and had to knock on the door to get help. Enzo opened the door and immediately reached for the box of strudel.

"Pastry!" shouted Enzo to the rest of the family.

"That one goes to the kitchen," she called, watching him runoff.

Tony was washing some glasses when Enzo charged in with the box. He looked up and said, "Pastry, you mentioned?"

"I think so and it smells really good," said Enzo.

Tony opened the box and found the strudel. "My favorite," he said, looking closely at it.

His mom had entered the kitchen and was looking distracted.

"Hey, Mom, where did you get the strudel?" Tony asked, keeping his voice even.

"I um. . . just picked it up on the way home," Mrs. Marella murmured.

"Picked up," he said quietly as he stared down at the box. The intricate design looked very familiar and then he tasted it. He immediately recognized the flavor. "Mom, you saw Emma. Where?" he demanded.

"Tony, you don't—"

"Where, Mom?" Tony asked determinedly.

"Outside," she said begrudgingly and, when he raised an eyebrow at her, she continued, "Just now."

"Just now. . ." He didn't delay in going after Emma. Grabbing his hat and jacket, he was out the door as his mother called for him to stop.

"I don't want you going after that girl. She doesn't care about you," she said loudly.

Tony stopped for a moment and turned back toward her. "Mom, you don't know what kind of a person she really is and how much she loves us. You might want to talk to Dad about what she did to help him and our family."

She watched him leave, turned toward Michael, and said, "What is he talking about?"

"Come, sit. We need to talk." She listened quietly and realized how wrong she was about Emma.

Tony went downstairs as fast as possible, slipping on the last ones, pulling himself up, and going outside. He looked left and then right. He saw her in the distance and started at a dead run toward her.

"Emma!" he called. She didn't turn at first. He called again, "Emma!"

She turned slowly and looked at him hesitantly.

"Why didn't you bring the strudel to the apartment?" Tony asked.

"I wasn't sure I would be welcomed, but I wanted to let you know how proud of you I am," she said, the words pouring out.

"Not welcome? You're always welcome," he said, eyes wide in shock.

She looked hurt and confused.

Immediately, Tony felt guilty about how he had acted toward her. "I know I've been behaving badly by avoiding you. I'm so sorry for that. My only excuse is that I needed some time to work out how I was feeling," he said.

"Tony." She reached out to him but started to pull her hand back before she made contact. He grabbed the retracting hand and pulled her closer.

"Emma, I'm sorry I made you feel like I didn't want to see you, when the truth is, I wanted to see you every day. I've missed our morning walks. Not to mention your pastries."

She blushed but continued to stay silent.

Tony continued, "Let's go back to where we were as friends."

She had thought about this for a while. "Tony, I don't want to go back."

He paled at this statement and gripped her hands tighter.

She winced a bit at the strong grip but continued. "I want to move forward instead."

When he looked confused, she said, "Tony, I want to be with you, but we'll have to move slowly."

He was grinning foolishly and said, "Really?" He grabbed her closer and gave her a long leisurely kiss. "Is that slow enough for you?"

"Tony," she said, blushing furiously, enjoying every second of the kiss.

He was still grinning. *Progress*, he thought.

They walked back to her house slowly, holding hands. They didn't talk much until they got to her stoop.

"I did enjoy the strudel," he said quietly, looking deeply into her eyes.

"I'm glad. Congratulations on the job. I'd like to hear more about it. "

"Tomorrow night," he promised.

"Come over for dinner and then we can walk and talk after. We need to catch up with each other." They kissed again and she wandered dreamily up the stairs into the house.

Dora was waiting for her, grabbed her hand, and dragged her into the kitchen.

"Tell me everything," she said, having seen the long kiss.

Emma started with how she went over to Tony's and ended up kissing him (twice!) on the way home.

Dora had many questions. "So, you are together now?"

Emma said simply, "Yes."

"And what about Tony's new job?" asked Dora.

Emma blinked and then laughed. "We didn't get around to talking about anything but us."

Dora laughed with her, knowing how that felt. "Okay, so where do you go from here?"

"Well, we continue as best friends but also with a special addition."

"Hmm, all right, Emma, but what about Tony's mom? She sounds like you may be on the outs with her."

Emma sat for a moment and thought about that problem. "Yes, I'll think of something to help with that."

"Is Tony going to tell her?"

She nodded. "We don't want to hide anything."

"When will you see him next?"

Emma blushed. "He'll be here tomorrow night for dinner and a walk. That is if you can add another person to the pot?" She waited for an answering nod. "We also discussed attending the fair this weekend."

"Don't be surprised if we start seeing him a bit more," murmured Dora with a smile.

"More?"

"Yes, it turns out that Tim and Tony like to spend time with us," Dora said with a smile.

Tony came over that next night to share his possible future at the museum. Emma caught Tony up on her cases. They were finding their way to a new future, together.

CHAPTER 22

*E*verything continued to stay quiet for Emma, both personally and in cases. The days moved forward with Emma seeing Tony, working deliveries with Tim, and working in the bakery.

On a delivery day, Tim dropped off Emma at the bakery so she could give Cousin their orders for tomorrow's deliveries. As she went in the back door, she saw Tony already there, putting in his orders for the next day. When he saw her, he sent her a wink.

Cousin saw the wink and spotted her. "Emma, after you turn in your delivery orders, I need to speak with you about a special order for tomorrow."

Tony nodded in her direction and headed out to the museum for his afternoon job.

"What's up, Cousin?" Emma asked, taking off her hat and undoing some of the tight braid in her hair. She handed him her delivery orders.

As he was glancing at them, he said, "We have an order of Chocolate Leaves with Asbach Uralt-Poached Pears and Grape-fruit-Lemon Quark Mousse that came in again this afternoon."

Emma squinted at him. "That is getting ordered a lot lately—"

Before she could finish, Cousin interrupted, "And only your Mama and you know how to make it the way this customer likes it."

She grimaced and explained, "I don't mind making it occasionally, but this is happening multiple times a week."

He got to the point quickly. "Will you be able to make it?"

Emma sighed and then nodded. "Yes, I can do that. Could you check the supplies for all of the ingredients?"

She jotted down the ingredients and Cousin surveyed the list. "I have all of this," said Cousin, "but the rose water. I can have some delivered before you start in the morning."

Emma noticed Chloe frowning at Cousin from her workstation. "What's up with you and Chloe?"

"There is no me and Chloe, and I don't want to talk about it," he said defensively and walked off, glaring at both Chloe and Emma.

She sidled up to Chloe and whispered, "What happened?"

"If he doesn't want to talk about it, then neither do I," Chloe said in a huff and went back to punching the dough she was working on.

Oh well, thought Emma, *not my business.*

Funny, she thought as she was walking home later, *no one orders that particular recipe outside of the holidays. I'll have to think about this development. Is it important or just a coincidence that Mama was at the bakery on the night she died because of that dessert?*

Continuing home, she took some shortcuts through the back streets and ran up the steps of the boarding house. "I'm home!" she called out as she sailed into the house.

"So, I hear," answered Dora from the dining room. "Change your shoes and clothes."

"Okay," Emma said, resigned to changing, and trudged

upstairs to wash up and put on her split skirt and blouse. Dora followed her up to hear about her day.

"Dora," she said as Dora helped pick up the dirty clothes. "Do you remember Mama making Chocolate Leaves with Asbach Uralt-Poached Pears and Grapefruit-Lemon Quark Mousse for a special customer? I remember Papa mentioning something about it the night Mama died."

Dora sank onto the bed, thinking intently about what Emma had said. "Now that you mention it, yes. Papa was so upset, he kept mentioning that, if she hadn't been at the bakery at that hour, she would still be alive. Why do you ask?"

"No real reason," Emma said truthfully. "I have gotten this special order more often than I would have expected this time of year and was curious about it."

Chocolate Leaves with Asbach Uralt-Poached Pears and Grapefruit-Lemon Quark Mousse
Ingredients:

- 8 ounces of semi-sweet German chocolate, chopped
- 2 cups of Gewürtztraminer
- 2/3 cup of sugar
- 1/4 cup of Asbach Uralt
- 4-star anise
- 3 firm Bartlett pears peeled, halved, and cored
- 1 and1/2 cups of quark
- 2 tablespoons of grapefruit juice
- 2 tablespoons of lemon juice
- 2 tablespoons of vanilla sugar
- 1/4 teaspoon of sea salt
- 4 tablespoons of cornstarch
- 1 and1/4 cups of confectioners' sugar
- 1 cup of heavy cream

- 6 egg whites
- 1 pint of raspberries
- 2-3 tablespoons of superfine sugar
- Chopped pistachios for garnish
- Berries for garnish
- Mint for garnish

Directions:

1. Melt the chocolate in a double boiler. Pour the melted chocolate onto a parchment-lined baking sheet and, with a palette knife, smooth to about 1/8 inch thick. Refrigerate until completely hardened, about 20 minutes. The chocolate may curl at the edges during the cooling process; this is normal.
2. Remove the chocolate from the refrigerator and let sit at room temperature for 45 seconds to 1 minute. Cut eight squares into the chocolate but do not remove the squares from the parchment. Place back in the refrigerator.
3. Cut a circle of parchment that is slightly smaller than the opening of the saucepan in which you will poach the pears. Cut a hole about 1 inch in diameter into the center of the parchment. Place all ingredients in a saucepan. Place the parchment directly over the ingredients so that the pears stay completely submerged in the liquid. Bring to a boil over high heat. Turn off heat and allow pears to infuse for 25-30 minutes. Remove parchment.
4. Mix the quark, grapefruit juice, lemon juice, vanilla sugar, and salt. Combine the cornstarch with a bit of water to create a thick slurry. Dust the quark mixture

with the confectioners' sugar and then gently mix it in by hand. Gently fold the cornstarch slurry into the quark mixture.

5. By hand or in a stand mixture, whip the cream to the stiff peak stage. By hand, whip the egg whites to the stiff peak stage. Gently fold the whipped egg whites into the whipped cream. Gently fold this mixture into the quark mixture.

6. Place the raspberries and 2 tablespoons of sugar on a cutting board and pound with the side of a knife or bottom of a glass. Add more sugar if necessary, to taste. Pass the puréed berries through a fine-mesh sieve to remove the seeds. It may be necessary to add a little water to thin the coulis. Refrigerate for up to 2 days.

7. Leaving the tops intact, slice the poached pears into fans and place them on the center of each serving plate. Remove the chocolate leaves from the refrigerator and gently peel them from the parchment. Place one leaf atop each pear and cover with the mousse. Place a second square atop the mousse. Garnish with raspberry coulis, berries, and mint.

"Well, nothing changes the fact Mama died in the fire," she said.

Emma nodded slowly, feeling like she had found an important puzzle piece but was unsure what puzzle it fits into.

"Sister." Dora waved her hand in front of Emma's face to get her attention. When Emma finally focused on her, she said, "Dinner in a few hours and homework."

Emma smiled. "I know. I'll check on my assignments Papa left for me. Where are the ladies this afternoon?"

"I understand they wanted to see a new exhibit opening at the museum. I think it involved old knives. I'm sure they'll talk to you about it tonight," Dora said over her shoulder as she exited the room.

Emma went down to the basement to check on Papa, who was back from his consulting trip. "Papa," she said softly.

"Sister, come over where I can see you. Did you have a grand adventure today?" Papa knew Emma was like her mama and got herself in tangles occasionally.

"What's my homework today?" she asked, hoping to move Papa off the topic of her day, which included Mama and her special dessert. She didn't want to upset him with her theories.

He didn't mind the change in topic. "I have another type of puzzler for you. I want you to read this engineering document and let me know what should be included in the structural drawings and what should not. Also, two chapters of reading—"

Emma interrupted, "Can it be an adventure novel?"

He smiled indulgently and said, "Yes, once you complete the task. Oh, and some calculations may stump you, so ask if you need me to help."

"Papa, I won't need help," she said confidently. She grabbed the work and took off at a run up the stairs, heading to the study.

Papa shook his head at his daughter and was back to work within moments of her exiting the room.

Emma pulled out her notes and started to evaluate the problems Papa had put together for her. He had added some red herrings to trick her, which she looked at thoughtfully. *There are additional unnecessary calculations that were put in to distract me. There is an easier method to figure the load on the concrete.* She made the correction and the problem came together.

She finished the engineering work, grabbed a book, and plopped herself into a large worn leather chair near the desk. Opening it eagerly, she started to read Jules Verne's *Around the*

World in Eighty Days. It was such fun to climb into other people's skin and live for a bit. *What would it be like to live so freely and go to New York or overseas by yourself?* It was her goal to be independent and travel, having adventures as she went.

She read for another hour and realized it was time to help with dinner. Dora could always use extra hands. The table, like at breakfast, filled fast with people, and platters of food were emptied as soon as they were placed on it. It was because Dora cooked beautifully and everyone knew it.

Dinner was noisy but Emma was quiet. She sat between Miss May and Miss Marjorie, listening to them chattering about their day at the museum.

"Do you want to come outside with me after dinner?" Emma asked the ladies after a break in the conversation.

"We can practice throwing and tell you about the knives we saw today," Miss Marjorie told her. Miss May and Miss Marjorie grinned at each other, knowing they would also get to hear of Emma's adventures on the delivery wagon.

Once outside, both ladies turned to Emma, and Miss Marjorie asked, "Anything to tell us about today?"

Emma teased with a question, delaying the answer a bit. "You want to hear about my day?"

"Yes," they replied together.

"It was quiet today," she said, thinking about that dessert.

"Quiet?" Miss May asked. "No new cases?"

"I don't think so." She hesitated. "I have some thoughts, but I'm not sure what they mean right now."

Miss Marjorie nodded at Miss May, and they started in on how the museum displayed the collection of knives. "I have to say," said Miss Marjorie, "in my younger days, that collection would have tempted me."

Miss May looked down when Miss Marjorie made that comment. Emma got worried. "Miss May, what's wrong?"

This made Miss May look up, and both Miss Marjorie and Emma saw something was bothering her.

"Well, I thought that Emma might want something from the museum," she said a bit defiantly.

"Oh, you got me a token from the gift shop? That was sweet of you," said Emma softly.

Miss Marjorie looked confused because they didn't go to the gift shop today.

Miss May, still in a defiant voice, said, "No, no, something else."

Emma and Miss Marjorie looked at her questioningly

She reached into her long coat and pulled out a wicked-looking knife with an ornate handle.

Miss Marjorie recognized it immediately. "Oh, May, what have you done? That is from the museum's collection. They are not for sale." She looked frantic and, for the first time since Emma had known her, seemed a bit helpless.

Emma was already thinking of ways to fix this problem. "Miss May, I think I have someone who can help us return this knife."

Miss May said, "But I don't need help. I wanted to give you a nice present to remember me. . . us by," she said, looking over at Miss Marjorie.

Emma took Miss May's hand in one hand and Miss Marjorie's in the other and looked into the woman's eyes. "Certainly, you must see that I can't keep something that doesn't belong to me?"

Miss May bristled visibly at this remark and said stiffly, "I don't want to give it back."

Miss Marjorie looked at Emma; they didn't want to wrestle it from her. Someone might get hurt in the process.

They continued to speak softly to her, giving her many reasons to return the knife. It was when they said that Emma could get arrested for knowingly taking stolen merchandise that Miss May finally relented and begrudgingly handed it to Emma.

She slid the knife under her coat. "I need to get this to a secure location as soon as possible." She headed back inside while the ladies quietly discussed what had happened.

She grabbed her hat and headed out to find Tony. He would be at home. She was nervous about going over; she hadn't been there since they had gotten back together. He had discussed Emma with his mom, but she wasn't as welcoming as he had hoped.

Emma continued to think about how she would respond to Mrs. Marella if she was home. She wasn't looking forward to that meeting, but she had to talk with Tony about the knife.

Tony was working afternoons at the museum, helping put together displays. He was hoping the part-time job would turn into a full-time position.

She made her way to his family's apartment. She raised her hand to knock and hesitated. Her nerves got the better of her at the thought of facing her, and she started to turn to leave. *Stop,* she told herself, *Be brave.* Her hand raised and she knocked forcefully on the door. It swung open quickly, unfortunately, it was Mrs. Marella.

"Hi, Mrs. Marella," Emma said awkwardly.

"Emma," she said stiffly. The lines around her mouth hardened when she saw who was at the door.

"Is Tony here?" Emma asked in a hopeful voice.

Mrs. Marella blocked her entry into the apartment.

When Tony realized who his mom was blocking, he scolded her lightly and kissed her cheek. When she still didn't move to let Emma in, he said in a more commanding voice, "Let her in." Then, to lighten the mood, he added, "Please."

Mrs. Marella sighed, and she moved to the side. She would do anything for Tony. "Please, come in," she said.

Emma stepped in and, as Tony grabbed her hand, she leaned into him and said, "Tony, we need to talk."

She sounded serious and Tony immediately said, "Mom, we need to go out for a little while."

"Fine, just not too far," she said in a worried voice.

"Sure, Mom." Tony understood she was concerned about him.

They headed downstairs together, holding hands. When they got to the street, Tony turned to face her. "What is it, Emma? Is something wrong?"

She looked very worried and a bit strained. Not knowing how to begin, she just blurted the situation out. "Miss May did something she shouldn't have done, and I think you're the only one who can help her."

Tony frowned. He had known Miss May as long as she had. He knew she meant the world to Emma. "You know I'd do anything for you."

She looked around to see if anyone was watching them. "Tony, look at this." She opened her coat and revealed the handle of the knife.

"But that. . ." he started, shocked at what was before him.

". . .is from the museum's collection," she confirmed. "Miss May thought I might want it, and she got it for me."

"She just took it?" he asked in disbelief.

"Yes, and now we need to find a way to return it," she said determinedly.

"Wow." He sat down for a moment on the stoop. "I guess this is where I test how important I am to the curator." He shook his head, thinking how things can change so quickly.

"Tony, I don't want to destroy your future. I can go in and explain, as best I can, what happened and try to keep Miss May out of jail."

"No, we said we're together and that means we want to protect both of our futures." He thought for a moment and said,

"I have an idea. Can you meet me here in the morning, early? You have off tomorrow for deliveries and the bakery?"

"No, I have a special order. I have to go in early and should have it completed by 8am. Is that early enough?" she asked, hoping there was a way out of this situation.

"Yes, I'll meet you there and we'll go to the museum together. I'll keep the knife with me until then." He indicated for her to hand it to him.

She looked around to make sure no one was watching and when it was safe, she reached in her coat, took out the knife, and handed it to him. He put it into his coat for safekeeping.

CHAPTER 23

They met early at the bakery the next morning, joined hands, and headed toward the museum. They made it there just as it was opening and went straight to the curator's office.

He looked a bit surprised, but was curious enough to inquire, "Tony, you're early, and who's this with you?"

"Mr. Johnson, this is Emma." He gestured to Emma at his side. "She's my friend. Emma, this is Mr. Johnson, the curator of the museum. Emma and I wanted to speak with you about something important."

"Emma Evans?" he asked curiously.

"Yes," she said, confused how he knew her name; she had never met him before this.

"I heard quite a bit about you and your adventures. Please, call me Philip," he said, his eyes lit up with excitement.

"From who? Tony?" asked Emma.

Tony shook his head and said, "No."

"No, from a few other sources." Mr. Johnson waved his hand to indicate it was unimportant. "What can I do for you? Is this about a case? Can I help you with it?"

"Well, not exactly a case, but there is something we need help with." She looked at Tony, and he removed the knife from his jacket and handed it gingerly to her.

Philip recognized it instantly. "Where did you get that? That's in our collection. Or, it's supposed to be." He took it carefully from Emma to examine.

"Well, there is a story there." She started to discuss Miss May and Miss Marjorie and their visit the day before. She also briefly explained their history and how they had reformed.

"I truly believe this was only a slip and with no malicious intent," she stressed.

Philip listened and didn't say anything until she finished.

"All of this happened yesterday and no one noticed?" He mulled this over. "Could you have Miss May and Miss Marjorie come to the museum to meet with me?"

"Oh no," said Emma, starting to get upset and, in turn, this upset Tony.

Philip noticed their distress and realized he hadn't been clear. "No, I don't want to get them in trouble. What I would like is for them to show me how we can improve our security around the exhibits."

"You won't turn them in for the theft?" she asked, hoping she had heard right.

Philip smiled suddenly and said, "What theft? I have everything that belongs to the museum."

Emma felt a wave of relief wash over her, and she reached for Tony's hand. He squeezed it and offered her a soft smile.

Tony breathed a silent sigh of relief and said to Philip, "I'm so appreciative of your patience in the matter."

He looked directly into Tony's eyes and said in a very serious voice, "Tony, we value you as an employee and would like to see you move into a full-time role here. Can you come in at your regular time today and we'll discuss your new hours?"

Tony nodded and said, "I would love to discuss a full-time role."

He turned his eyes back to Emma. "Emma, can you bring Miss May and Miss Marjorie in tomorrow afternoon?"

Emma answered, "Yes, I believe so, but I'll have to speak with them."

With that, they stood and started to take their leave. Philip stopped them. "Emma, I would like to hear about some of your adventures one day." She nodded as they filed out of the office. Both were dazed by the morning's events.

Tony and Emma were quiet as they headed out. They sat down on the steps outside the museum. "Wow," she said.

Still stunned, Tony said, "Yes, wow. We thought it could be the end of our careers and, instead, we seemed to have had a positive outcome."

"Well, it looks like I'll have to have a long talk with Miss May and Miss Marjorie," said Emma.

"It looks like I'll also have to have a long talk, but with Cousin," he said.

She leaned over and kissed him softly on the lips. "Thank you for being there for me today."

"Emma, I'll always be here for you," he said and kissed her again.

After a moment of looking into each other's eyes, he said, "I have to go finish the morning deliveries and come back here."

They went their separate ways, with Emma heading home and Tony to his deliveries.

First thing I need to do thought Emma *is to let the ladies know the police would not be coming to take Miss May to jail.* She got there and went to the sitting room. This was the lady's regular location this time of day.

They both looked up as she entered, looking apprehensive. She smiled to show it wasn't bad news. One look at her face and they seemed to relax.

Miss Marjorie said, "Sit with us," and patted the seat between her and Miss May. "Well, are we in trouble?"

Miss May said, stuttering, "No, no, it should be only me in trouble."

Emma continued to stand and held up her hands to stop further comments. She alleviated their concerns immediately. "No one is in trouble. Tony and I met with Mr. Johnson, the museum curator." She explained how the meeting went. "He would like to speak to both of you."

The apprehension was back, and both ladies began to speak at once. Emma gave them a second. Miss Marjorie went first, "Oh no, we can't. It might be a trap to get us."

Emma tried to get to the point fast. "But it isn't. I think they want to find out how you did it and how they can prevent it from happening in the future." With that, she left them to their discussion about security for the museum.

The idea of security consulting made her think of a business opportunity. She thought to herself, *I'm going to get with Tim before we go over. I have an idea about how to do this.*

That night, Tim, Dora, and Emma sat down to discuss her business idea.

"So, this type of thing would allow people to work for shorter terms? And we could have specialists available for different positions," Tim said consideringly.

Emma continued with her idea. "Yes, my thoughts are we could have different types of positions. Security to start, shop-keepers that need additional help at holidays, clerical, and others. I think we could set it up and have a fee that is paid to our business."

Tim was starting to get excited. "Emma, I think this might work. We would need to take it slow initially, and I'll still need to find an accounting position. I will work on developing this idea."

"But what about Miss May and Miss Marjorie now?" inquired Emma.

Tim conceded. "You're right. We'll do this short term and use it as a test case for future jobs. If you are all right with it, Emma." She nodded that she was. "I'll go over to the museum with them and help negotiate the position and responsibilities tomorrow."

He thought it best to go down to see one of his accounting professors for some advice on the appropriate amount of pay and get an idea of the paperwork and contracts that would be needed. He wanted to be organized before he presented his business proposition. He sent a note to the museum asking for a few more days and suggested a more formal meeting.

Tim would work hard to make sure his presentation and contracts were ready for submittal to Mr. Johnson. He would be ready.

The day of the meeting came around and, as Tim and Emma were eating lunch at the clubhouse, Tim indicated he needed to make one more private delivery before taking her home and picking up Miss May and Miss Marjorie. "Also, Tony wants to accompany us to the meeting. I'll bring him back with me.

"Okay, I can wait here. It shouldn't be long?" asked Emma, happy he was working with Miss May's and Miss Marjorie's new job opportunity.

Tim chucked her under the chin. "I won't be long," he said and headed out.

"Fine, I'll go over my observations of this morning's activities and wait for you here," she called after him.

Over the next hour, the other delivery boys filtered in and out, some in pairs and someone at a time until eventually, Emma was alone.

It was quiet and she was wrapped up in her writing. Another person entered the clubhouse, but she didn't look up to see who it was. She was enjoying her quiet time, sitting at the table with her legs swinging from the stool.

Bang! The "boy" slapped both of his hands- palms down in front of her, pressing his chest into her back.

It made her start and the hairs on her arms stood straight up. She tried to say casually, in a gruff voice, "What are you doing?"

And then he said something that Emma hadn't heard since the "incident" six years ago. He placed his wet lips on her right ear and whispered, "Want to play, little girl?"

Emma was well trained in how to respond to an attack, but she took a moment to clear her mind and remove any emotion from her response. By that one statement, he made it clear he knew who she was and wanted her to know who he was.

She made a distressed sound to distract him, much like she had that day he had grabbed her previously. He was too close for her to access her hidden knife, and she did not have her hat with her. She would have to use other methods to fight back and this time win!

The sharpened pencil was gripped in her hand, she didn't hesitate and rammed it into his like a sharp knife.

He hadn't expected the move and screamed in pain. Before he could pull back his arm, she had planned her next move. She elbowed him in the airway. This sent him backward, holding his injured hand to his neck and falling to the floor, coughing loudly.

She turned toward him and realized she knew him. That fact didn't affect her response.

He was up in seconds. He pulled the pencil out of his hand and started toward her. "You interfering little bitch, you think you can stop me this time? You think that notebook you're always carrying will save you?"

He brought his fist around and she wasn't able to miss the hit to her face. The blow threw her into the wall of the clubhouse.

He continued in a venomous voice. "You keep showing up in my life, writing in those damn little notebooks. And you keep ruining my plans. This time, I'm going to make sure you don't ever interfere again."

With that statement, she knew he would spare no mercy. She let the emotion she had been pushing down for so long boil over. Darting forward, she aimed two perfectly aimed sidekicks into him. Her pointed boot made immediate contact with his groin. He went down like a stone. She didn't hesitate and picked up a stool, slamming it repeatedly across his back until he stopped moving.

Her legs sank to the ground under her. Suddenly remembering her knife, she started to laugh. She took it out and held it in front of her in case he woke up. There would be no hesitation to use it.

She thought for a moment about who he was. She had recognized him as soon as she turned around. He was the man involved with both the department store burglaries and smuggling operations. He was also the man who had almost killed her six years ago. *What was his motivation back then?* she thought. *He had said she kept interfering in his life. Had she seen something that day, so long ago, that interfered with his plans enough that he needed to kill her? Did he have her notebook from back then?*

She thought it best to wait for Tony and Tim to come back and help clean up the mess. She also didn't want him to get away.

Her face was throbbing; her eye was probably going black and her ribs ached, but she still didn't move from her guard duty.

Tony and Tim were walking back in, discussing their deliveries and the afternoon meeting, when they noticed the room was tossed about. "Emma!" They looked frantically around, first seeing the man on the floor and then finding Emma next to him.

Tony ran over to Emma first, carefully removed the knife from her hand, and examined her face. "What happened? Are you—"

Emma interrupted him. "It was him."

Tony didn't need to ask who "him" was. His eyes went darker and his face paled.

Tim saw what was happening and cut him off. "Tony let me tie him up. You take care of her."

Tony realized she was shaking and pulled her into his arms.

Tim indicated he needed to go to the wagons for some rope. There was usually plenty left over from their deliveries. He came back in and tied up the assailant's hands and feet. Looking at Emma, he inquired with worry, "Are you okay? Your face is a bit worse for wear."

Emma started to nod and winced. "I'm okay."

"Let me check it," said Tony as he tilted her head back to get a good look. "It's going to be black. You'll need to put some cool cloths or ice on it today. Any other injuries?"

Emma didn't answer and kept staring at her assailant, half expecting him to spring back up. "Is he. . .?" she asked, leaving her question hanging in the air.

"Well, I wouldn't have tied him up if he were dead, would I?" Tim teased her gently. "He's still alive. You did a number on him. I'm proud of you."

"He's starting to come around," Tony observed. He went over to the man and picked up his head until he saw his eyes clear, then he pounded it into the ground. "Oops," he said. "Out again." He moved back to Emma's side.

"Okay, who do we contact to help with this?" inquired Tim.

Emma said simply, "Papa."

Tim nodded in agreement and took the wagon to get Ellis. Papa sent immediate word to Cole to help resolve whatever the situation might be.

Papa arrived and the first thing he did was go to her. He

didn't look at the attacker, afraid of what he might do. Cole arrived soon after and went directly to the man down on the floor, where he was able to determine him to still be alive.

Cole was talking directly to Tim and Tony. "What happened here? Fight get out of hand?"

Tim and Tony shook their heads. They told him who he was and then who took him down. Cole looked nonplussed for a moment when he realized Emma had done this.

The man groaned and tried to sit up.

Cole said to Papa, "Get her and the boys out of here. We'll work this out."

Papa, Emma, Tim, and Tony vacated the premises, loaded into the wagon, and moved slowly toward home. Tony held Emma all the way there.

They got back to the boarding house at about 3pm, just as people were starting to get home. The group agreed it would be best to go in the back door. Tim suddenly remembered the appointment they had missed and separated from the group to go in the front door. He needed to first speak with Miss May and Miss Marjorie about the delay.

He found them waiting in the sitting room. They were dressed nicely and thought they were about to leave. He quietly explained that there would be a delay because Emma had been in an accident.

They wanted to see her immediately, but he explained she was fine and would need some rest. They should give her some time before asking about what happened. They nodded, not happy with being excluded, but they understood.

He sat down and organized a note to be sent to Mr. Johnson at the museum. He asked for a delay until the next day for their meeting. He also thought to let him know Tony had a personal matter to attend to this afternoon.

While Tim was organizing the note, the family decided to bring Emma in through the kitchen. Papa had made sure only

Dora was in the room when they entered. Tony walked in with Emma close to his chest, hiding her face in his shirt.

Dora was shocked by everyone in her kitchen all at once. But once she saw Emma's face, she immediately went to get a cold compress. "Tell me what happened." She narrowed her eyes at Tim and Tony, looking for some answers. Tim had come in quietly from the dining room.

Emma spoke in a muffled voice. "Dora, it was him. He went after me again."

"But Emma got him this time," Tony said proudly.

Emma described the events and then asked if she could lie down. Dora took her arm and started to walk her to her room. Emma stopped, turned back to Tim, and asked, "Tim, can I go out with you tomorrow on deliveries?"

Tim considered this and shook his head. "How about in a few weeks? Just give yourself a chance to recover."

Emma nodded and said, "Sure. Can you see if you could get my notebook from the clubhouse?"

"Sure, Emma. I'll go back later tonight," he assured her.

Emma and Dora shuffled off upstairs.

Tim, Tony, and Papa sat for a moment. Tim told Tony he had taken care of the museum notifications. Tony nodded, not concerned about his job at this time; he was where he needed to be.

Tony looked at Papa and asked, "What happens next?"

"I trust Cole. He'll take care of it," stated Papa in a firm voice.

Back at Pinkerton's office

"Hassey, what did you find out?" Cole asked his lead investigator.

"The name is Zeke Jones. Looks like a lifetime criminal. He's tied to that gambling club and several burglaries in the area. He must know someone important since he has yet to go to jail here. We did find arrest warrants for him in New York and New Jersey. Looks like he likes to beat up women on a regular basis," said Hassey, completing his report.

Cole took a deep breath and released it before stating, "Good, then we don't have to include any of Ellis' family. Let's wrap this up. Take him to the doctor and get him patched up. I'll make notifications to the New York and New Jersey authorities. Let's keep this quiet and move him out as soon as he is stable."

Hassey nodded and made his way to the doctor treating Zeke. He was able to confirm he could be moved. They had him on the way to New York on the early train the next morning.

CHAPTER 24

*E*mma lay back in the tub as she let her aching shoulders get some heat and held a wet rag to her bruised face. She stayed there for a long time. When she finally had enough, she dried off and climbed into bed, her face and her ribs throbbing.

Dora came up with a tray and a towel wrapped around some ice a little while later, but Emma was fast asleep. She placed the towel on her face and took the tray back downstairs, not wanting to disturb her.

Later that evening Tim, Tony, and Papa were still in the kitchen. Dinner had come and gone. They kept information pertaining to the event within their small group. Her absence at dinner wasn't mentioned; it was common knowledge Emma would miss occasional meals due to the cases she was working on.

They also updated Miss May and Miss Marjorie that there had been an accident on Emma's delivery route, and she was fine. They asked the ladies to keep it quiet for now. They looked a bit dubious at this explanation but did not interfere.

Later that evening, Emma came down the back stairs to the kitchen and heard the group talking.

Tim said, "What are we going to do to keep Emma safe?"

She started to barge in when she heard that, but the next person to speak was Tony and he said, "I think she did an excellent job of that on her own this afternoon."

Emma surprised everyone when she came in, went directly to Tony, and hugged him. "Thanks, Tony." He hugged her tightly back.

He stood up and tilted her face to get a good look at the blackened eye. "Feeling better?"

She said quietly, adoring him with her eyes, "Yes."

"Emma," Papa said quietly, "could you stay down here with me for a moment?"

The statement had a clearing effect on the room. Tim and Tony found a reason to leave. Tim squeezed Dora's hand as he headed out. Dora excused herself and retired to her room.

That left Emma with Papa. "Emma, come sit by me," he said as he patted the chair beside him.

Emma moved over and sat down. "Papa, I'm okay."

"This isn't about that," he said. "I had already planned to have you around for the next few weeks. I have a large code project due and I need to have you here to evaluate and confirm my calculations."

Emma was silent, which was unusual. Papa continued with a smile and a twinkle in his eye. "It also has the added benefit of me keeping an eye on you."

Emma sat for a moment and admitted, "I would like to do that, Papa. I think I could use a break and some time at home."

Papa didn't know he was holding his breath until Emma agreed. He breathed out slowly. "All right then," he murmured.

"Emma," he said directly to her, "meet me in my lab after breakfast in the morning to get started on the drawing assessment." He knew she would want to keep busy.

"Yes, Papa, I'll be there," she responded.

Emma got another towel and some ice out of the icebox to place on her face. She slowly made her way upstairs, keeping her shaking hands on the towel. Once in her room, she laid it down and looked at her hands. The shaking continued through the rest of her body until she felt like she was breaking on the inside. Sinking down on the bed, she curled up into a ball and cried herself to sleep. Dora climbed in and held onto Emma through the night.

She woke up feeling refreshed and shook off any effects she might have been feeling. Looking over she saw that Dora had already gotten up and started her day.

She sat up, she moved her hair off of her forehead, and thought to herself, *I beat the devil I did, I beat him!* That made her straighten up her shoulders and know she could move on. It gave her a spring in her step as she washed up, got dressed in a light blue skirt and a frilly blouse. She started to put on her stockings when she caught a view of herself in the mirror.

She stood up slowly and approached it. She leaned forward to get a good look at her jaw and eye; both were black and blue. It was still sore as she touched it hesitantly. *Battle wounds*, she thought and moved back to the chair to put on her stockings and boots to head downstairs.

She noticed her notebook was on the side table. Tim must have brought it over early this morning. She hesitated for a moment, picked it up, and looked at the articles she had placed there. Maybe today was the day to ask Papa about them and why he had kept them. Folding them up, she placed them back into her notebook. She headed downstairs to help with breakfast. She pushed open the door and saw Amy and Dora in the kitchen. Dora was working on making bread.

"Well, you look quite nice today, Emma," said Amy. Then she noticed Emma's face. "Are you okay?" she asked in a worried voice.

"I am fine, just an accident during my deliveries yesterday," commented Emma. "Thanks for asking."

Dora squinted at Emma. "Sister, what are your plans for the day?"

"I'm taking a few weeks off at the bakery and deliveries to help Papa finish his project," stated Emma somewhat rigidly.

"But—" started Dora.

Emma interrupted, "I know what you're going to say, that I'm being irresponsible. Papa sent word to Cousin and Tim last night. They know not to expect me for a while."

"I know Cousin will miss you," Dora said absently, working her bread, folding it over and over in the flour on the kitchen table. "He mentioned that dessert has been ordered again this week."

"That dessert," said Emma in exasperation. "It seems all I do lately is make that dessert. Okay, for Cousin, I'll make it here." She mulled that over while she helped put together the morning meal.

After breakfast, she was still thinking about Cousin's request when she went to see Papa in the basement. For some reason, she always thought of the night of the fire when that dessert was ordered. She turned off that thought for now and called to Papa in the basement, "I'm here, Papa. I'm ready to work."

"Over here." The drawings were set up on the drafting table with a high stool. It was tilted and several gas lights were being utilized for the close work. She worked diligently through the morning, comparing the drawing to the required fire codes. It would be tedious work for the next two weeks, but it kept her occupied and she needed that for now.

CHAPTER 25

*L*ater that week, Cousin sent a special request for her to make the dessert for the next day's deliveries. He apologized and would send the ingredients to her. There would be a bonus expected for making it tonight.

Emma shrugged and said it would be okay if she could do this at home. She asked Dora if she could use the kitchen that evening.

"Sure," replied Dora. "I'll help, that way we can share gossip."

They both worked on the dessert and had it cooling on the kitchen table for delivery the next day. Emma sent a note to Tim to request help getting the special delivery to the customer tomorrow.

The next day, she was working code work for Papa when she noticed it was about time to take the special delivery to the customer. She got ready but did not switch into her boy clothes. She didn't expect to be out very long. Out of habit, when she dressed in her split skirt, she attached her sheath to her thigh and slid the knife in. She also grabbed her hat and made sure the larger knife was secure. She went downstairs to wait for Tim.

As he pulled up, he noticed she was in her girl clothes. "No delivery clothes today? Do you want me to take it for you?" he offered, knowing she was probably still sore.

"No, I'm good. It'll be nice to get some air, and it's just the one delivery." He jumped down and helped her up to the wagon seat. He handed her the box; she would carry it on her lap.

Tim had completed all of his deliveries for the bakery and had a few business items to do that afternoon.

"Tim, was Mr. Johnson all right with the delay? I'm sorry I caused problems with our new business."

Tim pulled the wagon over. "Emma, that was in no way your fault, and no apologies are necessary. Tony explained what happened to Mr. Johnson." She started to interrupt, worried someone outside of the family was involved.

Tim assured her, "No worries. Tony says we can trust him."

Emma knew Tony could read people and, if he trusted Mr. Johnson, then she trusted him.

"What about Tony missing time on his first full day?" she said worriedly. "He hasn't mentioned it to me."

"He's just being protective. I'm sure if you asked, he'll tell you."

"Yes," she said quietly, knowing Tony would do anything for her.

They both fell silent as they started moving again. A few minutes later, a boy ran up next to the wagon with a note for Tim.

He scanned it and said, "Emma, I have to leave you with the last delivery of the day. I think I have an interview for an accounting position. It says I need to apply in person, immediately."

She asked, puzzled, "At this very moment? Now?"

"Yes, I haven't had one yet. I guess it happens this way. Listen, I have to get going, I'll need to clean up some," he said as he pulled up to the final delivery location. He tied the reins up and jumped down to help her off the wagon. He reached back up and retrieved the dessert for her. The delivery was to a local shop, one she didn't think was opened as yet.

"Now, just don't go in. If needed, place it on the outside. Agreed?" he asked.

"Yes, it should be fine."

"How will you get back?" he asked, concerned she might need help.

"I can walk or take the trolley."

"Okay, good," he said, satisfied with that answer.

He handed her the large dessert and, once he was sure she could carry it, he climbed back on his wagon and waved. "See you."

"See you and good luck."

And off they went their separate ways.

Emma walked the next three blocks balancing the dessert.

Her watcher was still around. He was always on top of any deviation to schedule, especially around the gambler's road area. She walked past him. There was no mistaking what she was carrying and who it was for. *Why is she alone? Tim normally accompanies her,* he thought worriedly. He started to trail closer than he ever had. Something was up, and he had to intervene prior to that happening. It was time now for her to meet her watcher.

The streets were still busy with lunch traffic. She passed the large department store on her left and looked in the windows. The glass was shiny and created a mirror effect. She saw the watcher before she rounded the corner. She tossed the dessert to the ground and was ready for him when his arm came around her, pinning her against the alley. She stayed silent and watchful.

"Sister," he whispered. "I'm here to help."

Emma's eyes opened wide when she realized who was following her. He loosened his grip on her arm but did not let her go.

Immediately, images flooded into her mind. Seeing him in the alley by her house, doorways near the bakery, all along her delivery route. It was the little man who seemed to be everywhere, even at the church dance. She always knew he was around but never felt he was a threat to her. She had started leaving him a basket of food in the morning and pie in the evening.

She didn't feel threatened but questioned why with a raised brow. He grabbed her hand and answered simply, as he fast-walked her down the alley, "Your mama was my best friend."

She pulled him to a stop and snatched the hat off of his head. More memories flooded her senses. She could see him in front of her as he had been then, a small, compact man with reddish hair and a freckled face that would turn red when he talked to Mama.

"Thomas Callahan," she said finally. It came out in a little girl's voice, remembering how nice he had always been.

That man was very different now, his skin scarred from burns. Unfortunately, since the great fire, there were a large number of people walking around with similar scars. But behind all of that was the same eyes of the man who adored Mama all those years ago.

"I think you're being set up," Tom said in a worried voice.

"Why?" she said, still shocked at Tom's appearance at that moment, not realizing he was still pulling her with him.

"Because of that damn dessert. Trouble flows with that thing. When I realized it was being ordered continuingly, I knew that HE was around," said Tom hurriedly over his shoulder.

"Who is HE?" asked Emma, finally waking up a bit.

He continued his story, not answering her question. They had kept walking quickly, using back streets and alleys, but had not gotten out of the area where the social club was located. "I was in the front of the bakery when she was working on that special dessert in the back. I heard something in the kitchen and listened to see if she was okay. Before I knew it—"

He was interrupted by a deep, gravelly voice from farther down the alley. "And she was okay at that time, but she wouldn't listen." Tom stopped abruptly with Emma slamming into his back.

Two men stepped out of the shadows and blocked their exit. A third man came up behind him but stayed in the shadows.

"Wait," said Emma to the man she could see. "I recognize you. You sometimes pick up that dessert I make." There was no response.

"I knew," said Thomas in a hard tone. "I knew you were in town again when that dessert started being ordered. I've been looking for you. It's time for you to accept responsibility for what happened to Mary."

"Yes, that damn dessert. I do love it, though," the man with the gravelly voice said as he stepped out of the shadows, revealing his face for the first time. "Too bad we're going to have to get rid of you both, like we got rid of Mary. Maybe you can give me the recipe before I handle this situation."

Emma recognized John Harden as soon as she saw his face. He was infamous enough to have hand-drawn pictures of him scattered around local police offices. He had also been missing for years and was assumed dead in the big fire.

"Take them both." His two henchmen grabbed her and Tom. "Bring them to the tunnels. I'll meet you there. I can't afford to be seen with them."

The men holding her and Tom didn't know that Emma could defend herself. She had her two knives with her and she did not volunteer the information to them. The men tied up Tom but did not tie up Emma.

Stupid men, she thought to herself.

Tom had been watching her for a long time and knew she was up to something. He would wait and see if he could help. They were tossed into a covered cab.

With her hands-free, she reached up to grab her knife from her hat. The cab was made of a material that could be cut and she would have to be fast. She made a sign to Thomas to keep quiet and made a forward slashing motion with her knife to demonstrate her plan. First, she cut Tom's binding around his hands. Then she immediately turned to the side away from the men and cut with a long arc of her arm. The material gave as Thomas and Emma dove through it. When they hit the ground, they took off at a run down the street.

The buggy rocked, enough that one of the men said, "What are they trying to do, knock it over?"

The other man looked into the cab and saw a gaping hole. "Shit."

He glanced down the street just as Tom and Emma ducked into an alley. The men gave chase after them, both thinking, *The boss will not take kindly to the two getting loose.* They ran until they got to the alley where Emma and Tom had disappeared.

One of the henchmen grabbed the other by the arm to stop him. "So, I hear New York is a good place for businessmen like us."

The other nodded in agreement and both headed to the train station. They knew better than to stick around and be responsible for this mess. The two made it safely to the station and onto a train out of town before the boss found out what had occurred.

CHAPTER 26

*T*om and Emma kept running until she pulled him to a side street to catch their breaths. Emma thought to herself, *I have enough evidence and an eye witness to finally bring John Harden and his crew down. I know who we can use to help us.*

She looked around and determined the Tribune offices were the closest to their location. *I would rather get Cole, but we are too far and the danger is too close. It will have to be Daniel*, she thought. *He was there for Mama; he could be there for me also.* They exited the alley and she indicated he follow her. They quickly ran to the paper's offices. It was after hours, so there were only a few people around.

Emma hadn't told Tom where they were headed, and he appeared hesitant to enter the paper's office. She pulled on his arm to get him moving, and they entered the back entrance. The evening paper had already gone out and the reporters had finished their job for the day. The room was empty leading directly to Daniel's office. They ran for the door and were startled when Daniel opened it.

"Well, Emma, what a lovely surprise. Won't you come in?" He indicated for them to enter with a sweeping motion.

Odd, thought Emma, *he doesn't seem surprised I'm here.* She was too relieved to think about that for long.

"Sit, sit," he said to both of them. "Tell me why you have come to see me."

Tom seemed shocked and could only stare at him, but Emma attributed that to the excitement of being held captive.

She started describing what had happened to them and how it might be connected to the cases described in the original articles he and Mama worked on.

"So," he said, drumming his fingers on the desk, "you both know everything."

"Yes," Emma said. "I need to get a note to the Pinkertons."

"Well. . ." he said, but a knock on the door stopped him. "Ah, my other guest has arrived." He moved from behind the desk to open the door, only for John Harden to step into the room.

Emma sat as shocked as Thomas. She opened her mouth but words did not come out.

When Daniel saw her shock, he said, "I guess this is a lot to take in." He focused his next comment toward John. "I told you she would come here."

"Yes, you did," said John laconically. "What do we do with them now? Do we take them to the tunnels and out to the club?"

Emma watched their interaction, realizing the obvious person in charge was Daniel. Emma mulled over the facts silently and asked herself, *How long has this been going on? Did Mama know?*

"Yes, tie both of their hands this time." He looked pointedly at John. "This is Mary's daughter and she's just as clever as she was."

John seemed to be waiting for Daniel to take the lead. Emma tried to make sense of it all and said, "Daniel, I don't understand. You were Mama's friend. She was the source of your articles."

Daniel ignored her and looked at the gangster. "Bind their

mouths also. I'll go with you to the club basement."

Emma and Tom had their hands bound and their mouths covered as they made their way through the newspaper office to the basement. The tunnels at the paper connected to the ones at the social club. They made their way mostly in darkness. The men leading had a vast knowledge of the layout.

Smugglers, thought Emma, connecting even more cases with John and Daniel.

She recognized the tunnels they were in and was not surprised to be pushed into the social club basement. John said to his henchmen, "Grab those two chairs and move them over here." They moved the chairs and pushed Emma and Tom into them. They removed the binding around their mouths.

Daniel said briskly, "You can leave, I've got this."

John gave him a look and said, "Yeah, like last time. Just don't make a mess down here. By the way, what happened to Zeke? I thought you said he would take care of this for us.

Daniel seemed bored with the topic and said laconically, "Complications. Looks like we have a labor problem."

Another connection, thought Emma. *The man who attacked me was attached to this group. Were they connected to both attacks?*

John and his men went upstairs; he paused and leaned on the rail to say, "Daniel, you might want to remove her hat." Inclining his head toward her.

Daniel took his advice and, before Emma knew what was happening, he grabbed her hat and sent it flying across the room. "I think I'll take this. I'm aware that's where you keep that lethal knife you like so much."

Daniel had silently removed a pistol from his jacket and had it trained on Emma and Thomas. He kept it on both of them.

She was watching him closely. She was also working on loosening the ropes around her wrists. *Thank you, Miss May,* she thought.

"Are you going to tell me why you brought us here?" asked

Emma in a soft voice, continuing to work on her ropes.

Daniel's deep voice reverberated through the room. "You're turning out to be just like your mother, creating havoc in my businesses. We made such a team, her and I. She created an opportunity for me to get rich and I wanted it. I tried to include her in my plans for the future, but she disagreed."

"What do you mean disagreed? You discussed this with her?"

"Of course," he said. "By controlling crime and the news at the same time, I would be able to have anything in the world I wanted. I thought she could be part of this enterprise. She chose no and wanted to turn me and John into the authorities. We couldn't let that happen."

Emma frowned. "What do you mean?"

Tom chose that moment to lose control and yelled, "He killed her and tried to kill me that night!" His chair shook as he tried to untie his hands and get to Daniel.

Emma stopped moving when she heard Thomas' statement. She sent a frantic glance to him and he nodded an affirmative.

Daniel didn't react. He very calmly said, "The fire that night was fortuitous. We were able to use it as a cover. We were planning to take care of her eventually, but the fire started and moved up our schedule."

"But why?" asked Emma. "Why did you take her from us?"

"She was in my way," he said simply. "Your mama knew everything I knew about John's business operation."

"You mean crime organization," corrected Emma.

He acknowledged her with a nod. "Yes, crime organization." His voice started to take on a harder edge. "I tried to explain to her that we could manage it and clean it up while being part of it. I could already see that controlling the media would control the narrative the people saw and believed. I would control the narrative and John would move his operations underground."

"Mama saw through that," Emma guessed.

"Yes," Daniel acknowledged regretfully. "I met with John and we made a deal, we two. I would continue to move up at the paper, with him providing the occasional criminal element to use as a patsy. The plans changed after Mary died. We decided I would oversee operations here and he would go to New York to set up shop there."

"Was the fire in the plan?"

"No, no," he said shaking his head, "the fire happening was just a case of being at the right place at the right time. We were arguing with Mary when we noticed the room was hotter than normal. The beam became dislodged and almost hit us. I took the opportunity it provided and hit Mary on the back of the head with a rolling pin. We placed her under the beam and the room continued to fill with smoke. We got out just in time."

"Was my mother dead when you left her there? Did you even check?"

"No. She stood in my way and I couldn't allow that."

As he kept freely explaining the details of his business, Emma realized he didn't plan on keeping them alive. She kept a shocked expression on her face while continuing to work on the ropes. She got them loosened enough to let them fall off her hands. She just had to get to the knife strapped to her leg. *Daniel would not be walking out of here tonight.*

Thomas chose that moment to provide the distraction she needed and spit at Daniel. He started to shout, "You were always low, so low. You were never good enough for her. She was a better person than you."

Daniel, who had ignored Thomas until now, put his full focus on the man. "Why do you look familiar?" He snatched the hat off of his head. Like with Emma, Tom's ginger hair gave him away. "You! But you're dead!" he said as he wiped the spit off of his face, his calm demeanor dissolved. His hands started shaking and his face darkened. "You, a little nobody. You were always with her, her guardian angel. I couldn't take one step toward her without you there blocking me."

He seemed to be back in another time when Mama was alive and what stood in his way, again, was Thomas. He seemed to forget he had a gun in his hand and dropped it when he grabbed Thomas by the throat and started choking him. Tom's eyes bulged and his face turned purple.

Emma took that moment to slip her hand into her skirt and retrieve the knife from her leg sheath. She called out to Daniel, sounding eerily like her mother, "Daniel."

Daniel stopped choking Thomas for a moment and turned, expecting to see Mary. She didn't pause and threw with purpose. He hadn't expected a knife to be thrown his way and stood there looking incredulously at it lodged in his chest. He fell forward onto Thomas.

Emma ran over to remove his hands from Thomas's neck and pushed his prone body to the floor. Tom's head was rolling back against the wall. She propped him up and rubbed his face and neck. He was starting to come around. He looked at her and smiled as she untied him. "It's like being with your mama again."

The first door to open was the one from the tunnel, and the Pinkerton detectives flooded into the room with guns drawn. Cole and Jeremy led the charge and stopped abruptly when they saw the body on the floor. Cole glanced wryly at Emma. "I am a bit late to the party again?"

Emma nodded and asked in amazement, "How did you know we were here?"

A voice sounded behind Cole, "I saw them take you in the alley." She looked and saw it was Karl.

"Emma, are you okay?" asked Jeremy as he pulled her into a bear hug.

"Yes, but Thomas needs some help," she said, indicating him with her hand. She watched as the Pinkertons took over the scene.

Cole called out, "We need a doctor down here." After checking Daniel's pulse, he reported, "This man is dead."

The doctor was brought in and, as he checked Thomas, Emma was thinking, *I don't regret throwing the knife, and I'm glad he didn't survive. The world is better off without some people.*

At that moment, the door at the top of the stairs opened and police in blue flocked down the stairs.

She and Thomas tried to explain how they ended up there, who Daniel was and what he was involved in. The entire room went quiet when two dark figures showed up at the top of the stairs. One was closely followed by another.

The first man was John Harden, *He didn't get away,* thought Emma. She was relieved and she thought wryly, *I can finally stop making that dessert.*

More surprisingly, though, was that the police chief was escorting John Harden. He looked right at Emma and said, "I told you I would take care of it, girlie." And for the first time, he smiled.

She knew immediately who he favored; she looked at Karl and he sent her an identical smile. *Guess I was wrong about him. I had the good guys and the bad guys mixed up. I still have a lot to learn,* she thought.

She watched as Cole was speaking intently to the police chief, and realized they were working together. *A joint operation. The rumors about police corruption had come from the top.*

John Harden was in handcuffs and was waiting for the police officer to remove him from the premises. As he waited, he looked over at Emma and said softly, "You know, I really was only in the room when he killed her. I didn't participate."

"But you were there," Emma said, more of a statement than a question.

"Yes. I'm sorry for being involved even a little in the loss of your mama. I'm not sorry to be out from under Daniel's thumb. If you need anything, you come find me."

"Won't that be hard for a long time?"

"Well, you never know."

"No, you don't," she agreed softly.

The police chief escorted him back upstairs.

Papa and Dora arrived minutes later; Jeremy had sent out some men to pick them up.

Papa shook his head as if to clear it. "I don't understand. What happened here?" Dora hugged Emma close.

Emma spoke up. "Well, to answer that Papa, let me introduce you to my constant shadow." She pointed at Thomas. Papa had never gotten close enough to see the shadow's face. But now...

"Thomas?" he said brokenly. Seeing him brought back Mary. "You-you have been watching my Emma all along?"

Thomas wiped his hands across his eyes and said, "They took Mary away from us. I had to keep Emma safe. She's turning out just like her mama." He smiled as he took in the chaos of the room.

Emma continued the story and went on to tell Papa and Dora about Daniel and John Harden and how they worked together after Daniel killed Mama. When Papa heard it had not been the fire but murder, he felt an impotent range knowing Daniel was already dead.

"What about John Harden. What will happen to him?" Papa asked, thinking he could expend his rage on the man.

Cole saw Papa's response to the news that John was still available for retribution and wanted to stop it there. "Ellis, he'll be going to prison and will get what is coming to him. I've contacted state officials in the governor's office to send the special council down. This will be taken care of properly," he promised.

Emma could see the information noticeably calmed Papa. His hands unclenched and his mouth settled into a more relaxed line.

Papa and Cole headed upstairs to talk to the police chief about her role in the death and how to make sure she didn't get into any trouble.

CHAPTER 27

ony came to the boarding house as soon as he heard about the events at the social club. Later, he would tell her that Jeremy sent him to her. Emma hadn't reacted to the events that had taken place until Tony rushed into the boarding house, almost knocking Papa down as he went straight to her. Until that moment, the events had not penetrated her calm. But once she was in Tony's arms, she started to cry and cry. Papa shooed everyone out of the room and Dora pulled the sliding doors closed on the study to give them privacy.

When the tears slowed, Tony took out his handkerchief to blot her eyes. "Better now?" he asked quietly. "Did you have the adventure you always wanted?"

Emma nodded. "But it was a little more real than expected."

"What will you do now?" he asked.

"Sleep," she mumbled, tired.

"No, I mean long term," he said.

"Working at the bakery and delivery driving for now. I have some thoughts for the future, maybe school," she said, leaning against him.

"Any more casework?" he asked.

"I don't think I'll search it out, but if something comes up, then I'll see," she murmured.

Tony nodded, looking thoughtful. He had something for her but would give her some time to rest before bringing it up.

Their lives settled back to normal, and the days became routine. There was one positive change, Thomas walked next to her and Tony on their way to the bakery each morning. She had gotten him a job at the bakery and a room at the boarding house. He would still be close by if Emma needed him.

She admitted to herself, a few weeks later, that she was getting a bit bored. During their long evening walk, she mentioned to Tony she could use something to work on.

He stopped and looked at her consideringly. "I may have something for you to look into."

"Really?" she asked, her voice curious, not upset. "You're not usually wanting me to be involved in a case. What caused the change in attitude?"

"I was honestly scared you would get hurt, but after your last case, I see you can handle yourself," he explained.

"Thank you," she said sincerely.

He kissed her softly. She saw a bench up ahead and motioned with her hand. He nodded, and they sat down.

"Okay, what's the case?" she asked, wanting to hear more.

"It's Marco. He says there's something odd going on at a house where he, dad, and David are working."

"Odd in what way?" she asked.

He shrugged and said, "He isn't sure, just a weird feeling in the house. He thinks they're hiding something."

"I'm not that busy, and I am due some days off. Any idea how I can get into the house?" she asked, drumming her fingers on her lips.

"Dad and his crew are still working piping if you want to be a general helper," he suggested.

She crinkled her nose at him. "General helper? Is that cleanup duty?"

"Yeah, but Dad is aware of why you're going to be there," he assured her.

She came to a quick decision. "Okay, when do I start?"

He laughed. "I think Monday will be soon enough." They took the weekend to rest and relax.

Emma was getting ready for her dinner with Tony's family on Sunday night to discuss the case when she heard a knock on her bedroom door. She called, "Come in."

Dora entered, saying in a firm voice, "Emma, I need to talk with you."

Emma answered without looking over at her. "Dora, I don't have time. I'm going to Tony's for dinner to discuss a new case."

"You're avoiding me," Dora accused.

"No, I'm not," Emma said, trying to keep her voice level.

"You're not looking me in the eyes," Dora said, watching her closely.

A flash of anger went through Emma and she looked her directly in the eyes saying, "Is that better?"

"You're being obstinate. You know I want to talk about Mama and what happened with Daniel. Every time I ask about it, you're on your way out or you're too busy."

"Well, I don't want to talk about it," she muttered.

"Do you think that's fair?" asked Dora in a shrill voice, letting her emotions come through.

"I don't think anything about this situation was fair," Emma said honestly, hoping to end the conversation there. "Can we talk about this some other time?"

Dora took a deep breath and let it out slowly. "If I give you time, will you finally speak with me?"

Emma didn't want to commit to anything, not yet. "I'll try."

"Fine. Work your case," Dora said abruptly and left the room.

Emma sat heavily on the bed, looking down, wishing she could talk to Dora about what happened. She just wasn't ready. She hated when they fought. There had been times over the years when one sister would slight the other and arguments would ensue. They had always been resolved with one or the other admitting wrong. *But who was wrong in this case?*

She got up and finished getting ready, wiping a tear away. She shook her head and gathered her bag to head down to pick up the dessert she made earlier for Tony.

German Bee Sting Cake
Ingredients

- 2 cups of all-purpose flour
- 1/4 cup of granulated sugar
- 2 and 1/4 teaspoons (1 packet) of active dry yeast
- 1 teaspoon of salt
- 3/4 cup of milk, at room temperature
- 2 large eggs, at room temperature
- 4 tablespoons of butter, softened to room temperature
- 3 tablespoons of honey

Honey almond topping

- 6 tablespoons of butter
- 1/3 cup of granulated sugar
- 3 tablespoons of honey
- 2 tablespoons of heavy cream
- 1/4 teaspoon of salt
- 1 and 1/2 cups of sliced almonds

Filling

- 2 and 1/4 cups of heavy cream
- Vanilla pudding
- 1 teaspoon of pure vanilla extract

Directions:

1. Assemble ingredients and bring the eggs, butter, and milk to room temperature.
2. Add the flour, granulated sugar, yeast, and salt to a large bowl and mix to combine. Make a well in the center of the dry ingredients.
3. Add the eggs, milk, honey, and butter to the center of the well. Mix well with a wooden spoon until the mixture comes together to form a soft dough.
4. Cover the bowl with a kitchen towel and allow the dough to rest for 60 minutes. *Note - the dough will not rise much.
5. Generously butter a 9-inch round cake pan
6. Fit the bottom of the buttered cake pan with a disc of parchment paper coated with butter.
7. Add the cake dough to the pan and spread it out evenly.
8. Cover the pan with a kitchen towel and allow the dough to rise again for approximately 45 minutes.

Honey almond topping

1. Meanwhile, melt the butter, sugar, and honey in a heavy bottom saucepan over medium heat.
2. Stir well and allow the mixture to cook, stirring frequently until the mixture deepens in color and turns a golden brown.
3. Stir in the heavy cream, salt, and almonds.
4. Stir frequently and allow the mixture to deepen in color but not burn. You're looking for a light amber color.
5. Remove the honey almonds from the heat.
6. Spoon the honey almond mixture over the top of the unbaked cake, making sure to spoon the almonds to the edges of the cake.
7. Place the cake pan on a baking sheet and bake in a preheated 350F oven for 25-30 minutes or until a toothpick inserted in the center of the cake comes out clean.
8. Cool the cake completely on a wire rack.
9. Once cooled, invert the cake on a second wire rack. Remove the parchment paper from the bottom of the cake.
10. Invert the cake one more time so it sits almond side up.
11. Use a serrated knife to gently slice the cake evenly in half, lengthwise.

Vanilla cream filling

1. In a medium bowl, whisk heavy cream, vanilla pudding, and vanilla extract until it becomes thick and creamy.

2. Place the bottom half of the cake on a serving platter and drizzle honey liberally over the cake bottom.
3. Spoon and spread the pudding mixture in an even layer over the bottom half of the cake.
4. Gently place the top of the cake, almond side up, onto the cream layer and press gently.
5. Cover and refrigerate until ready to serve.

Dora was busy preparing dinner. She didn't look up to see who entered the kitchen, but commented, "It's in the box over there."

"Thanks for doing that for me," Emma said softly.

Dora just sent a muffled reply back, continuing to peel vegetables.

Emma wanted to say more and wished they were in a better place. She shrugged, picked up the box, and headed out to get her bike. Tony said his mom was making spaghetti for dinner and she was looking forward to it.

She loved the cold air on her face as she was riding over. She felt her mind clearing. At the apartment, she jumped off, put it on her shoulder, and carried the dessert by its strings with her other hand. She made her way into the apartment building and, when she knocked, Enzo ran to the door to let her in.

"Hi, Enzo," said Emma cheerfully.

"Hi, Emma. We're having spaghetti tonight," he said importantly.

"I heard that," she remarked wryly.

Tony came up and kissed her on the cheek. "Hi, Emma."

"Tony," she murmured back in greeting, looking into his eyes.

"Maybe we'll skip dinner," said Tony, seeing that look.

That thought was interrupted by Michael calling, "Tony, bring that girl in here. Dinner's almost ready."

"On our way in," he called back as he took the bike and put it in the hall closet.

He saw the box she was carrying and asked, "Dessert? What kind?"

"It's a Bee Sting cake," she answered.

"Well then, we might want to stay for dinner and then go for a long walk after," he teased.

He took the box in one hand and her hand in the other and walked her to the living room. Marco, Enzo, David, and Michael were on the couches and floor reading the paper.

Marco jumped up when he saw her enter. "Emma, thanks for helping with our job this week."

Tony broke off from the group to take the dessert to the kitchen and returned to Emma's side a moment later.

"I don't mind. I got time off from the bakery and delivery wagon." She looked over at Mr. Marella and said, "Michael, I hear I'm going to be helping out this week."

He smiled. "I don't think I'll have you pipefitting, but I can keep you busy." He held out his hand to her, saying, "It's very good to see you."

She smiled at him, taking his hand in hers. She was happy he was looking like himself again. She leaned over and kissed him on the cheek. "I'm looking forward to spending time with you all this week."

Mrs. Marella came into the room and smiled genuinely at Emma. "Emma, the dessert looks amazing." Their relationship had suffered when Emma and Tony stopped seeing each other, but the favor Emma did for Michael showed her that Emma truly loved her family.

Emma went over and hugged her. "I'm looking forward to your spaghetti."

"That's good because it is ready. Come over, everyone."

Mrs. Marella slipped an arm around Emma's waist and walked to the table with her. As they all sat down, blessings were said and they began eating. The food was wonderful and the conversation light.

After dinner, they moved back into the living room and sat down. Emma pulled out her notebook and turned to look at Michael, Marco, and David. "Tell me your concerns with the family."

Michael and David looked at Marco. He shrugged and said, "I don't know, it just doesn't feel right."

She thought about that, tapping her pencil on her notebook. "Okay, let's try this, who lives in the house?"

"Mr. Saunders owns the house and is paying us to upgrade it," said Michael.

"Don't forget about his son James coming back," commented David.

"Coming back?" asked Emma, curious about this family.

"Yes, James joined the Union Army and he was reported to have died in 1865 at the end of the war. His father had taken it badly and his wife died soon after they heard the news," David continued.

"It must be nice for him to have James back in his life," said Emma.

"Yes, you would think so," commented David.

She heard the caution in that statement and asked, "Have you seen James and Mr. Saunders talk or interact?"

"Not really. They only talk behind closed doors," said Michael.

"What has James done for work since he returned?" she asked, continuing to take notes.

"He doesn't seem to do much," answered David.

"Now, David, I disagree with that," said Michael slowly. "He's often working in the garden when Mr. Saunders isn't there."

"What is he doing in there?" asked Emma.

Michael considered the question for a moment and replied,

"I'm not sure, but he seems to be working with the individual plants."

"Okay, got it. Who else lives in the house?" she asked.

"Abigail, James' wife; Mara, their daughter; and Christopher, their son," listed Marco.

"Can you tell me about each one?" she asked, marking down the different names.

"What kinds of things?" asked Michael.

"What do they look like: hair color, height, and ages?"

David started, "Well, the son, Christopher, has brown eyes, dark brown hair, and is about twelve years old. He's sweet but seems different."

"Different how?" she inquired.

"I don't know, a little slow maybe? Cheerful kid, though," finished David.

"Yes," said Michael, "he always wants to help bring in supplies and will talk your ear off."

"Next?" she asked.

Michael answered, "Abigail, the mom, had dark brown hair like Christopher's, but the eyes are blue, I think. She is of average height, similarly to Doris," he gestured at Mrs. Marella, "and a similar build. Nice but keeps to herself. Oh, and she takes care of the cooking for the family."

"Is there help for the house?" asked Emma.

"Yes, a maid, Mandy. She's a small woman and kind of plain. Dark blonde hair, she doesn't seem to be able to brush it properly. She looks like she's in her thirties," commented Marco.

"There's a daughter?" asked Emma, looking down at her list.

David grinned and said, "You should ask Marco about her. I am sure he has all the details."

Marco went bright red at the teasing, but said, "She's about sixteen and she has long, lighter brown hair that curls on the sides of her face. . ." His voice drifted off and Emma cleared her throat to get his attention. "She's about 5'3", slim build." He finished up the description quickly.

Michael was smiling and shaking his head in response to Marco's description.

"Mr. Saunders?" she prompted the group.

Michael nodded. "His name is Walter. He's older but still very much mobile and very intelligent. I am honestly surprised that he stepped down from his job at the Pullman Cars factory as early as he did."

"Whose idea was the changes in the house you're working on?" Emma asked, wondering who was paying the bills for the family.

"They were Mr. Saunders' ideas. He wanted the best for his reunited family," answered Michael.

Marco and David nodded in agreement

"Does everyone get along? Is there any strife?" asked Emma.

Michael looked concerned when he said, "Initially, I would have said no. When he had me over to review the job, he talked about how happy he was his son had returned. How much he wished his wife had lived long enough to see their son had survived."

"Did something change?" she asked.

"I think you should go in and observe them, get your impressions," suggested Michael.

"Agreed," commented Emma as she closed her notebook and held out her hand to Tony. "Walk me home?"

He smiled at her, taking her hand in his. They said their goodbyes and they walked home. He walked her bike with him as they made their way there.

"What do you think?" asked Tony.

She hesitated a moment before saying, "Not much right now. It could be that the family is trying to adjust to being together after a long separation. I keep thinking what if my mom just showed up after we were told she was dead. I can't imagine the emotions going through them at this time."

"Yes." Tony had never experienced a loss like Emma's family and the Saunders family had experienced. He and Emma were quiet on the way home, lost in their thoughts.

They kissed and parted ways with Tony saying, "I'll put your bike up. Be sure to meet Dad and the boys at our house in the morning."

She nodded and said, "Goodnight." She entered the house, thinking about the case. Dora called to her from the sitting room.

"Hi, Dora. Up late?" Emma asked, trying to not start another fight.

"I thought I would wait for you," she answered, sounding more like herself.

"Hmmm," Emma murmured as she sat in a chair facing the couch where Dora sat.

"So, what is the new case about?" Dora asked.

Emma went over it briefly.

"What do you think?"

"I'm not sure right now. Every case is different. I'll have to be patient and observe," commented Emma.

"Well, you're good at that," Dora said with a quiet voice.

"Yes," Emma said in the same tone.

"Will you be undercover?" Dora asked.

"No, I'll wear work clothes but I'll be a girl on this job and no hiding of anything, including my name," said Emma.

"I'll have your lunch ready for you to take. What time will you be leaving?" Dora asked.

"I confirmed with Michael, since we don't want to disturb the family, we start at 9am. I'll meet them at Tony's house and ride over with Michael and the boys," Emma said as she stood up and started to leave the room.

Dora stopped her abruptly with a hand on her arm and said,

"You know I'm still angry with you about Mama, but. . ." When Emma started to interrupt, she frowned. "I'll give you some time to think before I ask again."

Emma thought a moment and said, "So, will you stay angry with me until I talk about what you want to talk about?"

"Emma." She sighed deeply. "My anger will eventually turn into disappointment. Disappointment that you won't share something personal to both of us. Will you please think about that?"

"I will." She felt suddenly lonely without her sister, even though she was next to her.

"I'm going up now," said Dora. "Will you be coming up soon?"

"In a moment," she said, sinking back down on the chair, thinking about what Dora said. *I'm just not yet ready to talk about what happened.*

CHAPTER 28

$\mathcal{T}$he next morning rolled around more slowly than most. Emma lay in bed, not wanting to face Dora downstairs. Her day began later than she was used to; both the bakery and the delivery jobs required a much earlier start time.

She rolled to the side of the bed and pulled on her wool socks to protect her feet from the cold floor. Taking a moment, she sat on the side of the bed and organized. Pushing herself to get dressed, she put on the pants and shirt for today's job. She didn't think she would need it, but she strapped on her knife out of habit. Pulling her hair into a ponytail, she braided it to hold it in place and keep it out of her way.

She put on her boots and made her way downstairs. As she descended, she noticed the house was louder than she was used to. The children were still home and getting ready to start their day. Breakfast was being moved into the dining room and the breakfast bell rung. People came from their rooms and down the stairs. She managed to get herself a biscuit and sausage as she listened absently to Miss May and Miss Marjorie talk about their security work at the museum. She got her fill and started to help clean off the table. She carried the first platter into the kitchen and saw Dora working rolls at her kitchen table.

"Good morning," said Dora a bit formally.

"Good morning. Thank you for breakfast. I can help clear, then I have to get going," Emma said, ready to help.

"We have it," she said, avoiding Emma's gaze. "Don't forget your lunch." She nodded to the table where it sat.

Emma reached out and took her lunch pail, staring at Dora, wanting to say something, but not knowing what. She finally nodded, grabbed a coat, and headed out of the back door to begin her day.

It was a nice spring day with a chill in the air. She was glad she had on Papa's coat. It was big and comfortable. She ambled along, looking forward to her day, and saw Tony walking toward her.

"You didn't have to meet me; I was on the way to your house."

"I like to see you without competing with my family," he teased. He noticed her distant expression and asked, "What's wrong?"

"Dora wants to talk about what happened with Thomas and Daniel. I'm just not ready yet."

Tony nodded. She hadn't discussed the case with him either. They walked toward his house, holding hands and talking about their day.

Enzo must have heard her on the stairs because he yanked open the door as she arrived. "Morning, Emma."

"Morning, Enzo. Having a good morning?" she asked, always happy to see him.

"Well, it would be if I could skip school," he said, sending his mom a winning smile.

She knew her boys and didn't let them manipulate her. She shook her finger at him, saying lightly, "None of that. You're going to school."

"Oh, Mom," Enzo groaned.

"Oh, Enzo," she mocked back. "Get your books." He nodded and ran off, knowing he wouldn't win this argument.

Michael came out of his bedroom and was pulling on his coat when he noticed her. "Emma, good to see you."

"You too," said Emma sincerely.

"Marco and David, get finished with your breakfast. Everyone is waiting for you," Mrs. Marella reminded them.

"Sure, Ma, we'll get ready," David said and tapped Marco, pointing to their room.

"Oh, okay," said Marco, his mouth full, and he followed his brother out of the dining room.

"Emma, they'll be ready soon," Mrs. Marella called as she cleared the table. "Would you like something to eat while you wait? I made pancakes this morning."

That is tempting, thought Emma. She said with a smile, "One would be nice."

Mrs. Marella grinned at her and got her a pancake. She was very happy Emma was back in their lives and with Tony.

Everyone piled into the living room at the same time. Tony was in a nice suit and everyone else wore work clothes.

"Here are your lunches," said Mrs. Marella, handing out lunch pails to each person. She looked over at Emma. "Do you have your lunch?"

"Dora took care of me this morning," she said, holding up her lunch pail.

They headed outside, and she saw David had gotten the wagon ready and was waiting for them. Tony helped Emma into the back, kissed her goodbye, and said, "See you later."

"Yes, bye," she said as she watched him walk away. She waited and he turned to grin and wave at her. She grinned and waved back. The wagon pulled away, giving her a jerk. She turned toward the front and noticed Marco patting his hair down and buttoning his shirt. David was grinning but he didn't say anything. Emma smiled and looked around as Michael drove them to the job.

They were slowing down and she turned to see where she would be spending her days. She started her observation of the house. *It is a large Victorian-style home, mostly blue and white. The other houses in the neighborhood appear to be better maintained,* she thought, noticing the sagging porch and missing shingles. *He must not have wanted to work on the house after his son was declared dead and his wife died. What a sad thought, going through the motions of living and not really living.*

The boys and Emma jumped down and Michael handed over their tools. Michael looked at Emma and said, "We're working all over the house, so make yourself generally useful: moving trash, cleaning up jobs, and toting materials as needed." Emma nodded, knowing she needed to appear to be a working member of the team.

They carried their lunch pails and tools to the door. As Marco knocked, they heard a sound of scurrying steps that reminded her of Enzo. The door was thrown open by a small boy.

This must be Christopher, thought Emma.

Christopher focused on Marco and said loudly, "Marco!"

"Hey, Christopher, how are you?"

"I'm good. Do you want breakfast? Can I help you with your work today?" And the questions continued. Marco was extremely patient with him.

Emma noticed the intricate craftsmanship in the house as they walked through the foyer. There were hardwood floors, dark paneling, and a lovely curving staircase.

"We're in the back," indicated Michael.

Emma trailed the group as she glanced around the house and documented as much as she could. *Very clean, polished even.* She didn't see the maid mentioned earlier. *She might be helping in the kitchen.*

She heard something behind her, a swishing of a skirt. She turned and saw a girl about her age on the stairs.

"Who are you?" the girl asked.

"Emma," she said, trying to determine what the other girl's tone was.

"You're a girl," the girl exclaimed.

This must be Mara, she thought and replied to her question, "Yes."

"And you're working in plumbing and gas pipes?" she continued.

"Yes." She kept her answers short, trying to get a read on the girl. She could see why Marco was so taken with her. She was very beautiful.

She surprised Emma with her next statement. "I want to learn to do something useful."

Emma was about to respond when Michael called her back.

"Have to go," she said to Mara.

"Can we talk sometime about your job?" she asked.

"Sure, that would be nice," replied Emma.

She nodded her head at Mara and headed back to where Michael and the boys were setting up. She saw Christopher was keeping Marco company. He was able to work as Christopher continued to talk.

Mara came in and reminded Christopher that he was supposed to be with her working on his schoolwork. He went with her begrudgingly.

"I will see you soon, Christopher," promised Marco.

Christopher grinned in response and left with Mara.

"Emma," Michael said, seeing her attention had wandered. "Move those pipes to the next room. We'll be starting there next."

"Okay," she said putting on her gloves and started moving the pile of pipes; they weren't heavy just bulky. She noticed the room they were upgrading was the main sitting room.

Michael had commented that they had completed the family bedrooms.

The morning went by quickly and she stayed busy moving materials and cleaning up. When they paused for lunch, she was ready for the break but admitted to herself the physical labor felt good and kept her mind off her sister.

They sat out in the garden eating lunch. Michael and Emma sat in chairs at a table. Marco and David were resting on the patio with their backs against the house.

Marco kept looking around and Emma noticed. "I think I saw her in the library," she said casually.

"Oh, I think I need to check the gas lines in that room," he said and headed inside.

"Marco," Michael called, "we already completed that room."

"I'll check to see if they're working properly," he said quickly.

"Careful there," Michael warned him softly.

"I get it, Dad," Marco said quietly, understanding they were employees at the house.

Michael nodded and waved him on.

As Marco was leaving, a very attractive older woman in a dark blue dress came out with a pitcher of lemonade. "Would you like something to drink?" she asked the group.

"I would," said Emma. "Thank you." David also stood up and walked over to get some lemonade.

"How is the sitting room progressing?" Abigail asked.

"It's going well if you would like to review the details with me," said Michael, standing up.

"Thank you." They headed back in to inspect the improvements.

"She seems nice," Emma commented to David as they left.

"More so than her husband. At least she talks to us. I get the idea the husband would rather we weren't around," David commented softly.

"Why do you say that?" she asked, curious about this man she had not met.

"He's just not friendly. You'll see when he comes home this afternoon."

"Where's the older Mr. Saunders?" asked Emma.

"He's working in his garden, seems to be his favorite place," said David.

"So, he's active?"

He smiled and said, "You need to meet him. We have a few minutes if you want to go back to the garden."

"That would be nice." They made their way to the back of the house and entered the garden area. It was a greenhouse, attached to the house. Glass windows surrounded the structure. Lush greenery covered the lower windows. They saw an older gentleman who looked to be in good shape.

David said as they approached him, "Mr. Saunders, how are you?"

"David," he said and smiled. "How are you today? Is this a new helper?"

"Yes, this is Emma Evans. She's working with us this week."

"What are you helping with, my dear?" asked Mr. Saunders in a kindly voice.

"I am cleaning up and helping where needed," she replied.

"Sounds interesting," he said with a smile.

"Grandpa!" came a yell from Christopher as he came in running and hugged his grandfather's knees. He rubbed Christopher's hair and tilted his head up saying, "Hi, Christopher. How are your studies going?"

Christopher frowned and said, "I hate school."

"But you will try some more for me? Mara is doing her best to help you," he said softly.

"Yes, I know," he said, shuffling his feet. "Can I work out here with you?"

"How about this, another hour with Mara and then you can

come out and help me with my planting. Do we have a deal?" he asked.

"Yes, sir," he said grudgingly.

"Great. Now, get back to Mara and finish your schoolwork."

He grinned up at his grandpa and ran back into the house.

"He's always at full speed. Hates to sit still," commented Walter.

He caught Emma's considering glance and she decided to comment and see his reaction. "I heard about your son returning after being missing. That is such a wonderful thing."

His expression went more serious. He looked down at the plants as he replied, "Yes, yes, it is. Shouldn't you be getting back to work?"

David motioned to Emma for them to leave. She nodded and said to Walter, "Yes, it was nice to meet you."

"Hmm," he murmured and went back to his gardening.

Emma and David joined Marco and Michael in the sitting room. They finished piping the room and kept to themselves.

As they were packing up for the day, Emma noticed a man standing in the doorway. She started walking toward him, but he turned and moved away without speaking.

She didn't think it too odd that James seemed withdrawn. Men back from the war sometimes returned changed and uncommunicative. He had so much to be thankful for, being home and no loss of limbs. In town, many men had returned home missing arms, legs, some were addicted to morphine trying to control the pain.

She mentally went through notes on the people she had met today.

- Mara – lovely, wants to be useful; something there between Marco and Mara.
- Christopher – amazing kid, a little different, but

friendly and fun to be around; obviously, a favorite of Walter.

- Abigail – mother, quiet but seemed nice and ran the house efficiently.
- James – Father, war veteran, withdrawn; unsure of him at this time.
- Walter – grandfather, a very happy man when involved in garden and grandchildren; unhappy with questions about his returned son.
- Maid – keeps to herself cleaning or helping in the kitchen.

She continued to make notes in the wagon on the way home when Marco said something interesting. "Something odd happened."

"What," asked Emma, looking at him.

Marco continued, "I was calling Mara's name over and over, and she didn't respond until I got close to her."

Emma documented this and continued to write. She looked up as they slowed and realized they had stopped in front of the boarding house. "Oh, you didn't have to bring me home."

"It is the least we could do. You did good work today," commented Michael.

"See you in the morning?" asked Marco hopefully.

"Definitely. Meet you at the apartment in the morning," she said as he hopped down to help her off the wagon. She was grateful for the help after the long day. Waving goodbye to them, she headed into the boarding house.

"Emma," she heard a call from Dora as she entered.

"Yes, I'm here," Emma said absently, thinking that she needed to go to the library in town to check for any articles on James' return. It would have made a good human-interest story. She was drumming her fingers on her lips, thinking.

Dora came into the foyer, from the dining room and asked, "Long day?"

"Not too long and the work was interesting," Emma replied.

"Is there a case there?" she asked, curious about the family.

"I am still not sure, but there is an interesting story there. Boy leaves for war and returns as a man with a family," Emma stated.

"Have you seen him?" asked Dora.

"James?" She nodded, saying, "Just a glance. The other members of the family are really nice people. Though I did feel an undercurrent with the grandfather when I asked about James returning."

"Walk me back to the kitchen," Dora suggested.

Emma slipped her hand into her sisters' elbow and accompanied her to the kitchen. Emma laid her head on Dora's shoulder as they walked, glad they could still be close even when they disagreed.

When they entered, Amy was stirring a wonderful smelling soup. Emma commented, "That smells good, Amy." She nodded, smiled, and went back to her stirring.

"Dora, I think I need to go to the library after dinner."

"All right, why don't you ask Thomas to go with you? He would probably enjoy riding with you," Dora suggested.

"Instead of following me, you mean," she said with a grin.

Dora nodded and turned back to her pastry. She wanted to confront Emma again but promised her she could have some time. Instead, she said, "He is in the study if you want to ask him."

"I will," said Emma and she walked quickly to find him.

"Hi, Thomas." He looked up from his book and smiled, always happy to see her. "Would you like to go to the library with me? You can sit with me on the cable car," she teased lightly.

"Sure, that would be nice. Now?" He sat up, ready to go.

"No, we can go after dinner," she said with a chuckle. "I need to get washed up."

"You are carrying some dirt with you," he said, noticing her work clothes.

"Agreed." She laughed and headed upstairs to change and wash up.

After she finished her bath, she put on her red slit skirt and white blouse. The ponytail was giving her a headache, she brushed her hair out and left it down; and headed downstairs to help with dinner. Dora was still unhappy with Emma not sharing, but she wasn't ready for that conversation. She would continue to channel her energy into the current case.

Dinner was prepared and everyone moved into the dining room. Emma was hungry from the physical labor. Miss May and Miss Marjorie tried to get her to talk, but she was distracted and didn't say much. She helped clean up and asked Thomas, "Ready?"

"Yes, let me grab my hat and coat," replied Thomas.

They waved bye to Dora and Amy as they headed out the kitchen door.

Quietly talking, they headed to the cable car and into the library. "I will be over here," she said as she headed toward the area where the older newspapers were kept.

She looked through them for the date she knew James had shown up with his family. She found what she was looking for; the article was smaller than she expected. The article did detail James had come back home and had not died in the war. What was surprising was what was not in the article. She noted the writer's name and made up her mind to see him early the next day.

Their walk home was nice, Thomas talked about his bakery job and people he'd met that day. When she got home, she put together a note telling Tony's family she would meet them at the house a bit later the next day.

CHAPTER 29

The next morning, she made her way to the newspaper office. She was unsure of how she felt about going into the building but noticed the editor's office seemed to be occupied. "I guess they have replaced Daniel. Things must keep moving forward." Going up to one of the writer's desk, she asked about the location of the writer of the article she was researching.

He grunted, not looking up from his typewriter. "He is over there." He waved in the direction with his right hand.

She approached the desk he'd indicated and saw he was a young man. She asked him, "Are you the writer who wrote the article about James Saunders returning home?"

"Yes, that was me. Did you like it?" he asked, hoping he had a fan in this young lady.

Without answering, she pulled out her notebook and pencil.

"Is this an interview?" he asked with a smile.

"Kind of. The article was so brief for a personal interest story? Wouldn't a story of this type normally have included information about the family, where the returning person had been living, and how they were going to move forward?"

He didn't say anything. Instead, he sat back in his chair, causing it to squeak loudly. He took off his glasses to clean them, not answering any of her questions.

She continued, "Did you interview the family?"

"I did actually," he finally said as he considered her.

"Mara, Christopher, Abigail, James, and Walter?" she asked, going down her list of people.

"Yes, to each—except James. He wasn't home yet when I started the interview." Remembering that day, he said with a sudden laugh, "That Christopher is a real pistol."

That made her laugh. "Talked your ear off, did he?"

"Yes." He got very serious when he said, "Okay, yes I did interview everyone. And Mara and Abigail were very nice but didn't share much except they were glad they were there."

"Walter?" she asked curiously.

"He was also quiet but seemed very happy to have his family with him."

"Christopher?"

"Well, I got a moment alone with him and he told me some things the others didn't."

Emma waited, sure this would answer some questions. He paused and looked around. "Let's take a quick walk to the dock." She nodded and followed him. It was empty at that time of day and would give them some privacy.

She waited for him to start again. He continued to talk about Christopher. "He indicated they weren't from the south at all and had been living only a few towns over from Chicago. He also said he had a new name and he liked it better than his last one."

"A different name and place. Did you find out anything else? Weren't you curious?" she asked, knowing she would have looked harder into the family.

"I was," he admitted.

"What happened? Something must have because the article didn't reflect any of this information," she commented.

"James returned home and realized I had been alone with Christopher," he said simply.

"What was his mood? Was he angry?" she asked.

"I don't think anger is the right word. He appeared more scared or panicked," he said.

Emma thought, *A large number of soldiers returned from the war troubled by the intensity of the fighting. They were fighting helplessness, panic, and dealing with sleep deprivation.* "What happened?" she asked, wrapped up in the story.

"I explained the article and he wanted to see what I had planned to publish." He paused before saying, "That is when he offered me money to limit the article."

"Did he say why?" she asked.

"He just said they were trying to form a new family and he didn't want outsiders in their business."

"Did you think he was telling the truth?"

"To a point," he admitted, "but I thought there was something up then. And now."

"But you took the money?" she pointed out.

"Yeah, I did. I am not perfect and I could use it. It was more than I would see in six months here. And who was I hurting by publishing a shorter article?"

"Hmm," she said, taking down what she had learned. Christopher wasn't his real name; they came from Johnsonville. "Did Christopher mention what his dad did for a job in Johnsonville?"

"Yes," he said, looking at his notes. "He wasn't working. Abigail was. She worked for an influential family, the Lewison's."

"Thanks for the information," she said, closing her notebook.

"Please, don't mention my role in this to anyone," he warned softly.

"I won't," she promised. "Thanks for telling me."

As she walked away from the newspaper dock, she got her bike from under the stairs, thinking, *The police chief. I will see if he can check some facts out for me.*

She went to the police station and upstairs to the chief's office. "Emma," said the secretary. "Welcome."

It is certainly different than the first time I was here, she thought wryly and said out loud, "Does the chief have time for me?"

"I think he will make time. Let me check." He got up, knocked on the door, and was called in. He came out a moment later and said, "Emma, you can go in now. The chief will see you."

"Thanks," she said sincerely as she walked past his desk and entered the office.

"Emma," the chief said, standing up and going around the desk to greet her. He took her hand in his and said, "Please, sit."

They sat on his couch and she pulled out the familiar notebook. "Ahh, you are here on business," he commented, curious but not upset.

"Yes, I hope you don't mind?" When he indicated for her to continue, she described her current case. "I was hoping you could send a telegram over to the chief there and ask if he is aware of the family. Abigail worked at the Lewison's when they lived there. I am unsure of the names they were using but I can give you a description and when they were probably there.

"I can send a telegram," he said. "We should hear something later today or tomorrow morning."

She gave him notes on the family, thanked him, and headed downstairs to the veteran's administration office. The office was nearby, so she got her bike and walked it there. She asked the clerk for the service record for James Saunders. Pension records were accessible since 1868. "Can I also get a list of people in his regiment?" she asked, thinking she was on to something.

She took the information and made her way to the boarding house. When she got there, the police chief had sent a note over with a telegram enclosed. It confirmed that the description matched the family of Doug Gregg. His wife's name was Martha Gregg when she worked at the Lewison's. That rang a bell and she pulled up her list of people from the regiment. Doug Gregg was on the list. *So, Doug did know James.* Looking further down in the note, she saw the Gregg family had left on good terms, owing no money to anyone.

Okay, now I have the information, but when do I communicate it? She sent a note over to Michael at the worksite to tell them she would be there tomorrow.

The next morning, she met Tony halfway to his apartment. "Meeting me again?" she teased.

"Yes, we missed you yesterday," he said as he leaned over to kiss her.

"Me too, but I made progress in the case," she said.

"Anything you can share?"

"Not yet. I would like to continue observing the family before I say anything," she said.

He nodded. "I understand."

Meeting Michael and the boys at the apartment, she told them she was still working on the case but was making progress. Michael said, "Let's go. David, get the wagon ready."

As they walked down, Emma asked Marco, "What room are we in today?"

"We've moved to the dining room," he replied.

"That is a large room," she commented.

"Yes, should take 3-4 days to get the room piped and walls repaired. We have cleaned up the previous room. You can work on some final debris removal and help with wall preparation," Michael commented.

"Okay," she said, thinking that would give her time to evaluate about next steps.

They made their way to the house and knocked on the door. Christopher once again let their crew in. "Emma, you're back!"

"I am. I had some stuff to do yesterday," Emma replied.

Once again, Christopher accompanied Marco. "Mara made something special for you," Christopher whispered loudly. "It is a secret, though."

"Really?" said Marco, pleased Mara was thinking of him.

Their group continued to talk and moved into the dining room.

Michael motioned to David and Emma. "You two finish up in the sitting room. David, let Emma know what she needs to do."

David nodded and said, "Will do."

Emma and David went into the room and started picking up debris left from the previous day. After a while, he said, "I will check the texture on the wall. We should be able to paint." Emma nodded and kept working on taking debris piles outside.

She was walking back inside when she noticed James in the yard with his face up to the sun. He seemed very tired. She was curious about this man. He had managed to change his family's life by taking on someone else's identity but did not seem to be there for nefarious reasons. "Mr. Saunders, is there something I can help you with?" asked Emma."

"What?" he said, distracted. "No, no."

"It is a lovely day, isn't it?" she asked, trying to get to know this man.

"Yes," he said, still holding his face up to the sun.

"I need to head back in now," she said when he didn't talk more.

"Yes," he commented softly.

She headed back in; so many men came back for the war angry, broken. This man seemed to be more distracted than angry. She wondered if he had hurt his head in some way or maybe this was just his way of coping.

She continued to make several trips, cleaning up the room while David started painting. When she finished the debris removal, she asked him, "Can I help?"

"Sure, grab a paintbrush and start on that wall. Don't get too close to the windows. I will do the detail work." She nodded, grabbing a brush and dipping it into the paint. They worked on the room and were finished by lunch.

"Emma, good job," said David, looking over her work. "You should be about to move into the dining room to help out there next." He laughed and said, "You have some paint on your face." He reached over to wipe it off.

"Thanks," she said. "That was fun."

"Your shoulders may bother you a bit tonight, so take a hot bath and soak them," he cautioned.

"I will," she promised, rolling her shoulders.

They grabbed their lunch pails and headed outside. Marco and Michael were waiting for them before they started their lunch.

Abigail brought out lemonade and Mara carried a platter of cut slices of cake. Emma tried the cake and said, "Hmm, this is good. Can I get the recipe?"

"Yes," Mara commented happily. "It is a Molasses Cake."

Molasses Cake

Ingredients:

- 1/2 cup of shortening
- 2 eggs
- 1/4 teaspoon of ginger
- 1/4 teaspoon of allspice
- 1/4 teaspoon of cinnamon
- 3 cups of flour
- 1 cup of sugar

- 1 cup of dark molasses
- 1 teaspoon of baking soda dissolved in 1 cup strong hot coffee

Directions:

1. Bake at 350F for 30-40 minutes.
2. Cream sugar with shortening; add eggs, molasses, spices, and flour.
3. Mix thoroughly; add coffee with soda dissolved. Pour into greased pan.
4. Test with a toothpick in the center; when it comes out clean, it is ready.
5. Frost with a white butter frosting.

Mara glanced over and asked shyly, "Marco, do you like it?"

"I do. It is wonderful," he said honestly.

She blushed and said, "Well, I am going back in."

"Would you like to stay for a moment and talk?" asked Marco.

"That would be lovely," she said as she sat down next to him with her back to the house. They each enjoyed their cake and the afternoon sun.

Once again, Emma noticed James walking around. He appeared to be going toward the greenhouse.

"Mara?" asked Emma, watching him.

"Yes," she said, not looking away from Marco.

"Your father? Is he well?" Emma asked carefully.

That got Mara's attention, and she focused her gaze on Emma. "You mean the absentmindedness?"

"Yes," she said.

"When he wants, he can focus. It's just that I think memories of the war can overwhelm him," she said. "Mama said he is very different from when they first married."

"Does he work? Or have something he is interested in?" Emma asked.

"He hasn't held a job in a while, but he loves the dirt and working with plants."

"He must come to that naturally from his father. He seems to also really enjoy gardening."

She averted her gaze and said, "Well, yes. I do wish they would work together, but Papa doesn't go in there when Grandfather is there." Emma noticed the hesitation and made a mental note of it.

"What else does he focus on?" she asked.

"Us," she said simply. "He wants to make sure we are safe and secure."

That sounds right. thought Emma. This situation, taking another identity, maybe because he needed to protect his family. Securing a new name and life for them.

"Michael, when will we be finished in the house?" asked Emma.

"The dining room is the last room; we have the rest of the week and we should be done."

"Okay," said Emma. She wouldn't jeopardize their job but planned on communicating the information to the family soon.

CHAPTER 30

*T*he week went by quickly and the rooms were well lit with gas lights. They were testing the lights and doing a final walkthrough with Walter.

Emma said to Michael, "It looks like the job is complete?"

"Yes," he said absently.

"Mr. Saunders," she said after they completed their inspection.

"Yes, Emma," Walter commented, looking from the lamps to her.

"Could I meet with you and your family?" she asked.

"I don't understand. Why would you need to meet with us?" asked Walter, bewildered by the request.

Michael and the boys stood silent while Emma talked with him.

"I would like to go over some information with you all," she stated.

Curious, he said, "In the sitting room. I will call the family." He turned to his grandson. "Christopher, please, go get your father."

"I will," he said and ran off to find him.

The family gathered in the dining room. Michael and his boys made themselves absent, knowing Emma would handle things from here. "Emma, we will be outside if you need us," said Michael as they went out the front door.

Emma went in and sat down. She pulled out her notebook and started. "You know my name is Emma. My full name is Emma Evans. I work as an investigator occasionally." She paused a moment when Abigail gasped. Emma tried to ignore the response and continued. "Someone I know asked me to look into your family," she said formally. When she saw Walter was going to interrupt, she said quickly, "It wasn't meant to be malicious. They were worried about you. I will continue if that is all right."

Abigail, Mara, and James looked very uncomfortable. She thought it best to lay it out in an abrupt manner and turned to James. "I know you're are not James, but rather Doug Gregg, and you are all from Johnsonville." The quiet was deafening in the room as she continued to speak directly to James. "I also believe you assumed the identity so you could move your family here to protect them."

James, aka Doug, looked defeated and the women scared, but oddly, Walter didn't seem surprised.

James looked at Walter and asked, "You knew?"

"You think I don't know what my son looks like? Where did you get the picture?" Walter asked in a neutral voice. James/Doug had provided the small handheld painting of James' mom as proof of who he was.

James/Doug said, "You probably won't believe this, but I did know him. We were in the same regiment—"

Emma interrupted him, saying, "I can confirm that fact." She thought about how many men Illinois had contributed to the Union Army. Over 250,000 had volunteered and several thousand died.

James/Doug watched her and waited a moment before going

on. "I was there when he died in the battle at the Potomac and he asked me to take the picture back to you."

"You chose an odd way to do that," Walter commented, his voice not betraying any emotion.

"Yes, when I got here with my family, it was so easy to just be James instead of telling you how he died," he said simply.

"How did he die?" asked Walter hoarsely.

James made an indication with his head for his wife to take the kids out of the room. Emma stayed; they had forgotten she was there.

"So many people died immediately. I was with James and it seemed everyone was dying around us. We were walking through the blood and brains of our friends. I still can't sleep because of the dreams." He took a deep breath. "James took a bullet in the chest. I did the best I could to help him and carried him to the doctor's tent. He talked all the way to the medical tent about you and your wife. He went so quiet, and when I finally got a doctor to look at him, they told me he was dead. I didn't believe them, and I just stayed and stayed until they made me go back to my regiment."

Walter let his emotions take over and he cried. He finally looked up and said to James, "Call your wife and daughter back in."

When they returned, James/Doug said, "I will take my family and myself and clear out."

Abigail turned to Walter. "I am sorry if we hurt you."

Walter said, "No, you are not going anywhere."

They looked shocked at his statement and stayed still. "I love having you here with me." He turned to look at Emma and said, "Emma, it was time to have this out, so thank you for that. But I think this information needs to stay inside my family. Can you keep that secret for me, for us?"

"I can. I am very glad you found each other," said Emma sincerely.

"James," said Walter, showing that he would continue to use the alias. "Would you like to come to the garden with me? I can show you what I am working on."

He looked startled but happy and said, "That would be nice." He followed him out.

Abigail and Mara were hugging and crying. Abigail looked at Emma and said, "We are so relieved. James. . . Doug couldn't work, and he just wanted to make sure we had somewhere safe to live."

"I understand. I will leave you and your family to your privacy," she said and exited the room.

Emma headed out of the house and saw that Michael and the boys had waited for her. She briefly told them what had happened in the meeting. "Please, keep this quiet. This family needs each other," she told them softly.

"We will," said Michael. "Everyone okay with that?" They nodded and he turned around to move the wagon forward.

On their way home, Emma thought about how the case had ended. There were no deaths or fights this time, but a group of people choosing to be with one another. She kept thinking about the family members, growing apart because they didn't share more of themselves.

Dora, she thought as they pulled up to the boarding house. She jumped out without waiting for assistance and said a quick, "Bye." She took off at a run up the stoop and flew through the door, catching Dora, who was checking the mail in the foyer, unawares.

"What is wrong? Has something happened?" Dora asked, concerned.

"Yes," Emma said. "So many things. Can we talk?"

"Yes, let's go to the study," said Dora in a worried voice. She closed the doors behind them and sat next to her.

Emma took Dora's hands, looking her deep in the eyes. "I

want to say I am sorry that I haven't been more open to talking with you about Mama."

Dora hadn't realized this was about Mama. She took a deep breath and said, "What caused this change?"

Emma told her about the case she was working on and how it ended. "I realized that, by not telling you about Mama, I was putting a wall between us. I never wanted that." She went on to describe how Mama's case had come together. She detailed how Daniel had tried to make her into the same kind of people they were and, when she resisted, they killed her.

"How?" Dora asked in a shaky voice, wiping her eyes.

"They got to the bakery that night. They *said* they were there to talk to her one more time, but they decided she was a liability. Daniel hit her with a rolling pin and then laid her under a beam that had fallen."

Dora knew the rest. She felt calmer learning what had happened. "Emma, you try to protect me from the harsh realities of life. I am stronger than that," she said quietly.

"I do know that," Emma said earnestly," but I have one more thing to share."

Dora was wiping her eyes and said, "Oh, what else could there be?"

"Emma, when I found out Daniel killed Mama, I made up my mind that I would kill him," she said, not breaking eye contact.

"But you killed him to protect Thomas," she said, feeling a little lost.

"Yes, but I would have thrown that knife anyway. I knew how it was going to end," she said simply.

"Oh," said Dora, unsure of what to say.

"Dora, I didn't tell you because I didn't want you to think I was a monster," she explained, looking down for the first time.

Dora immediately grabbed her shoulder and shook her

lightly. "No, I know who the monsters here are. You killed one. You are never to think of yourself that way. Do you hear me?"

"Yes," Emma said, tears thickening her response.

"I love you and I always will, no matter what," stated Dora.

"I worry you feel things more than I do," Emma said.

"I don't think I do. I just show mine more. You have been hurting, holding this in, and not being able to talk about it," Dora said.

Emma nodded.

"We will try to do better," Dora said, more as a statement of fact than a question.

"We will," Emma said as she laid her head on Dora's shoulder.

WANT MORE OF THE NOTEBOOK
MYSTERIES SERIES?

PREORDERS MAY 2021

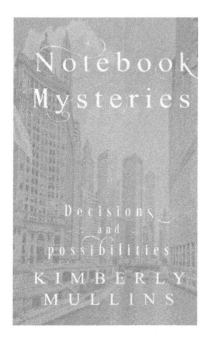

ABOUT THE AUTHOR

Kimberly Mullins is the author of series of books titled "Notebook Mysteries". Her stories are based on historical events occurring in 1871 Chicago. She holds a BS in Biology and a MBA in Business. She lives in Texas with her husband and son. When she is not writing she is working as a Process Safety Engineer at a large chemical company. You can connect with her on her website www.kimberlymullinsauthor.com.

Photo Credit: Blessings of Faith Photography

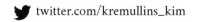 twitter.com/kremullins_kim